THE BECKONING DOOR

BY MABEL SEELEY

MYSTERIES

The Listening House (1938)

The Crying Sisters (1939)

The Whispering Cup (1940)

The Chuckling Fingers (1941)

Eleven Came Back (1943)

The Beckoning Door (1950)

The Whistling Shadow (1954)

NOVELS

Woman of Property (1947)

The Stranger Beside Me (1951)

THE BECKONING DOOR

DOOR

A MYSTERY

MABEL SEELEY

Afton Historical Society Press
Afton, Minnesota

Designed by Barbara J. Arney

This first Afton Historical Society Press
reprint edition is limited to
two thousand copies.

Library of Congress Cataloging-in-Publication Data

Seeley, Mabel, 1903–1991
    The Beckoning Door / Mabel Seeley.
        p.   cm.
    ISBN 1-890434-07-8 (hardcover)
    I. Title
    PS3537.E2826B43   1998   98-36993
    813'.54--dc21   CIP

Printed in Canada

The Afton Historical Society Press is a non-profit
organization that takes pride and pleasure in publishing
fine books on Minnesota subjects.

W. Duncan MacMillan   Patricia Condon Johnston
        president   publisher

Afton Historical Society Press
P.O. Box 100
Afton, MN 55001
800-436-8443

THE BECKONING DOOR

I WONDER how many other people have looked at a face they knew or thought they knew, and seen fixed on it the tight, still smile that meant death was near. Sylvia did, I know that; or Sylvia and probably old Hector too; for Sylvia and for Hector there weren't any afterthoughts— or maybe there were; maybe the little instant they had was enough; maybe they too, in their instant, saw the world turn over, revealing its underside.

That, I think, is what's happened to me; I don't understand it, entirely; I don't yet, entirely, know what I feel. Other people—people I read about, especially—seem always to know what they're thinking or feeling; they're exasperated or happy or loving or sad, just the one thing at a time, and so clearly. For me, it's almost never that way; I'm more apt to be unclear and mixed. Sylvia, for instance. I know too much now about Sylvia; I know things about Sylvia I wish I had never needed to know about anyone. But even then—even then—I don't know. Maybe what I feel toward Sylvia is the dislike and resentment the people of Long Meadow have for so long taken it for granted I felt. Maybe I hold her in abhorrence—if the codes I've lived by are right, that's what I'm supposed to do. Or maybe—in the night when I wake up I feel it— maybe in spite of what Sylvia was and what Sylvia did I'm still linked to her; maybe in some way she's part of myself.

Of course I had known my cousin Sylvia was home from New York for the summer; in a town the size of Long Meadow—even when it's swelled by resorters—you can scarcely miss a circumstance so

1

whetting to the local tongues. But my path and Sylvia's didn't cross often—not of late, anyway; it wasn't until a night toward the middle of August that I so much as saw her, and then only passingly, at the distance of sidewalk to street.

I was, I remember, coming out of Pete's Kitchen—not a circumstance at all remarkable; I drop in at Pete's for coffee half the nights of my life. The only thing at all out of the ordinary, that night, was that Russ Bennert was with me. It was, perhaps, nine then, or shortly before it, because that's the routine—around eight-thirty when we're through with admissions and the rush of evening visitors is over I push back my books in the hospital office for a ten-minute break, while the night nurse on main peels an ear for the phone. Often Doris Orfelt drops in to go with me, but that night she'd been busy; as I went down the side corridor past the common room Russ Bennert had lifted his head from the building plans spread on the common-room table; he'd said, "Alone tonight, Cathy? Then I'm going too."

I'd answered as shortly as possible, "That's not the least necessary," but he had unfolded his big body anyway; he'd said, "I've known you since you were seven, Cathy; there's no reason—is there?—why we can't be friends."

And so I had let him come with me, humiliated because being near him was at once a pain and its opposite, wishing—as I so often had wished—that he was away again as he'd been during the war, wishing I could be anywhere but in Long Meadow, where I couldn't escape seeing him. Carefully speaking of nothing but the weather and the proposed new hospital, we walked the half block to the Kitchen; still carefully distant, we sat at the long counter served by Mrs. Haushofer, having some of Pete's spring-water coffee and his freshly fried doughnuts. While we were doing so Hector LeClerque ambled in; Hector, as usual by that time of evening, was well in need of a sobering snack, and Russ bought him one. I was taking coffee back for Dr.

2

Diebuhr too; I remember my hands were full as Russ opened the door for me, and I stepped through to the side porch which used to give entry to a country-style house but which now takes the traffic of Pete's bouncing young enterprise.

It was then that the car came by, drifting lazily up from the darkness behind it—a long gray convertible with its top, down, announced not so much by its whispering motor as by the shafts of its lights and the swell of its radio. During the moment it passed under the nearest street light the four people in it were framed in an obscure and leaf-edged relief—Sylvia driving, her head a little forward, her long light hair loose on the shoulders of a misty white blouse, her hands high on the wheel. At her side, arm along her back and dark head bent toward her, sat Pete Fenrood, his long young body holding something of the poise and balance of a ready leopard; in the back seat—bald head surmounting thick shoulders in a much too young plaid sport shirt—Clint Boyce slouched beside his red-haired wife.

Abreast of Pete's place of business they all, except Sylvia, turned; Pete, straightening a little, called, "Hi, you!"; Clint Boyce, too, lifted a careless hand. Then they were past us, the car floating forward into darkness the same way it had floated up from it, trailing the receding wink of its taillights, the receding drift of its music, the echo of Sylvia's husky low laugh.

Beside me, Russ spoke quietly. "They must have left Ada with Lucy. . . . It looks as if Sylvia's making a play for Pete Fenrood. I wondered, when she loaned him that money. I'm sorry, Cathy."

I said, "There's nothing at all to be sorry about."

He answered, "There ought to be, Cathy. Sooner or later I've got to be sorry about someone."

Of the replies to that there were none I could make, not without too much betrayal. I went on down the walk, but as I did so—willy-nilly and fight as I would—I was shaken by compulsions I seldom allow

MABEL SEELEY

myself, not when I'm waking. I couldn't envy Sylvia, I couldn't let myself be covetous, but there she went in this town she so fitfully visited only because the spirit moved her, there she went in a car that for me would be ransom, there she went pleasure-bent, there she went, free. While here on the walk in front of Pete's Kitchen was I, one hand bearing a wax container of coffee, the other a brown paper bag with two doughnuts, caged in a town I despaired to be gone from, mortgaged to a job with no past and no future, bound by debt, bound by duty, bound—most unbreakably of all— by my own doubts and incapacities; no door ever opened for me. Here I was, beside the man who had begun blinding me to all other men when I was in pigtails and he seventeen—out on a basketball floor in a kind of blaze, big even then, so tall he could tip the ball into the basket, streaking down the middle with his blond head back and the ball slapping up to his hand, meeting interference or ignoring it with the same sure power. A man different from anyone else in Long Meadow—strong and quick and authoritative, openhanded and ambitious, getting a start in state politics, making his mark as a construction engineer.

A man I couldn't so much as think of loving, because he was married to somebody else. Married to Sylvia's sister and my one other cousin, Ada.

The thrust of that rebellion washed up, washed over me, and then washed away, leaving an ebb that was older and drearier. When I came back to the night and the ordinary we were still only halfway to the hospital, and a murmur was sounding behind me.

"That M'selle Gainer, she is of the rich who do not care for the poor."

Hector. I hadn't heard him come after us, but when I turned he was right in back of me, padding along in his moccasins, his black French-Canadian eyes plaintive, even his long mustache drooping.

"Oh, go along, Hector," Russ told him indulgently. "You've had three too many; get back to that shack of yours."

4

Hector persisted. "My friend John Gainer, he does not forget. Always he has for Hector a little money for bread, a little money for wine. But this Ma'amselle, nothing."

"Applesauce," Russ told him more rudely. "She's slipped you a fistful more times than you can count—if she hasn't, why are you always out trailing her? Cut along now, sleep it off."

For still a few steps the old man kept after us. What he had in mind, all too probably, was following me to the office, where he would have sat by my desk in the new-patient's chair for the rest of the evening, retelling his wrongs. But Russ was a major of engineers during the war and his tone carries authority; at the edge of the hospital grounds the seedy old lumberjack came to a halt, rocking gently as he stood to watch us go.

"Poor bastard," Russ muttered as we edged past Dr. Diebuhr's red Studebaker—parked, as usual, head on toward the side entrance— "it's too bad your grandfather didn't leave him a little. Too bad your grandfather didn't do a few other things too. I'll have to hunt Hector a job somewhere——"

He fell silent, after that, as I remained; at the door of the common room he said good night a trifle absently; I went on to my desk alone.

And that was all there was, then, to that brief glance of Sylvia; all that there was to the circumstances surrounding it. Perhaps, as I walked on up the corridor, my neck should have prickled; perhaps I should have felt some sixth sense of prescience, perhaps I should have been touched by my nearness to that other dread presence which even then must have been riding hooded and cloaked in the car I had seen. But I was too self-absorbed; what filled the center of my mind, as I went on up that hall, was the coffee I must get to Dr. Diebuhr, the tedious last hour I must put in on the hospital books, the peppermint ice cream I mustn't forget to pick up on the way home, because Mother had phoned to say Agatha Pence and Rose Gamble had dropped in. And if my other thoughts were

5

taken up it wasn't by anything concerning Sylvia, or Hector, or even, directly, Russ. It was, instead, by the dreary old question concerning myself. "Will I ever get away from this? Will I ever get away?"

The next time I saw Sylvia, though, it was different. Not enough different so I could possibly have guessed what was ripening, but enough so that I was, at least, taken aback. Because Sylvia, that time, came to see me, and Sylvia's coming to my house to see me was very nearly in a category with the Duchess of Windsor hopping a ride in a freight car.

The hour she chose for her descent was two o'clock, on a day toward the end of August. Since my worktime begins at three I was doing what I most regularly do about then—I was upstairs dressing. Maybe Sylvia knocked before she opened the front door of our small forty-year-old house, or maybe, as I was later on to believe, she moved quietly through the rooms downstairs, looking for me or for something else. At any rate my first hint of her presence came when she called from the front hall.

"Cathy, you around here?" The voice drifted up, casual, scarcely raised, so much at home yet so out of place that for a while I could scarcely believe my ears. Mother, that day, was away at a Methodist bazaar; I'd thought myself not only alone in the house but certain to stay that way. Probably I met my own eyes incredulously in the mirror for as long as a minute before I even reached for the seersucker robe I had thrown on the bed. It was hot that afternoon, dry hot, the way August in Minnesota can be even as far north as we were, and I wasn't wearing much.

"Cathy, aren't you home?"

After that second call I managed an answer, and got out through my bedroom door. Hall windows don't come in local houses of the size and vintage of ours, but there was light enough in the well below for me to verify, from the stairhead, that she actually stood there.

"Sylvia." I was stupid about it. "What're you——" because that, of course, was what I thought first: she'd never have been there without some reason.

She laughed, throwing my own broken-off query back at me. "What am I doing here? Sweet, aren't you my only cousin?" That hazy, husky, slightly jerky drawl wasn't any native way of speech, but she could make it be mesmerizing.

I started forward. "I'll be right——"

"Oh, why bother? I can join you up there." The fronts of my housecoat, as I discovered by that time, had gotten rolled in the belt; I was still tugging at them, trying to get myself decently covered, when she came level with me, rising lithely up through the dim well of the stairs, hands out-stretched and lips smiling, as if she truly were moved by an eagerness to see me.

"M-m-m," she continued. "You should play up those curves of yours, Cathy; too bad you ever wear clothes. Why haven't you been up to see me? There I've been, all alone in my piece of the old Gainer home-stead—can't you even say anything welcoming? You needn't mean it."

Hands light on my elbows, she rocked me a little, affectionate, ironical as if I were a loved younger sister. Under the circumstances I couldn't very well produce the obvious, which was that I had never in my life entered her home, any more than she had previously entered mine.

"It's nice of you to be so unorthodox," I managed instead. "It ought to set at least some of Long Meadow by the ears. If you'll wait till I——"

"I'll watch while you dress."

I began resisting, but opposition to her highhandedness was one thing and getting anywhere was another; she stood waiting, cool, brows sweetly lifted, and after another quick glance at her I gave in over a point that couldn't be worth struggling about anyway and led the way back to my room. Once there, while I went on with my hair, she immediately and airily flopped on the bed. I was by that time a little wary, or maybe—along with my other responses—I had been wary from the first; you never quite knew, with Sylvia, whether good was going to pop from her or ill. She was gotten up, that afternoon, in an ankle-long velveteen, not beige, not orange, but somewhere between the two. Probably the dress was a Dior; her head, her shoulders, and most of her bosom rose out of the low roll of collar; the bodice hugged, the skirt artfully flared. The hat that went with this was wide, very wide, in the same velveteen, the front brim folding back to be held by a staggering three-foot-long quill. On the night I had seen her in the car, with her hair down, she might, in the darkness, have been seventeen; today for the incongruous setting of my angle-ceiled bedroom she had chosen to look what she was, twenty-nine, a schooled cosmopolite who could enjoy the full irony of sitting dressed as she was on a worn chenille bedspread, sables loose on her lap, brown suéde gloves and handbag thrown beside her, one long leg carelessly swinging. Not beautiful maybe—the cheekbones were a little too high and angular, the gray eyes a little too small for beauty. But beauty wasn't important in Sylvia, any more than it would have been in a timber wolf.

"Say it, darling," she urged me. "How nice for me that I've got Long Meadow to startle, when it's so hard to stand New York on its head with mere clothes. I've been at the bazaar."

Mockery for me, because she was reading me. But mockery too for herself.

For as far back as I could remember, I had been supposed to detest and hate her. "Your cousin Sylvia, the one with the money." It wasn't from Mother or Father I had gotten that whisper, but surely it had come from most of the rest of Long Meadow. So long ago that my feet in yellow socks and black slippers still stuck straight out in front of me in a church pew, I was already aware of that whisper; across from me in another pew had been that other child, four years older and four years bigger, who had been Sylvia Gainer, and always around me the whisper was sibilant. Not "That's her grandfather Gainer, who disowned her mother for marrying Carl Kingman's son." Not "That's her cousin Ada"—Ada was so much older than I that there wasn't any comparison; when I was four Ada must have been thirteen. Just always "That's her cousin Sylvia." Around me, tight and pressing, had crowded all the angers and animosities I had been supposed to feel; I had felt myself home along on the current, but at the same time, curiously, I had felt a kind of linking—the gray eyes under the blond hair and the slightly knobby forehead had looked at me as if they knew me.

Later on, too, in spite of the bad fortune that so often seemed to result from her sporadic offers of friendship, things had stayed the same way. There'd been the time when I was six or so, and she had suddenly appeared beside me in a neighbor's yard. "Here, you can have these," she had said, thrusting at me a large bag of marbles. "I won 'em off Lucy Hague, and I'll show how you play." For the rest of that June afternoon she had squatted beside me, painstakingly drawing out lines in the dust, painstakingly guiding my inexpert fingers. Lucy Hague's mother, afterward, had turned up to storm at me frighteningly, saying I'd stolen the marbles and wrenching them back, but I had always believed it was Lucy, not Sylvia, who lied. There'd been the time I almost ran away with her. There'd been the time I was a high school freshman and she got me elected to a society I had wretchedly had to turn down because I couldn't afford it. Always the eyes with which she met mine had held the same look—detached, perhaps, but keeping their sure inner knowledge. They'd met mine that way the day she walked down a church aisle as a bridesmaid behind her sister Ada and Russ Bennett, and that gaze was the one she turned on me now. Against it I might continue to be wary, but I couldn't be wholly hostile.

"Oh," I replied to what she had just said, "the bazaar. When I thought you'd been fishing,"

The wriggle she gave in return to my tartness was one of pure pleasure.

"See?" she asked, and she was, then, entirely smiling. "I love you, Cathy. I love you, I love you. All those years, Grandfather Gainer threatening to disinherit me too if I so much as spoke to you, but— you're like your mother. She just read my palm for me, at the bazaar."

Abrupt change of subject, but abruptness was what you tuned yourself to, around Sylvia.

"Mother can't sew much any more, not with her hands." I was careful, an increase of wariness telling me that Sylvia might be approaching what she'd come for. "So she's taken up palmistry. In Long Meadow you've got to have some talent to offer up at bazaars."

"Oh, don't apologize." It was light but, I thought, temporizing. "Aunt Julia's good at it. Too good. She told me I was inconstant and ruthless. She said I was erratically selfish and erratically generous, and she didn't know which was worse. She said I should have been spanked——"

I laughed. "Old residents usually come away from Mother's booth looking a bit strained."

"So I should think. She can be—well, she hits close." This was much less airy, and I thought, "Here it comes." "She told me I'd meet a tall man with dark hair and blue eyes. Well, I've met him. Anyway, I think I've met him. Cathy, last winter—this spring until I got home— how much did you see of Pete Fenrood?"

Back toward her, I let myself pull a cotton dress over my head before I answered, thinking, "That's it, that's why she's come." I was visited by a little, relaxing relief. Ever since her arrival I had—hadn't I?— half expected it might be something else, and here it was only Pete Fenrood. I repeated cautiously after her—Sylvia like Mother can hit close, and when you're most at ease with her may be just the time to be most on your guard—"Pete Fenrood? Oh, I used to see him around town; I rather liked him awhile——"

"Until he began seeing me, until he got a reputation for being a hothead and turning up drunk on your porch."

"All right, until he got into the fight with Clint Boyce, even if they do seem to have made up. And until he started drinking too much. In Long Meadow——"

"You're provincial."

Maybe it wasn't supercilious; maybe it was thrown at me as a flat statement and nothing more, but resentment flared.

"All right, I'm provincial." I wouldn't add to it.

"Let's not fight. I'm sorry I said that. You were seeing him quite often, though, weren't you? He took you out——"

"A dance or two; a few movies."

"That's not what I heard." She was sitting up straight by that time, not being airy any more. And I wasn't fiddling with clothes, either; we were facing each other as belligerents.

"From confessions?"

"He calls you Miss Glacier of '49. He'd scarcely do that if he hadn't made tries."

"I'd imagine that Pete's always trying. You can't have missed hearing about his womanless stretch on Saipan."

"Now you're being flip, Cathy."

"Why not? If he's your dark tall man, quick take him. For a wolf he's not too bad. A little easygoing——"

She said, "I'm twenty-nine." And then suddenly she wasn't an antagonist any longer; not in the same way; she didn't slump either; it was impossible for Sylvia to slump. She just sat there looking cool, shrewd, and sober in her elegant clothes, the foot in the brown platform pump no longer swinging. "As your mother would so brutally say, it's time I cut such losses as I may have and settled down." Then, in another quick shift, "Cathy, what about you? You needn't stick around here in this town any longer, now that your father's gone—why are you? Is it Russ Bennert?"

That was what I had shrunk from; that was what I had been afraid she might ask.

CHAPTER TWO

MY LADDER-BACK ROCKER with the tied-on plaid cushions was there close beside me; I moved to get behind it; I stood there holding it, feeling the burn, feeling the rise and fall of heat in my chest, forcing myself to look at Sylvia steadily and when I could speak making that steady too, even if nothing inside me was steady, with that heat gushing up, falling back.

I said, "To anyone who'd trouble to think about me at all, it ought to be fairly apparent why I've got to stay on in Long Meadow. Before Father died he'd been helpless for almost six years. I owe the hospital and Dr. Diebuhr so much money it'll take me half the rest of my life to pay it off. I quit school as a junior because Father couldn't work any more; I'm not skilled at anything, not trained at anything. Every penny we can squeeze goes for debts—I break the law by not carrying insurance on Father's old car—you'd probably think it incredible that two people can get by on what Mother and I live on. I want so much to get out of this town that I—that's what I—that's all I dream about, just getting away. Getting away where I might have some job training. Getting away where I wouldn't be yours and Ada's impoverished cousin. Getting away where I don't owe debts. And all right, if you want this too—more than anything else I want to get out of this town because then I can't see Russ Bennert—I want to get so far away I don't ever have to think or hear of him again."

It couldn't help to get it said. And yet, in a way, it did help too. The heat was still there in my breast, but the burn that it left was just aching, not fiery. After I had quit speaking Sylvia sat on for a moment,

13

looking across at me steadily as I looked at her, and then, for the first time since she'd entered the room, she stood up, swinging forward to me, her one hand, the one with the star sapphire, reaching to grip my arm.

She said, "You're sure of that, Cathy."

"Of course I'm sure of it."

"My dear sister Ada may have more use for a man like Lucy Hague than she does for Russ, but she'll never give up anything she's got."

"For me she'll never be asked to."

"You could sell this house, Cathy. Move to some place big enough——"

"For this house we'd get maybe enough to pay off the mortgage. Moving means a break of time between the job I've got and another—a break when we wouldn't be eating."

"Then you should—oh, why do I go into this?" As abruptly as she had flung herself into my life and my troubles she flung herself out of them, whirling herself swiftly about. To herself rather than to me she went on rather bitterly, "I know what I ought to do, don't I? I should let you get a little out of Grandfather's money—but I haven't it, Cathy. Every penny I've gotten, with the income tax I pay, with other things I've got into—oh, I know I'm prodigal, I know I've wasted it—maybe I'm changing."

Once more she turned about, and this time too she was different; entirely different than I had ever seen her; she might have been quietly and intently brooding.

"Maybe I'm going to do just what your mother said—cut my losses. It's hard to decide, though. It's——" She broke this, too, to stand cut off and distant. That ended on a little shiver; abruptly, then, she was back at being herself, lifting her shoulders in a self-deprecatory shrug.

She asked, "Why do I ever get serious?" Then, as her glance fell to her wrist, "Heavens! Two-forty! You'll need to be hurrying, won't you? And I'm so horribly thirsty. Herring, baked beans, and cole slaw, that's what I had for lunch. I went to that bazaar with Pete, and he's still hunting cooks for his glorified delicatessen."

Whatever she had come to accomplish—whether completed or not—was now, or at least so her manner said, over. From the chair knobs I was still gripping I could let my hands fall, relaxing; even if she plunged into something else she could scarcely intrude quite so painfully again.

From that harbor I offered politely, "I've got cokes in the ice-box——"

"You'd save my life, darling; you'd save all of my life."

In the release of my safety I ran downstairs. Any other girl but Sylvia, I was already beginning to think by that time, turning from an encounter past to the necessity of getting to work on time, would have come along to the kitchen, we'd have had the cokes there. In the relief of evading her, though, I was almost willing that she should be Sylvia, staying upstairs to smooth already smooth brows at my mirror, with a little finger she had licked as a cat licks.

Since she was Sylvia I not only dug out the cokes, but also two glasses, ice chips, and napkins. When I got back upstairs with my tray-ful she had turned from the mirror to something else—the toy merry-go-round she had once sent me. I keep that merry-go-round in its original shiny red box on my sewing machine, but she had it out on the dresser and was winding it by the key in its painted octagonal base.

She said amusedly, "I see you've still got it; I see it even still runs."

Among the incidents in Sylvia's past of which you'd think she wouldn't want to be reminded, certainly the episode of which that merry-go-round is a memento should have been one. She had been four-teen at the time of that escapade, I had been ten, and for some perverse reason she had been having one of the times when she sued for my com-pany. A carnival had been in town, and for almost two weeks, there, we had haunted it, prowling the penny arcade and the fun house, eating innumerable hot dogs and cones of fluff candy, riding the ferris wheel, riding—this more than anything else—on the merry-go-round. Just when in the two weeks I began noticing that some special acquaintance existed between Sylvia and the man who ran that merry-go-round I don't quite know, but gradually I became aware of it—aware of the unvoiced strike in his eyes when he saw her, aware of the lingering with which he lifted her to a pony, aware of the almost sullen and taunting set of her lips as she looked at him. I can doubt, now, whether he was much more than a boy—eighteen, perhaps, perhaps only seventeen. But to me then, and probably to Sylvia too, he was entirely a man, experienced, disturbing. I can remember exactly how he looked, tall but negligent, standing with hips and shoulders both slouched forward, so that his chest, in the shining royal blue satin blouse, looked almost concave, and his face had a look of secretive, sharp, forward-reaching. Things he said were, in the beginning, perhaps merely boastful—"For a hick town I never saw this place beat; you ought to see cities I get to—Frisco, that's the town you can have a good time in; you ought to get around in the joints they've got there. N'Orleans and St. Louey—they're big towns too—people get around in N'Orleans and St. Louey, people know what they're doing."

These generalities, after a while, grew more pointed; from somewhere and someone he had found out who Sylvia was. "Girl like you—grandfather like you got—you could have a lot of fun, even in an outfit like this one; I could get you a job selling tickets. All you'd need is a little dough, that's all, say a couple of hundred, dough you could pick up easy around a grandfather like you got—just enough for a start. We'll be going along to St. Cloud, after that Brainerd; sure, bring the kid if you want to; she's cute too. Don't forget your dough, though. St. Cloud, Brainerd——"

There must have been more to it, but that was what I heard.

Always, around him, there had been the carnival lights and the carnival sounds and the carnival color; there had been a beckoning toward things illicit and forbidden and unknown.

It was at the time when, in my own family, Father was discovering the doom of his illness, Mother was walking about white and stricken, I was experiencing my own first need for getting away. Three days after the carnival left town Sylvia and I got out on the highway and pointed our thumbs toward St. Cloud. Only in the end it had been Sylvia alone who went; when the rattletrap Ford stopped and the genial old farmer leaned out—"You girls going a piece?" I had been visited by terror, wanting nothing but to get back to the home I had left. Sylvia, though, had gone on. To meet "That guy? He ain't here no more. He got fired. Where'd you come from?" And then the St. Cloud police and the scandal, her first.

It was years later, after Ada and Russ Bennert had married, after Grandfather Gainer was dead, after she'd gone to New York, that Sylvia had sent me the merry-go-round, in what mood and in what fitful moment of memory only she could know. As she stood beside it now, as the music box in the base began twanging out its scratchy little tune, "Some think the world is made for fun and frolic, and so do I, and so do I," as the gaily painted circus-tent top twirled and the gaily painted riders on their gaily painted ponies galloped up and down, around and around, there was almost nothing but a reminiscent fondness in her eyes and on her mouth. When the toy slowed she put out a finger to the Italianate, mustachioed, waving little man affixed to the edge of the platform by one foot. "See, it's even got a man to run it . . . he's not at all like, is he? Hardly at all. Yet"—her voice and her smile both faded—"sometimes I think that's what I've been looking for, all the rest of my life—that man who ran the merry-go-round."

Then, briskly, she was done with that too; she said, "Oh, my coke. Good." But there was about her, then, a restless impatience as if she

17

now couldn't wait to be gone; I didn't find it at all unexpected when she put down her glass after little more than a swallow.

"You should have heard Grandfather roar when I got back from St. Cloud that time. He said I'd never have a penny of his, never. Then look what he did. I've got to dash quick—no, no, don't come down with me."

As unceremoniously as that she appeared to be leaving me, but in the doorway she hesitated, not glancing back, just rearranging over one arm the furs she had picked up with her gloves and her bag from my bed.

"Don't be surprised if I call you someday; there's something—well there's a little something I may want to take up with you. I might even—no, I won't say it. Just don't be surprised if I call you."

With that she was really gone; I went after her; in Long Meadow it's not considered polite not to follow a guest to the door. But as I did so, as she breezed past me to the porch with no more than a careless "Good-by now," I couldn't help feeling, in addition to the dregs of all the other emotions to which she had treated me, some exasperation. During the next five minutes, as I hustled the merry-go-round back to its box, grabbed for my handbag, and got out the car, I allowed myself to simmer. That was like Sylvia, coming here unannounced, pulling me through a cakewalk that meant heaven knew what and got nowhere, then leaving me with this teaser, suggesting she had something to tell me but not telling it, suggesting she might offer me some kind of help—which I might have to be too proud to accept—but not actually offering it.

"Oh bother," I told myself, trying to swab down the itch of aroused curiosity. "It was a whim of hers; she won't ever call me. Just one more thing leading to nothing."

Only I was wrong there; nothing was scarcely what that visit led to. And Sylvia did call me, even if, at the time, the call brought no more enlightenment than the visit. She called me that very next week at the hospital on a day which, as I have all too good reason for remembering, was Friday the second of September.

When I got to work that day Pete Fenrood was there in the hospital office, lounging with one elbow on the counter as if it were a bar, kidding with Doris Orfelt, who keeps the desk the first half of the day. It hadn't been unusual, last winter and last spring, for Pete to turn up in that position, but that hadn't been lately.

"No smoking," Doris told him as soon as she saw me. "Remember? We're a firetrap."

Grinning, Pete swung around to me. Then he lifted one foot, ground the cigarette with exaggerated care against the sole of his shoe, and deposited the stub in the breast pocket of his tan sport shirt. There'd been times, when Pete first came to town and was giving me a rush, when I'd tried to do more than like him, times when I'd tried to forget not just my indebtedness but everything else behind me. And for a while it had almost seemed to work—maybe because Pete's eyes are so intense and deep a blue, maybe because his eyebrows twist up to little peaks in the middle like the ends of a waxed mustache, maybe because he can be so terribly impudent, maybe because his mouth can sometimes be as comfort-asking as a small boy's, just as it sometimes can be demanding, outrageous, and hard, maybe because he's dark-haired and tall, with the kind of man's body that looks fragile but, when you come up against it, isn't. I had found out, last winter, that I could be more peaceful out riding with a keg of dynamite. But then one day I'd seen him with Russ, and the contrast had been too much for me. Beside Russ Bennert's blond, clean, forceful authority, Pete had looked lazy and wavering. Besides, as I was beginning to remind myself despairingly, falling in love could do me no good; I could never load anyone else with my debts. I had given Pete up in my mind long before he began seeing Sylvia. It was months since we'd had a date, but he greeted me as if it hadn't been.

19

"Sweet little Miss Law and Order. The widest brown eyes in Long Meadow, and always so friendly and giving."

I couldn't let him disturb me. "It wouldn't be friendly," I pointed out reasonably, "to set sixty-eight patients on fire. You'd get awfully tired of carrying out bodies."

"Oh, you two." Doris, as she so often says, finds me impossible to understand; Doris wants to get married, almost to any fairly nice-looking man who turns up, and she doesn't mind making it apparent. With an eye to the main chance she lingered on at the desk, fluffing her extravagant dark bangs at her compact mirror, brushing up the extravagant lashes that go with her equally extravagant dark eyes, lipsticking her mouth. "Did you ever think it could be this hot in September?" she kept the road open. "I'm stopping at Finn's for a soda."

When Pete didn't offer she tossed out a blithe "Well, good-by, both; you'll fight better when I'm gone," and then she tap-tapped her way in high heels across the asphalt tiles to the front door.

Except for Pete and Doris the lobby had been empty as I came in, but I was still moving around to the desk when it wasn't—an obviously panic-stricken woman rushed in, thrusting toward me a screaming small boy. Emergencies, in a hospital, are part of the routine; ten minutes later, when I got back to the office, the boy was in surgery and Pete, at the telephone, was being smugly efficient.

"No, no, Mrs. Harrisburg," he was intoning cheerfully, "a day or two, now, and we'll have your aunt Stella out of here. That's right—out of here in a day or two." He hung up and finished, "Right on her padded fat fanny."

Toward me he tilted a grin. "Good, huh? Kid all set? There was another call too. Sylvia."

"Oh," I said. Up to then I had still been a little immersed in the assurances I had been giving—assurances that five-year-olds seldom died while a leg was being set. At Pete's last word, though, I surfaced rapidly. "Sylvia? Did she say what——"

He leaned back, creaking distance, in the desk chair, one hand wandering toward his shirt pocket, grin intensifying.

"She was darned surprised to get me, I'll say that."

"No smoking," I produced automatically. "I'll call her right back." But it was only when I pointedly waited that he began pulling himself, something like a slide rule picking itself up by its second hinge, from the desk chair.

"Can't wait for me to be gone, can you, Cathy? I was being darn useful here, too." The hard edge that could come around his mouth was breaking up the grin, although his tone stayed light. "Did I ever tell you I dreamed you up, Cathy? Two things I drooled about, those months on Saipan—smoked spareribs and you. A girl with brown eyes, that's what I said to myself, nice big brown eyes I can fall down and drown in. A little girl, holding size, but she'll never need falsies and she'll never need a bustle. Sort of lightish brown hair, too, just like yours, held back by a ribbon and curling under in the neck. I knew exactly——"

"You knew exactly," I took it up, "what size my feet would be, and that I'd like crackerjack better than candy." I didn't look at him. "Why're we doing this?"

"Okay," he said, "I just thought I'd bring up once more that I still don't know what happened that night I went to sleep on your porch; all I'd had was three drinks."

"You probably don't know what happens when you get in fights either."

A hot blue light came up behind his eyes and his lips drew tight. "All right, I know what I'm doing when I fight. If you're going to hold one good——"

I turned away from him. "What's the use, Pete?"

He had been standing, a little bent, at the corner of the desk,

21

the rest of his body as tight as his mouth. At my last reply, though, he loosened and straightened.

"All right," he said tonelessly, "it was just a try. Should be a big night tonight—the final water show. We'd have made a good triangle—you, me, and Sylvia."

He catfooted, after that, out past the counter and across the lobby, and for a bent minute, while he was doing so, I could almost have called him back; it's easy to soften toward a man who begs. But then I once more turned away from it; Pete wasn't for me, any more than any other man was. Instead, as soon as the door closed behind him, I reached for the phone. At least, if Sylvia was calling me, I might get to know what it was she had hinted at.

As I should have expected, however, Sylvia was no more informative by phone than she'd been in my room.

"Oh, Cathy, yes." Her jerky drawl, when she answered, was a little petulant, as if she'd found it annoying of me not to be right at hand when she'd wanted me. She brushed aside explanation—"Of course, I understand about hospitals. I was just letting you know that I really do want to take this matter up with you. We could make it ten in the morning, up here at the house. Ring the bell hard if I don't answer right away; I might be at Ada's for breakfast."

Just that, all of it spoken in the same petulance, and it sounded as if she were done. If I'd had any determinations when I took up the phone, certainly one had been that I wouldn't let her discompose me again, but in spite of any such resolution I was nettled; it isn't pleasant to take quite such brusque orders.

"Look," I protested, "I don't seem to know much what this is about. If you'd give me some idea——"

She said, "I'll do that tomorrow." Then more slowly, "At least I think I'll do that tomorrow." For the first time, in this particular conversation, petulance ebbed from her tone to be replaced by something that made me see her sitting very straight, very quiet, as she had been for a while that afternoon in my room. What she said next was almost inflectionless: "You'll probably be hearing about a railroad ticket I found last night under my pillow."

I repeated, "A railroad ticket? But what possible——" only it was no use asking; in my ear was the crackle that ensues when a French receiver is dropped on its base.

"A railroad ticket," I repeated to myself, still confounded. What had she meant by that? "Really do want to take this matter up with you"—that sounded almost as if . . .

I sat back, pushing the phone away from me, and as I did so I think a light sweat broke out all over me; I could feel the damp coolness even under my knees. On the afternoon Sylvia visited me she had said, "I know what I ought to do, don't I? I should let you get a little out of Grandfather's money. . . ." Only I had scarcely given ear to it then; she hadn't spoken as if it were anything she actually contemplated; she'd added, "But I haven't it, Cathy; I haven't it," and that was the part I had been able to believe. Royalty rights in two iron mines were what she had inherited from Grandfather Gainer, but the way she spent money she could have little over.

This phone call, though. "Just letting you know that I really do want to take this matter up with you"—and a railroad ticket.

In a way it wasn't just once Mother and I had been excluded from that particular wealth which had been Grandfather Gainer's, it was twice. It was through a none too straight land deal that Grandfather Gainer got most of his holdings—he sold land near Ely to my other grandfather, Carl Kingman, retaining for himself—in small print—the mineral rights which later meant iron and a thick river of profit. Grandfather Kingman had stripped himself bare of his own fortune, trying to cut in on that river. That didn't mean, though, that people hadn't said, "You can't tell me some smart lawyer sometime——"

Mother, who had been roared from her father's house when she married his worst enemy's son, had warned me never to let any such possibility start eating me. Father had said so too. Just the same . . .

Or suppose it wasn't that. Suppose it was just one more whim of Sylvia's, as capricious as hundreds of others she'd had. I couldn't want her to give me money, but suppose she offered me a loan. Enough so I could get to a business college. Enough to tide me over until I could find a better job. In some warmer climate, for Mother's sake. Not a big loan—just enough to be an open door. I could pay her back, pay off the other debts . . .

Queer, when you want something desperately. What you want can obscure almost everything else.

CHAPTER THREE

IF I STILL RETAINED any of my wild hope next morning it had been cut down to something at least a little more reasonable. Sylvia, I had been able to remind myself by that time, might be given to outbursts of generosity, but not unless she had an ax to grind. And if I hadn't gotten around to these more sober second thoughts Mother would have supplied them for me, at the breakfast table.

"For heaven's sake, Cathy." Mother, in fact, seemed more disturbed even than I'd thought she'd be. Most of the time, in the unexpressed way that seems natural for a mother and daughter living together, we are quite fond of each other, but there are obvious moments when she finds me lacking, just as—even if this is one of the things you are never supposed to admit—there are times when she irritates me. Mother and I are supposed to look alike; we both have brown eyes and brown hair. Only where I don't need padding anywhere, Mother could use it all over. I can remember when Mother was gay and witty, when she moved with a kind of shine around her, but that was before Father got sick. Now she's sometimes impatient and bitter; the glance she flicked at me across the toaster and the coffeepot wondered to heaven when I would collect sense.

"Sylvia's a will-o'-the-wisp. If you think anything different——"

"She seemed a little changed, though, Mother. Oh, I know it's impossible, but we could use money; look at your knuckles, against that coffeepot."

At that we should have detoured into the side road we so often travel; there are things to do for arthritis, things such as getting shots and keeping out of hot water and trying New Mexico for a winter, but Mother, who thought no sum too big for Father's care, won't spare a penny for herself. This morning, though, she just dismissed it—"Bother my knuckles"—to return, in a troubled kind of way, to my proposed visit.

"I wish you weren't going there, Cathy. We'll make out somehow; we'll have to think up something I can do. Maybe I could work too. . . .

"I wish you weren't going." She even waited to repeat it when I came downstairs again, dressed. "A girl like Sylvia—you can't tell what she's up to. Her life must be full of things we don't know about. I'd rather you still didn't have anything to do with her."

That, of course, was a reference to an old decree laid down after I came so close to running away; from the look on Mother's face, right then, it might almost have been coming alive again.

"For goodness' sake, Mother," I had to remind her, "Sylvia can't exactly be leading me up any alley; I'm twenty-five."

"Oh, I know." She agreed to that. "It's only . . . it's—well . . ." Before I could forestall her she had my pink summer coat out of the closet and stood holding it for me with her swollen hands. What followed came in an abruptly halted rush. "It's just that I read her palm for her, at the bazaar. I don't believe in my palm reading, you know that, Cathy. But——"

"But what?" I swung around to her, astonishment creeping in on me from this different source. Was this Mother?

"Oh, I know." Her eyes avoided mine. "It was just—well, an impression. I got—I feel as if Sylvia might even be in danger. Or dangerous."

I repeated, "In danger? Or dangerous?" By that time I was wholly incredulous. "Mother. This is me. Sylvia. Long Meadow."

"Oh, I know," she replied, subdued. For still an instant, though, the look on her face was one of resistance. She let it go, after a while, but she was at the door watching me, her hands on the spring of the screen, when I ran down the back steps.

That was the time I should have listened.

Driving is one of the things in which I can usually lose myself; it's not the physical aspects of the place I live in that I find so hard to bear. Long Meadow is set in a country that's high, clear, and quiet—not wild, exactly, but free and with an undercurrent of harshness. Near by are the Hauteurs, that dividing ridge that's the core of the continent and from which the continent's rivers run north, south, east and west; not far away, too, is Lake Hernando de Soto, the Mississippi's great ultimate reservoir; it's hard to drive for two miles in any direction without meeting water—a big lake or a little one, deep or shallow, but always tree-rimmed, always blue and rustling, always filled with water that lies clear and cold in a clean pebbled bed. In between there are rolling fields, thick woodlands, patches of brush, and low bumpy hills, the roadsides are edged by pine, birch, and Oak, by scrub brush, sumac, milkweed, gold-enrod, chokecherries, daisies, and poison ivy. It's a country of stormy white winters, late springs, too fervent summers, and chill threatening autumns; Pete Fenrood said once that anyone could live in California, but that to live in Minnesota you had to be tough. Maybe he's right; it's not the toughness I mind so much as being caged in it.

This morning, though, as I made my way across town, I had little thought for climate or country or my place inside it; I had little attention for the snug small white houses centered so neatly on their green lawns, no eye for the salvias and zinnias edging the front porches; I was barely aware of the clamorous jam-packed helter-skelter traffic downtown; I scarcely even noticed when Sixth Street opened into the spaciousness of the Shore Road. If the ideas I'd had about Sylvia were ridiculous, I was tartly thinking, then surely what Mother had brought up was more so. Maybe forty-eight was no more an age of wisdom than twenty-five.

Only when I woke to where I was, just in time to turn the Pontiac's nose up the Gainer driveway toward the Gainer cedars, did I shake off the froth of that small family friction to focus on what was ahead. For the first time in my life, now—and this alone might have set my blood racing—I was about to set foot in Gainer House.

If Sylvia has meant certain things to me all of my life, so too has Gainer House. Often and often I've driven out of my way just to see it, sitting great, soft, white, and nested at the top of its terrace, with the rippling expanse of Meadow Lake, on the other side of the Shore Road, to light it, and the immense deep blue clumps of its cedars to shadow it. John Gainer built that house at the time of his marriage, more than sixty years ago, and even though I'd never been inside it, Mother had grown up in it; almost as if I myself had lived there I knew the deep-cushioned couches inside its bay windows, I knew the cedar-green light shaking across its beds in the morning, I knew the bayberry smell of its candlelit festivities—for all the modernizing Sylvia and Ada had done, they hadn't thrown out the original candle set and crystal-hung chandeliers. At the front of the house stand two wide fluted pillars, resting on the lowest of the simple, semicircular front steps and supporting not a second-floor porch or a balcony but the roof; the door set within this approach is as simple as the steps, paneled and white but surrounded by delicate ironwork in a glass frame; the windowed wings fling out far to each side, to be lost in the cedars.

When John Gainer built the house his parents had been living; for them he had walled off a separate apartment in the left wing, and it was this small domicile Sylvia kept for herself, leaving the main house to her sister and Russ Bennert. I had heard a little of what to expect from Sylvia's apartment; Sylvia's crowd in Long Meadow wasn't sparing of tongue. Just the same, it would be something to see it, and when I parked the Pontiac in a wide graveled area before the remodeled barn at the rear and walked toward the side of the house my lips kept on getting dry; right at that moment I think I was almost as exercised by the entry I was about to make as I was by the prospect of finding out, finally, what Sylvia so elusively had been driving toward; certainly I had dismissed Mother's small worry.

The door at the south side, approached by flagstones set into the grass, and thickly hedged by the cedars, was a smaller replica of the one at the front; I stood in the sun on its single white doorstep and ran the palm of my right hand down the side of my fuzzy pink coat before I lifted it to the brass knocker centered on the door.

The sound the knocker made was sharp but quickly swallowed; the brisk rap-rap seemed to vanish, drowning in a thickness inside. What was it Sylvia had said? "Ring the bell hard . . ." Behind an intruding whisk brush of cedar needles I found the small pearly Circle; the chimes it set off ran musically but distinctly inside the house. "I might be at Ada's for breakfast," Sylvia also had said, or she might, as far as that went, be asleep yet. I could imagine her upstairs in her opulent bed, drowsing and stretching, frowning at the chimes, forgetting, remembering, groaning to herself, "Why did I?" and then being insolently and dawdlingly slow about getting herself from bed to negligee to bathroom to mirror to door. I could afford to wait, though; right then, for some reason, I felt tolerant toward her; the air around me was water-clear, water-cool, and smelled sweetly of cedar; even if I got nothing else out of this visit, I told myself, trying to keep expectation down, I was at least having this moment of anticipation.

No sound whatever, though, came from behind the door I was facing, and after a minute or two it began to seem that the air about me was almost too quiet. A bird or two cheeped somewhere, a saw rasped far away, on the Shore Road below the terrace cars announced themselves, crescendo and diminuendo. Once more I pressed thumb to button, considering, this time, as the chimes again sounded, that it might very well be only five or six hours since Sylvia got to bed. "We'd make a good triangle—you, me, and Sylvia." Sylvia, of course, had been out with Pete last night, at the water show. She might, in addition to the sapphire, be wearing a new ring this morning. . . .

When I pressed the button that third time the chimes inside jangled. Sylvia, after all, was the one who had asked me here, she was the one who had insisted she wanted to see me; sleepy or not, at breakfast or not, she needn't leave me on the doorstep forever. Then, when the door before me still gave out no sound, I was abruptly aware of a feeling of emptiness. As if Sylvia wasn't and never had been in the bed upstairs, as if the chimes rang for no ears, as if the very sun I stood in was empty and its warmth wasn't supposed to be felt, as if even the scent of the cedars was empty and wasn't supposed to be smelled.

Intensely aware of that emptiness, I stood there hesitating. I could go home: Sylvia might have forgotten she had asked me. She might—and this was all too likely—have capriciously reversed herself, deciding she had nothing for me after all.

Or—and this of course was the more reasonable action—I could go looking for her. Russ, by this time, would be at his office downtown. Ada wouldn't welcome me. Florence Squires, though, in her kitchen . . .

That, then, was where I went, stepping back along the flagstones to the wide trellised porch at the rear. Florence, when I tapped at the screen door, stood at the sink in the east wall, washing dishes, but she came immediately, wiping leathery brown arms on her apron, to let me in.

"Miss Kingman, don't see you often up here." The words might carry a small curiosity but the voice didn't; Florence, in spite of the Indian mixture that gives her coarse pulled-back black hair and small darting black eyes, is New England Yankee enough to be hard to shake.

At my explanation she snorted. "Sylvia? Just asleep, that's what she is. Likely got plenty to sleep off. Go on back and keep ringing. You'll get her."

"Florence, is that the bakery—oh."

I might have guessed, I thought wordlessly as a swinging door behind Florence thrust open, that I shouldn't have expected to penetrate even as much as an inch into this house without rousing Ada.

30

Of the things I sometimes struggle against, sometimes give way to, one is a fairly vehement dislike for Ada. Not because she's Russ Bennert's wife, though if I'm to be honest I suppose that must enter into it; still I hope I can be fair enough to know it's not her fault that she reached marrying age at the same time as Russ; I can't hold it against her that she loved him and wanted to marry him. I don't count it against her that she keeps Lucy Hague at her heels. What I dislike about Ada is something personal—a kind of harsh, unhappy grasping. That she has causes for discontent everyone knows; it isn't any secret that up to the day he died Grandfather Gainer made her his pet; she was the one who had the pony and groom, she had the trip to Europe when she was a junior in college; Sylvia, always in hot water, teetered on the edge of being thrown out just as Mother had been. If it had been a shock to everyone else when John Gainer left only twenty-five thousand to Ada and all the rest of his holdings to Sylvia, it must have been a good deal more than that to Ada. Sylvia had been generous with her, making her an allowance, letting her have the house, but that didn't mean Ada was satisfied. "Nice for me," she said openly, "my own sister's hanger-on." With Russ too—anywhere, over a bridge table or to his business associates—she was peevishly dissatisfied. "All this building, I can't say it brings in too much." "If he's going into politics why doesn't he get somewhere; all he does so far is throw around money. I get more company out of Lucy." Yet at the same time she complained she clung: "No one else is giving Sylvia's going-away party, I am." "Maybe"—this was while Russ was in the Army—"there aren't any living quarters around this camp he's building in Vermont, but I'm going." Some people think she's good-looking—slight, with a dark, gypsyish, somehow clever face, but in the past half dozen years she's looked more and more restless, as if she were driven by some force that kept her feet forever hurrying, her hands forever gesturing, her eyes forever burning.

31

Certainly they burned as they caught sight of me. Any time Ada has a chance to snub me she makes a good job of it.

"Oh," she said again, "oh." Each "oh" was a little more brittle than the last "I didn't know," she went on in a sharp rush to Florence, "that you had anyone up here wanting anything. Excuse me for intruding. But when the bakery man gets here I'd like to know it, please."

She would have sailed out on that, but I couldn't quite let her.

"Sylvia asked me here," I offered, straight down the center. "I'm in your kitchen only because she doesn't answer her door."

"Of course, I should have known it was Sylvia," Ada tossed back, "Sylvia has the queerest tastes of anyone I know." And before I could answer that one she had herself around the door.

Getting angry with Ada didn't get anyone anywhere, but I stood where I was, breathing hard.

Florence helped me. "Nice feelings," she commented costively, "that's one of the things we got most of, around here. Look, Miss Kingman, if it wasn't we had that bridge party last night, and all the county commissioners coming for a big dinner tonight, I'd go around with you; all the time, up here, we got to have parties. But you go on back there, see if the door's open; Sylvia's a log to wake up; go on in."

"Thanks," I said, swallowing part, at least, of what I had to swallow.

As I went back by the way I had come, though, I was certain of one thing: Sylvia, if she ever wanted to see me again, could good and well see me elsewhere. When I looked over at my car, sitting nose out in front of the barn, the sun on its battered fenders sending out splinters of light, I was gripped by such an impulse to throw the whole thing up that I don't know myself what kept me—maybe some inherited streak of doggedness, maybe perversity, maybe not wanting to explain lamely later, "Well, you didn't answer, so I left." Besides, curiosity still itched; I wanted to know about that railroad ticket; I wanted to know what Sylvia had been driving at. Her car wasn't gone—that was one thing; I could see it parked in the old barn, beside Ada's black Buick.

So I went back to Sylvia's door. Once more I rang at it. And when, still again, there was no answer, I turned the doorknob, pushed open the unlocked door, and stepped through to the room beyond.

As I had half expected, the room into which I then entered was at once strange and not strange. The size of it I knew—"fifty feet if it's an inch"—the huge crystal chandelier overhead, the graceful stairway curving upward at the right, with its mahogany rail and delicate white spindles, the purple-gray carpet—"Come on over here to this store window, Cathy; that's the same carpet your cousin Sylvia is getting in her place." I knew the ceiling-high, wall-wide, feather-print draperies at the huge picture window Sylvia had had installed in her lake-facing wall, I knew the low black lacquer tables, the soft low striped chairs, the glass-block and chromium bar, the flagstone wall of the fireplace. Only I would never have guessed that, in morning and with the draperies all pulled, it would be so dim and so quiet. With the door closed all that water-clear light from outside was cut off, so were all near sounds of living, all the known company of Florence Squires and even Ada. Within that room there was nothing but quiet—deep-piled, foot-swallowing, enclosed.

I called, "Sylvia, you around here?" The same words she had used in calling me. My voice died in small jerky echoes.

More loudly I called again, "Sylvia, you around here?" Still no answer.

And then once more I was seized by that sense of emptiness I had had on the doorstep outside; I turned, my hand on the brass of the doorknob, wanting to be gone from there, not caring, right then, whether the questions with which I had come were ever answered or not. But I couldn't quite go either; my feet swung me around again; my feet advanced me of their own accord into the shades of the room. I seemed to be saying to myself, "I can't run. I can't just turn and run." My feet found the carpeted stairs and began mounting them; I felt myself rising through the quiet; I felt myself numbing.

The room upstairs was lighter, a little; the pink velvet draperies over the white nylon curtains were thinner; light pricked out pink velvet chairs.

I stepped toward the bundle on the bed.

Maybe the first movement I made, standing there, looking down, was to try to cover myself more completely with the stuff of my coat. Because I was wearing a thin white peasant blouse and a full black peasant skirt that day too, just as Sylvia was.

Only I was alive in mine. Sylvia wasn't, in hers.

CHAPTER FOUR

I HADN'T ANY DOUBT she was dead; there couldn't be any doubt she was dead. After a while I began to be conscious that in the room which had been so quiet there was a horrible deep sound of breathing, my breathing. There wasn't much room in me, yet, for full fright, but fright was beginning; I shut my eyes, wondering if against the screen of my eyelids I would see the same sight: purple-gray satin quilt, and over the foot of it . . .

It was the gasp of my breathing that made fear grow bigger. That and the kick of a need to hear quiet shattered. I reached to touch the blond hair, reached to touch the bare arm flung almost to the floor; under my fingers the cold flesh seemed to move. I bent further, automatically, to pick something up from the floor.

"No, I mustn't." The, whisper was voiced, but seemed to come from a monitor outside me. "I'll have to get the sheriff. I can't help her. She's dead."

I ran then, ran soundlessly, as if something pursued me, until I got to the bottom of the stair. The big living room still swam in its murk; the whisper said, "It's not true; I'm seeing things," and I half turned to run back upstairs, as if at a second intrusion I would find things different—Sylvia at the dressing table, brush to hair, or coming from her bathroom. But then I knew, in the first surge of being past paralysis, that what I had seen was the way things were. In addition to my breathing I could hear my heart thudding; one hand against my throat was icy.

"A phone," I thought. "Where is it? But maybe I mustn't use it—not the phone in here." Ahead of me, like a beacon, appeared the image of Florence Squires. . . .

Later, and not too much later, walking what seemed endlessly up and down in the main living room of the Gainer house, I could reproach myself for inadequacy. The last thing I should have done was to run for the kitchen. When I'd reached there Ada had been there again too, with the man from the bakery. I'd blurted, "Sylvia, she's——" and after that it had already been too late to do better; Ada had stared at me, the dark skin of her intense thin face drawing visibly closer to the bones, and then she'd run past me. When the rest of us caught up with her she had dragged Sylvia higher on the bed and was senselessly shaking her, slapping at the terrible blue of the face, beating at the hands. It was only after we'd gotten her back to this house that we'd even been able to call the sheriff.

At the front door, every so often, Emil Hasko, one of the sheriff's men, said, "Sorry, Mrs. Balfanz, sorry, Mrs. Yelland, sorry, Mr. Paradoux, I guess it's better you don't come in. Sorry, Mr. Hague, sure I know you're a friend of the family, but the sheriff told me who he wanted in here, and he didn't say you." From front and side windows I could see the changing, growing crowd on the lawn. From the south wall behind me there came, or seemed to come, sounds of the slamming arrival of cars, the tramp of loud feet, the rumble of men's death-awed and low-ered voices. Sheriff Waslewski, town police, state police—they were all here by this time; Waslewski had already spoken to me shortly as he came in. They were all busy, on the other side of that wall, deciding how Sylvia had come by her death. They would walk in here, after a while, to tell Ada . . .

When the door finally opened I whirled to it, but it wasn't the sheriff or anyone from the police, it was Russ. This was his setting, but it was one in which I didn't know him. He stood just inside the doorway, his head with its glinting crisp hair held well back, and his big body as erect and solid as ever, but his gray eyes looked shock-sick, and his gen-erous long mouth seemed to have slacked and loosened. Always, when I see him, I'm shaken by an impulse toward him before I can create its opposite; I'd probably have given five years of my life if I could have walked openly to rest my face against his shoulder. But there were the years of discipline—and Emil Hasko in the hall—to remind me I couldn't.

As if he were echoing my thought and my feeling of strangeness, he asked, "Cathy, what are you doing here?" He stepped forward, both hands reaching toward me, clasping the hands I had to return to him, then dropping them as he too remembered.

He said, "I've just come from over there. I can't believe it. Not right here in the house. Not Sylvia." His lips twisted, and there was a movement in his body as if he would have liked to sink down, taking me with him. He continued, "You know, there was a while I——"

He didn't have to go on; I knew what he meant. For a while, just after he'd gotten out of college, there'd been a time when he had gaily squired Sylvia almost as much as Ada; Long Meadow gossip had wondered which one would get him.

Head lowering, he went on slowly, almost laboriously, "I don't know, I—get fond of people. It's sometimes hard to distinguish—Cathy, if you remember that evening——"

He didn't have to particularize there either; the evening of which he spoke is going to stay sharp in my memory no matter what else fades away. It was an evening shortly before his marriage to Ada, when he had carelessly halted his whistling way past our house to talk to me a moment as I sat alone in the porch swing. As he was leaving he'd looked at me with the amused, elder-brother affection he'd for so long shown toward me; he'd bumped under my chin with the back of his hand and said, "I'm going to hate the guy that gets you, Cathy." I'd lost my head; I'd clung to him, crying, "You, Russ, you; don't marry Ada, you can't marry Ada," and he'd stood tightly holding me, rubbing his cheek against my hair, he'd whispered as if he were amazed and lost, "But you're too young for me, Cathy, too sweet . . ." Only I hadn't been too young.

He said now, low, "I was wrong that night, Cathy; I should have waited for you. Only it's no good now, either, I see that forever; it's your right to start out with someone who hasn't been—used." His mouth at the last twisted with a more cruel bitterness than I'd ever seen on it, but when I made a swift movement toward him he drew as swiftly away from me, his shoulders rising, his head jerking back.

"I'd never have told you that, Cathy, if I weren't so shaken; I've been fighting myself not to say it." His right hand moved over his face, and when it had passed he looked almost composed—no more than haggard, no more than heavily troubled. He said, "Sometimes I think—everything goes. Ada. I'll have to get to her. I suppose she's upstairs."

I nodded, finding it hard to make my voice carry words, though at last it did. "With Dr. Diebuhr. I'm sorry, Russ. Sorry I did it so badly."

"Oh," he said. "Then you found her. I'll go on up—Waslewski told me he'd be in soon. He'll want to see all of us."

He moved away from me, his straight, wide-shouldered back receding evenly, directly, across the hall and up the stairs. In the living room where he had left me I stood in my old and my ever new torment; hearing him say, now at last, that he loved me—that was balm such as no other balm could be. But at the same time despair freshened: I could only look forward, as he did, not to what I might want but to the way things were.

After a while I went back to my pacing. I had already given up the questions with which I had come; whatever it was Sylvia had had to tell me, I'd never know it now, not from her. If Sylvia had been opening a door for me, I'd never know that either, not now. From the first instant I had looked at her there on her bed I had known without thinking, known without comprehending, that hers was no normal death; she had been thrown, a deed done, to the place where she lay. Yet somehow I had blindly expected that this was a horror that must resolve itself quickly; death in Long Meadow, no matter what shock or what grief it might bring in as freight, usually resolved itself soon. I had thought that Waslewski or some other officer, entering, must make clear not just how Sylvia died, but who had killed her. Now, shrinkingly, reminded of the tangle of my own life, I began to have a different perception. I myself had seen that room in which Sylvia lay; I'd seen nothing to point a finger. Maybe finding out who killed Sylvia wouldn't be simple; maybe it would go on and on, producing what troubles I could only guess.

By the time Nick Waslewski did lumber into the living room, a clear-cheeked young man in the belted brown khaki uniform of the state police unobtrusively behind him, I was pulled taut by waiting, and a single glance at Nick's orange-red face was enough to tell me my second idea must be closer to truth than my first; his was no air of successful completion. If anything he looked disgruntled, his hat pushed far back on the stubble of his red hair, his bleached brows pulled inward in a frown, the lower lip of his small mouth—small anyway in the expanse it punctuated—thrust crossly forward.

"Here's a nice thing," he said. "Rich young girl—mess like that."

Disgust, I thought. Now there's an emotion I wouldn't have expected, not from a sheriff in relation to murder. For a moment, hysterically, I could almost have laughed. But then Nick glanced across at me, hitching his brown corduroys toward his thick waist as he did so, settling his shoulders in the rubbed leather jacket, and there was a getting set in the movements, there was a careful, weighing speculativeness in his pale aquamarine eyes, that made any impulse toward laughter drain swiftly away.

He said, "Miss Kingman, you were Sylvia Gainer's first cousin, that right?"

It didn't take him long to accomplish. When he stepped in he had been one person in that room, I'd been another; now he was an inquisitor and I his subject, or maybe there was a closer analogy—his might have been the eyes looking into a microscope and I might have been the bug on the slide.

"Yes," I agreed, and then, sharply, because I didn't want to accept the position into which he was forcing me, "Have you found out at all yet what happened—who killed her?"

His thick forefinger pointed out an overstuffed chair in green leather before the big window.

"Sit down, Miss Kingman. Who killed Sylvia Gainer—that's something we're starting right now to find out. Not too good blood between her and you, was there?"

In the chair to which I had obediently dropped—a chair so deep I left relatively few traces—I struggled to the forward edge and sucked in a deep breath. Of the ideas I had covered while I waited, somehow I hadn't reached to this, that I might be suspect. Finding out I could be was like being tossed into a winter-cold lake.

"You mean you suspect *me?*" I produced squeakily. "But you can't." Self-defensive logic got its machinery going with a whirr, and one of its by-products was heat. "Go back and look at her. She's been dead for hours—even I know that much. The congestion. I got here at ten o'clock——"

"Slow down, Miss Kingman. I'm just asking questions. Know anyone else had it in for her?"

"No, I don't. Yes—well, I suppose there must be lots of people——" I floundered with it, still too much on the defensive to do any seeking outside myself, though it was a little calming to find suspicion seemed general rather than specific. "You know how Sylvia was."

"Uh." He acknowledged that with a grunt and a short spurt of silence. Then, "You didn't answer that question I was getting at, about what you had to do with Miss Gainer."

My mouth opened, then closed. It wasn't just the three times I'd seen her this summer that came into my mind; it was all I'd known of her—the child across the aisle in church, the girl who'd brought me the marbles—suddenly it hit me that what I had had of Sylvia was all there'd be. I hadn't wanted to cry when I looked at her dead, I had been too filled then by shock and horror; I hadn't wanted to cry when I was talking to Russ. But now tears stung the insides of my eyelids and through my body pressed the suffocation of a grief that couldn't be less heavy because I would never have expected to feel it.

Waslewski gave me a minute, no more. He pressed, "You didn't answer."

I said, blinking, "I guess I liked her. In a way, anyhow. I——" I couldn't tell him what I myself didn't know.

He let it pass. "You must of had some reason for coming up here."

So thin, so far away, so blocked off now by other emotions, why had I come here? I began, "She asked me to——"

So far the young state patrolman had been wandering, apparently aimlessly, about the long room; now I was aware that a second pair of weighing and judicious eyes was on me. Stumblingly I brought out what there was—yesterday's phone call, the rather disordered visit behind that. When I had dredged up everything that seemed in any way applicable the two men stood silent a moment, and the next question—or statement—came not from Nick but from the state policeman.

"You have no idea, at all, then, what Miss Gainer may have wanted to talk to you about."

I shook my head. "She didn't say anything at all specific. She mentioned that railroad ticket——"

"We didn't find any such railroad ticket in her apartment. You're sure she said railroad ticket?"

"I couldn't have been wrong about that."

"Try repeating Miss Gainer's exact words, please."

I did so, carefully; after all there hadn't been so many of them.

"Hm." The young state patrolman uttered a syllable of admission. "Didn't you even guess what she was driving at?"

"Well . . ." I had been guilty of a small concealment, but abruptly I gave it up. "I thought it might possibly have been about money. Sylvia knew I was anxious to get out of Long Meadow——"

"So this morning you turn up here at ten o'clock, expecting nothing but that Miss Gainer might hand out a check."

"Oh no. I mean I—I thought only of a loan. I'm her cousin——"

"Go over what happened this morning."

I seemed to have covered a good many answers already; my lips felt harsh and dry, my hand closed for support and comfort on the car keys in my lap. Carefully, though, I did as bidden. My first efforts at Sylvia's door, my trip to the kitchen, the return.

"You say it was Mrs. Bennert dragged the body up on the bed. Where was it when you found it?"

I told that too.

"Look at her at all?" Both men seemed to have drawn back from me, but not to lessen their scrutiny; it was more as if they drew back to tighten it.

"I touched her hair—I don't know why. Then I knew I ought to phone, but I thought of fingerprints——"

"Look at her neck?"

I said, "No," but I was being visited with a fresh inrush of horror. Her neck. That meant it was broken, or she was strangled. I seemed to have to go on talking, even if it meant nothing. "I think her blouse had fallen down over her throat, a little. It was thin white and embroidered in flowers, red flowers. Her skirt was black, but it was embroidered too, in a wide band of red flowers around the bottom. Hand-embroidered. I was wearing—I'm wearing——"

My hands rose once again to tug at my coat.

Nick said, "Uh. I noticed." He took a half turn away from me to let his sharp gaze rest for a moment on the man beside him before he turned it back.

"Miss Kingman, while you were upstairs in that apartment, did you look at anything else beside Miss Gainer?"

Anything else? I tried to build honesty in that answer too.

"Not in particular. I got a general impression—shades drawn, and several pink chairs, and a door on the other side to a bathroom——"

"Nothing specific?"

What had gone before was sharply focused, but I had a feeling that what was being asked now had a different focus, had a kind of gathering in. Against it I could only draw myself together, armoring myself with a blanket expectancy.

"I can't remember—no."

"You didn't look at the desk."

Swiftly but unrewardingly I sought back.

"I don't even remember there was a desk."

"Between the two windows. Miss Kingman, when you guessed Miss Gainer might be speaking to you about money, you're sure you didn't have something more concrete to go on?"

At least the third time that question had been gotten at in one form or another; I could only repeat what I'd said before.

"Neither you nor your mother have performed any service for which Miss Gainer might be paying you?"

When I'd shaken my head both men once more stood silent in their deliberative scrutiny, then the state patrolman shot another question.

"Perhaps you or your mother knew something about Miss Gainer that she'd rather have kept concealed."

My mouth opened on that one; perhaps I again began shaking my head, but contrary emotions intervened. So far—for a long time, anyway—I had been replying to everything asked of me in a sort of docility. As the implications of the last query struck me, though, impulses I'd been repressing boiled over.

"Are you trying to infer that Mother or I might have been *blackmailing* Sylvia? If you are, it's the most ridiculous, the most impossible— if you're just hitting around in the dark on this——"

"Sit down again, Miss Kingman." This time it wasn't Nick Waslewski's finger that pointed me back. "We're not hitting in the dark. Up there on top of Miss Gainer's desk—very openly on top of Miss Gainer's desk—we found her checkbook. There's a completed check there, on top of the pad, signed by Miss Gainer and made out to a Julia Kingman, who I understand is your mother. A check for six thousand dollars."

I stared at him, that was all I could do; stared while the blood drained away from my skin and my mind, leaving both of them chill; stared until slowly, that same blood came warmingly back. Sylvia had meant it, then; she had meant what she said; she had wanted to help me; she had been opening a door for me; she had intended letting me have a loan. No, not a loan; if the check were made out to Mother that sounded more like a gift—repairing, to that extent at least, Mother's disinheritance.

At first, what I felt as I faced it was a fresh access of grief.

I said miserably, "We don't have it coming. Neither Mother nor I thought she really intended——"

Nick didn't loosen.

"Listen, Miss Kingman. I don't know entirely how this works. Maybe since that check wasn't given to you it's no good at all. I think I know this much—checks made out by people who turn up dead don't get cashed—not until they've gone through probate, and unless you can prove you've got six thousand coming I doubt if you'll get it under any circumstances—not if I know Mrs. Bennert. All right, then. Wouldn't you like to turn up a reason or two why that check was made out?"

I could only shake my head. This check, then, would be like

almost everything else in my life—it would go glimmering before I even had it. Waslewski had only to say, "Not if I know Mrs. Bennert," to make a contrary wind blow hot in the face of my self-reproach, but I couldn't manufacture reasons.

"I've told you all there is."

This too was received in silence. After a minute or two Nick shook himself slightly, and now he did loosen, as if the check had been a card up his sleeve he had played for nothing. His hands thrust deep into his pockets, his gaze grew more ruminative than piercing, before he swung about to his partner.

"Anything else you'd like to ask?"

"I think so." The state patrolman stood very still one arm across his chest, the other holding a cigarette. His eyes, as they kept up their gaze at me, had a round, almost ingenuous look; his forehead was as smooth, his cheeks as freshly colored, as if he were a five-year-old, but I didn't need to be told he was no kindergartner.

"You work in a hospital Miss Kingman."

"That's right."

"Many emergencies?"

"Some."

"Usually lose your head?"

"Not often any more."

"Don't you rather think you did, today?"

"Yes," I admitted, and then, finding the pressure uncomfortable again, "Our emergencies don't usually run to murder."

"And you were quite sure, right away, that what you were look-ing at was murder, weren't you, Miss Kingman? Not a heart attack. Not suicide, from sleeping pills, let's say. But murder."

"Yes, I was certain." Maybe I hadn't been, not that clearly. But it hadn't taken me long.

What he might have said next I don't know; he was building up tension again, and certainly he must have had some purpose. But that tension snapped short—snapped to a jumble of voices at the door, and then Emil Hasko being emphatic and distinguishable.

"They sure do want you, Pete; you go right in."

CHAPTER FIVE

USUALLY WHEN I'VE SEEN PETE he's been rather devil-may-care, but he wasn't being devil-may-care then. The shock that had shaken and loosened Russ had tightened Pete; he walked into the room with his eyes whipping swiftly around it, the muscles of his long body obviously tight, as if he were a fighter advancing from cover into enemy territory.

He said flatly, "I was out in the country; I came up as soon as I heard. It doesn't seem possible—she was perfectly all right when I left her last night." He halted, apparently swallowing something else. "Any idea what happened?"

Nick's big head shook slowly. "We know she got choked to death," he admitted. "Not too much more. I guess you were a friend of hers."

"Yes," Pete said. "Yes. Guess I was." He dropped into a chair, his thin shoulders sagging a little as he ran his hands over his face. When he went on his voice was still lower, but a little less strained. "In the Army you expect it. But a thing like this, and a girl——" His hands dropped and he looked over from his chair to mine, nodding. "Hello, Cathy."

"Hello," I said. I still sat where I was, in the chaos and confusion to which my questioning and the revelation of the check had brought me, torn still by self-reproach, ruffled still by the small contrary wind which Waslewski so artfully had fanned, not yet oriented to the fact that my inquisitors were leaving me to turn their attention to Pete, although I could see why they'd do so—he might have been the last person to see her alive.

"This here is Lieutenant Kopp," Nick offered an introduction he hadn't considered necessary for me, and slowly Pete got to his feet again.

"We don't want to make it hard for anybody—not unnecessarily hard." Lieutenant Kopp might almost have been any young man, affably holding out his hand to another. "You're a newcomer here in Long Meadow—meet Miss Gainer here?"

"New York." Once up, Pete stayed up, accepting the light Lieutenant Kopp offered his inevitable cigarette.

"Long ago?"

"Year and a half."

"You can understand why we've got to ask questions like this—see much of her there?"

"Date or two." Pete was still being laconic, but when his questioner waited he amplified. "Met at a party—guy I'd known in the Army. I had this idea of running sort of a community kitchen—place where the kitchen would support me and I could hunt and fish. What she told me about Long Meadow sounded good."

"You'd never heard of Long Meadow except through Miss Gainer."

"That's right. I'd been working for a place in New York—Wernick's Catering."

My muscles, by this time, had begun to uncramp; I hadn't realized, until I tried moving, how tight I had gotten. Held as I still was by the snarls inside me, I yet had to feel mental tentacles reaching out for these other questions and these other answers. Waslewski and Lieutenant Kopp were now regarding Pete with the same dispassionate but in-cutting scrutiny they had accorded me, and even as I recognized it I recoiled with at least part of the rejection I had felt for suspicion against myself—whoever had killed Sylvia, it couldn't be Pete, whom I had almost grown fond of. As the interrogation continued I found myself listening with a purpose that could only be divided—wanting desperately to hear, in Pete's answers, some clue to the perplexities into which I'd been plunged, dreading to hear something that might be incriminating.

Lieutenant Kopp gave an effect of asking his next question casually.

"You may have been—more than a friend of Miss Gainer's?"

Pete's eyes glinted darkly toward me.

"Not yet."

"At the time you came out here, then, you were just friends."

"Hardly that much. We got more friendly this summer. When I met her she seemed to be busy in a few other directions. A girl like Miss Gainer, with all that money, can have a fair-size crew around her in New York, if she wants it."

"Any of those friends out here now, besides yourself?"

In return Pete asked carefully, "Ash tray? Yeah, I see one," and moved past Nick to a table, where with equal care he ground out his only partially smoked cigarette in a crystal oak leaf.

Nick interjected, "If you're thinking about the Boyces you don't need to hold back; we know she got them out here too. She seem especially friendly with Clint Boyce?"

"Not too much." For the first time, as he moved back toward his questioners, the taut lines of Pete's dark face relaxed slightly. "Not damn near as friendly as Clint would have liked," he said.

"Uh." Nick put in another of his grunts. "You started up that joint of yours—middle of last summer, wasn't it? Much dough of your own?"

Pete dropped to the arm of the chair he had previously sat in, stretching his long legs.

"Enough to get started. You're going to find this out anyway—probably you know it already. Sylvia loaned me three thousand early this summer—that's how I got the new stoves and the freezers. She's got a demand note for it around."

That news had been a riffle in Long Meadow, but whether Waslewski had heard it couldn't be told from his face.

"Miss Gainer show any signs of wanting her money back?"

"Not to me. In fact, lately I've——" It began being light, but sobered and dropped. Death can be stifling to lighter emotions, even, apparently, to pride of conquest.

"Yeah," Nick said, "I've seen you around with her. Anything seem to be bothering her lately?"

"Not that she brought up with me."

"She ever mention anything serious she might want to talk to you about—or to Miss Kingman?"

"Something serious she wanted to talk to *Cathy* about?" Pete sat up more stiffly. "No, did she have anything?"

Nick produced only another question, "About money, say. About feeling she ought to make the Kingmans some kind of settlement out of her grandfather's estate."

Pete's face showed conflicting emotions. "No—I'd have been all for it if she had."

Nick let a pause fall and then changed tack abruptly; even at my distance I couldn't help being aware that preliminaries with Pete were now over and he was moving in closer.

"This date you had with Miss Gainer last night—what was it?"

Pete too must have felt the increased incisiveness; as soon as Nick had the last question out he got to his feet again, moving away from the men to the back of his chair, where he stood with his hands stretched wide over the stuffed back, his gaze on the chair, not the men.

He said, "I can see you've got to get this. We had dinner at the Shore Inn—I'd say we got there around six-thirty and stayed until close to eight. We had a couple of drinks."

"Anything at all out of the usual?"

Pete's face remained set in its in-looking lines, and his fingers pressed into the chair back.

He said slowly, "That's not easy to answer. I was darned peeved, I'll say that much. At first, and while we were having the drinks, Sylvia seemed much as usual. While we were eating, though, she sort of clammed up. Now that I know about—this, I can guess she might have had something to clam up about. All I knew then was that she got harder and harder to talk to, and when we were done eating she said the drinks had given her a headache and she better go home. We had a little fight. I had these tickets for the water show—I wanted to see who got the cup for the outboard races—all those kids drop in at my place a good deal."

The intentness in the room was so great that when he stopped the room seemed filled by the murmur and hum from outside. These were the last hours of Sylvia's life we were hearing about now, and no detail could be too small for a possible importance.

When Pete didn't go on Lieutenant Kopp prodded, "You took Miss Gainer home?"

Pete took it up again, in the same reflective, sober tone. "She wouldn't have it any other way. She was—well, I didn't believe in the headache. I began suspecting she had another date for the rest of the evening. She handed me that line about couldn't I trust her"—the hands left the chair back to gesture upward— "you know how it goes. Anyway I said the heck with it; if she wanted it that way she could have it. I brought her back here—it must have been around eight-thirty. I was in the house maybe two minutes. Then I slammed out; later I went to the water show by myself; I was kind of down."

Again a pause, with the outside sounds drumming in. Then Lieutenant Kopp, quietly, "Those two minutes you were in Miss Gainer's apartment—those might be rather important. Remember just what you did?"

"Well, I . . ." Fleetingly the expression on Pete's angular dark face was one of being pushed beyond exasperation; the pointed eyebrows jerked high. He said coolly, "If you have to know everything, I asked to use Miss Gainer's bathroom. We'd had those drinks."

Swift reaction. "The bathroom upstairs off her bedroom?"

"Only one she had, that I know of." Pete was standing stiffly now, eying his inquisitors with a kind of defiance as they edged, like two sparring cocks, toward him. He went on quickly, "Don't get ideas. Miss Gainer stayed downstairs in her living room. That's where she was when I went upstairs, that's where she was when I came down, that's where she was when I left her."

That time, in the pause, I could hear not only the sounds from beyond but the near sounds of breathing, including my own. Lieutenant Kopp broke it softly.

"I don't mind telling you, fella," he said, "you've got yourself in there. We don't know yet when Miss Gainer died, but my guess is it wasn't too late in the evening. Maybe we better go over this again. Pin your times down when you can."

"Okay." Pete's hands pressed deep dents in the chair back. By now he was sweating; light glistened along his forehead. "It's the same as before, though. You can check on when we left the Shore Inn, but it must have been close to eight. We stopped just once on the way home, one of those lookouts along the lake, west side. We——"

"Anyone else there?"

A headshake. "Kids would be at the show."

"See anyone when you got here?"

"There were lights on in the living room—this living room. I remember I looked in the back window over there; Mrs. Bennert and the Boyces and Lucy Hague were sitting around a card table set up in front of the fireplace. Sylvia didn't stop, though."

Nick got in one more of his grunts.

"She ask you in, or you go in?"

"She didn't ask me. I said, 'Don't I even get asked in?' She was up on her high horse; she said, 'Can you think of any reason you should?' That was when I said, 'Well, I could use the bathroom.'"

"She just stand back to let you past?"

"No, she——" Pete again halted, looking down at his hands on the chair, and the hard edge around his mouth once more softened. "I suppose you have to know everything. All of a sudden she wasn't cross any more. But I'm damned if I hand on what she said, it's none of your business."

Nick began, "It's got to——" but Lieutenant Kopp cut across him.

"Let it slide. Just give us the idea."

"After a minute she gave me a push toward the stairs. She said, 'I'll be nicer tomorrow, just run along now.'"

"And you did."

"I ran upstairs like I said; I was down in two jerks. She'd gotten a cigarette out and was smoking it——"

"Lights on?"

A nod, then slowly, "Quite a few. Maybe that was one reason——"

"One reason what?"

"I'd gotten over being sore. But then I got a little mad again, because there for a minute I'd almost believed about the headache, but when I saw her coming back from the front window as if she'd been there looking around for someone it started me up again. I said, 'I'm going, but don't think you're getting away with anything,' and pushed out. She started to say something, she was walking toward me, but I didn't stop to hear it."

"That's the last you saw of her?"

Again a pause, and what followed sounded as if it came with difficulty.

"That's the last. She was wearing a dress with a thin white top and a wide black skirt, trimmed with red. Her hair was down around her shoulders, the way she wore it when she wasn't going anywhere much . . ."

It dropped off into silence, a silence in which this time even the sounds from outside seemed muted, and in which breath fell lingeringly. A last picture of Sylvia. What had come after that—would we ever know it?

As I sat there, I began to feel pushed by a strong and thirsting necessity that was at the same time a part of grief and separate from it—I wanted to know what had happened from then on. As I stirred, so did Waslewski.

He growled, "What you've given us had better be the dope, Pete, because we'll sure as hell find out if it isn't."

For a while longer he stood glowering, as if about to push it further; then he turned to his cohort.

"We don't know enough; we ain't hardly got started. We better get on to the Bennerts."

After no more dismissal and no more conclusion than that he stalked toward the hall; he was out of the living room before I had adjusted myself to the idea he might possibly be leaving.

"What about me," I got in. "Am I supposed to stay here?"

"Go on home if you want," he threw back at me. "I know where to find you. I'll be wanting to see your mother about that check. Pete, stick around awhile."

After him up the stairs, no more words spoken, went Lieutenant Kopp.

In the living room they had left there was not only cessation of speech but cessation of movement. Once more, after a while, slowly and with difficulty, I began unsnarling myself from my chair. My whole body, I found, had stiffened; my legs protested achingly as I rose.

Pete said, "It still—doesn't make sense. It seems more like a nightmare." His tone now was flat and dull; he dropped into the chair he seemed to have picked for support, bending far forward, his long fingers threading his hair.

I said, "Only it doesn't seem to be the kind of nightmare you wake up from. I found her."

The hands fell to his knees as his face lifted.

"Good Lord. I'm sorry, Cathy." He pulled himself up to step toward me, but when I drew back he stopped. "Don't get into it more than you can help," he advised me. "Something tells me it's not going to be—pleasant."

I went home after that, not saying I was already too far in it to get myself out of it, not saying how impelled I felt, or that I already knew I could never be easy again until this horror was solved.

I went home—checked out by Emil Hasko, watched by at least two hundred pairs of eyes as I skirted the house to my car at the rear, watched again as I maneuvered in low past the taffy-thick knots of people and cars in the driveway, caught by a queer sense of emergence but no freedom as I got out into the more unobstructed, September-sunny streets of Long Meadow.

I went home to be met at the back door by Rose Gamble's heaving bulk.

"I felt somebody ought to stay around here," she told me, her asthmatic voice swaddled in at least twenty blankets of meaning. "It didn't seem right I should go off and leave your mother alone in the house, the way she fainted."

THIS, IT SEEMED, was a day when one shock was far from enough. Not long ago I had been staring, confounded, at Lieutenant Kopp and his news of the check; now I stared in equal bemusement at Mrs. Gamble— at the little red veinings in her puffed, wine-dark cheeks, at the perfect finger waves of her iron-gray hair, at the protruding, water-colored eyes which, right then, somehow reminded me of quicksilver. Mrs. Gamble has lived next door for at least twenty years; in my childhood I'd had more slices of bread and jelly out of her kitchen than I can ever count; she was the one who helped most with Father. But now there was, somewhere inside her, a withdrawal which made her partly a stranger. Not that she had gone so far—yet—as to suspect us, but that, as she'd have put it in her own words, there certainly were some queer goings on around here.

I said flatly, "But Mother never faints." Then, as I brushed past, "Where is she?"

"She's resting. I've got her——"

I beat her to Mother's room, downstairs off the dining room. Mother, when I reached there, had gotten herself out of bed, her dress over her head but not quite pulled down, her body bent as she fumbled under her bed for her slippers. The face she turned upward was both startled and strained, but as soon as she saw me deliverance washed over it.

"Catherine. You're finally back."

Support of any kind is something she has hardly ever asked of me, but now as she hesitantly stepped toward me I reached to get a hand at her back and then to put an arm around her sustainingly; she was shaking, and her eyes seemed to have hollowed. She wasn't too over-come, though, to be rueful.

"I don't know how I could have been so—silly." She began answering the questions in my face before I got any of them out. "Don't make anything of it; it was just—when Rose told me—I used to live there, I was still living there when Sylvia was a baby. And that you should have been the one who had to find her, Cathy—I guess I forget how you've grown up."

In the relief of finding things no worse than this, it took me awhile to grasp that she wasn't speaking for me, or at least not entirely; she hadn't missed the reserve in Rose Gamble's attitude any more than I had. I realized I was going to have to say the right thing too.

"Finding her was bad enough," I put in soberly. "It's a good thing I've worked in the hospital. Mother, are you sure you're all right?"

"Yes," she said, and there was no disparagement in it; at least I'd been adequate. "I'm perfectly all right. It was kind of you to stay, Rose, and you haven't even had lunch. Now Catherine's here, though——"

Beside me Mrs. Gamble panted more heavily; the last thing she could want was to be shunted aside from anything going on, especially in the lives of her friends.

"Lunch! I forgot about lunch! As you say, you—it wouldn't take a minute, though, I'd scratch together something——"

After another glance at us she must have seen that nothing else was going to be said while she was there, nothing of importance any-way; her face felt only to relift immediately.

"I'll run along home, that's what I'll do; give you a chance for a word or two. But I'll be right back, I'll bring your lunch with me—no, no, not a word. I insist——"

Full of renewed good cheer, she at once bustled off. In the dining room, when we were alone in it, Mother sank to a chair. The gaze she lifted to me was long and level; it held trouble, it held what might have been regret, it held some kind of pity. For quite a while that was all that went on, Mother looking up at me, I looking down at Mother. I thought, "She probably knows almost as much as I about what happened; the grapevine will have taken care of that. But she won't know about the check." I felt an apathetic reluctance, as if I would rather not have told her about the check.

She was the one who broke the look; her glance fell to the brush she held quiet in her lap.

She said, "I'm afraid there's going to be much more trouble than this, Catherine, before this is over."

Because I couldn't stay where I was I moved around behind her, picking up the brush from her lap, taking the pins from her tumbled hair.

"Yes," I said. "Much more trouble. Sylvia left us a check, Mother. One for six thousand dollars. It was on her desk still in her checkbook. The sheriff has it."

"Catherine." For a second the head under my hands held itself rigidly quiet, and then Mother had risen, twisting around to me, on her face the same recession of thought and blood I had experienced when I first heard. Slowly, too just as it had for me, thought and blood began returning.

She whispered, "Six thousand. Cathy. But that would be enough . . ." I had known, before, that she wanted me freed of our debts and our bondage; I couldn't have realized, until I saw it naked in her face, how fiercely equal that desire was to mine. Then she began recovering herself. She said, "I suppose, before, if Sylvia'd been living, I'd hardly have wanted to take it. Now it's almost a legacy. I'd never have believed——"

I said, "I told you wrong, Mother." But I knew I hadn't, or if I had, then the wrong was deliberate; I had wanted to tell her exactly as I had. "Waslewski says we probably won't get it. The check never was given us; it would have to go into court and Ada can contest it. We won't get it unless we can prove we—have it coming."

58

She had been facing me, but she sank back. "Oh. Ada. And of course we haven't it coming; it wasn't any debt Sylvia owed."

She sat then with her head bent. I looked down at the little valley in the back of her neck, from which I had brushed up her hair. I went on, "It was to you the check was made out, Mother, not to me."

As soon as I'd said that, though, I was sorry I had; the words sounded almost like Waslewski and Lieutenant Kopp. I knew too why I'd phrased what I said as I had: somewhere in my mind, ticking and unavoidable, had been what perhaps was hope—*suppose there had been something between Mother and Sylvia . . .*

As if she knew what I was thinking, Mother said quietly, "I'm sorry, Catherine. My fainting must have made you wonder; I don't blame you at all. It's hard—I should have kept you from going to Sylvia's this morning; I knew it. That day when I read Sylvia's hand—I'd never seen anything like it. Her life line broke off—broke off in a sort of splattering star, no more than a third of the way down her palm. I thought, 'If there's one word of truth in what hands say, then she ought to be gone, right now.' I thought, 'If there's any truth in it, she must be crowding death.' I asked her about being in danger. And she didn't answer for a minute, the kind of minute when people look startled and queer, before they cover up. She said 'Danger? But of course not, Aunt Julia.' She called me Aunt Julia. And then she laughed; she said, 'Heavens, Aunt Julia, what makes you say so?' I couldn't point out the star; I just said she had a small sign of danger. I went on with the rest of it—now I don't know. Suppose I had told her. She might have believed, then, and taken care of herself. I think that's why I fainted. I feel—responsible. And then—it must have been right after that, Cathy, that she came here to you. Maybe that's what bothers me most. I can't believe about the other—no, I'm lying. That bothers me too."

It faded out. But while she was telling it I had a minute of my own, a minute in which I looked on at the two of us, Mother and I, standing there facing each other beside the round fumed-oak table. Light struck in at us through the blue-ball-fringed pongee curtains Mother made twenty years ago and that apparently are going to wear on forever; sunlight lay on the ferns and the African violets and the gloxinias in pots on the old table leaves set into the window sills, sunlight hit the old couch and the glass cabinet holding Grandmother Kingman's thistle-pattern, shell-handle Haviland. The room was straight enough, Mother and I were straight enough, but everything else was topsy-turvy.

I said, "You told her about danger, and she came here to me. Forget about what her palm said or didn't say; any coincidence like that can happen. What Sylvia did, though, isn't coincidence. Because you must by accident have been right, Mother; she must have been in danger or she wouldn't be dead. She came here to *me*. Only there wasn't anything——"

For the first time since Sylvia's death, then, as I was to do so often again, I thought over that visit she'd made me. All of it. But what had there been?

"She sat on my bed, talking, while I dressed. She reproached me for not coming up to see her, as if I ever had. She asked—substantially she asked if I'd care if she took over Pete Fenrood. She asked why I didn't move out of this place, and I told her. She wanted a coke, and when I got back with it she'd wound up the merry-go-round—there was just nothing to indicate she wanted help of me." I took a swift turn up and down before the flowerpots. "If I could see anything in it——"

Mother reminded, "She told you she might want to see you."

"Yes, she did." I whirled about again. "But that sounded more like help for *me*. She said she ought to give me enough out of Grandfather's money so we could get away from here. She also said she didn't have it. And that phone call—just that she wanted to see me, that probably I'd hear about a railroad ticket she'd found under her pillow. Of all things that can never make sense——"

"Did Waslewski mention that ticket?"

"I told him, but they haven't found it. Not yet. It's—oh, it's a quagmire. Why come to me, of all people? What could I do to protect her? What was there ever between us that she should have picked me? I've scarcely seen her these last years at all."

I said, "I can't figure it. I don't see light through it at all."

When Rose Gamble had edged out the door I had wanted only to be rid of her. Within thirty minutes I was willing enough to welcome her back, not because of the big bowl of tuna, pea, and still warm macaroni salad she came bearing, but because any break meant a quieting of the whips with which I was flailing myself. If anything more had been learned about Sylvia's death, too, Mrs. Gamble would know it.

That I was to be disappointed at least in this last was soon apparent; Mrs. Gamble had little to tell, a fact she tried to conceal even from herself by an excess of words. Her first care as we ate, of course, was to elicit from me every crumb I might have that she didn't; only after that did she settle into a recounting of what she had managed to pick up in the interstices of cooking macaroni and opening cans.

"I hear they haven't found any will, and nobody believes there is any will, either. A young girl like Sylvia, why would she think she was going to die? That'll mean Ada inherits. There's a lot of people say Ada was jealous, and I guess you can't blame her; she won't have so much to be jealous over now."

The slightly bulging quicksilver eyes moved from Mother to me, the slightly wheezing voice seemed to stick to us too. "You were John Gainer's own daughter," the eyes said even if the voice didn't. "I wonder, now, just how you're feeling about this." That, though, was a question even she couldn't ask; she went on.

"I was talking it over with Agatha Pence, you can imagine what it's like down there on the paper, reporters flying up from St. Paul and Minneapolis, probably from Chicago. Charley Reed's so busy sending out telegrams he can't do anything else. I guess Dr. Diebuhr's going to do one of those autopsies; it just don't seem decent to go poking around that way in the dead, but a thing like this, you can see why they got to. The way Dr. Diebuhr's so absent-minded he can't even remember where he lays his hat and coat when he comes on a call, it's funny the way you put stock in him, but I guess he can't be beat on doctoring."

All that had come in a breath, while her face, with its speculative, inquisitive hope, still turned alternately from Mother to me. When we didn't offer anything she took off again.

"I hear he stayed up there with Ada over two hours; they say Ada went all to pieces, screaming just something awful. You don't think, do you, that Ada's the one who *did* it? That's what everybody's bound to think first, with her getting the money; it would be a terrible thing, her own sister—they say Sylvia got choked with some thin kind of thing like a belt or a rope—all that shows on her neck is a sort of red line. They got men all over the Gainer place looking for something it could have been done with; when they get done up there they'll be going around other places; you can depend on it they'll be down here. I'm thankful to heaven, that's all I can say, that I didn't know any of those Gainers——"

A quick double glance, fast as a two-step, gave emphasis to this last, although she didn't allow that to break her off either.

"There's times when you're better off *not* knowing some people. Imagine the job that sheriff's got, trying to find something—it might be like a piece of clothesline—all over a whole town. They'll never do it, that's what I say, not till they find out who did it. If it wasn't Ada, then it'll be a man or some grudge——"

From there she passed so entirely into the realm of the speculative that I quit listening with more than a fraction of an ear; already, obviously, she had produced the few nuggets she had. That Ada would inherit—so much I had taken for granted, as Waslewski had; no more than Mrs. Gamble did I believe Sylvia would have made a will. Even if

Sylvia had known she was in danger, as from Mother's account it appeared she did, her response would have been to outmaneuver, to strike back, never to give up and expect to die. Striking back and outmaneuvering had somehow involved me, but going back to that puzzle now could get me nowhere. Dr. Diebuhr would do an autopsy—that was routine. Sylvia had been strangled by something like a piece of clothesline—that was new, but what good could knowing it do me? I was still in an alley as blind as before. The only thing that had emerged from Rose's recital was the direction that suspicion in Long Meadow was beginning to take. Ada inherited, so Ada, naturally, would be suspected first. Ada had screamed with what had sounded like incredulous horror when she first saw Sylvia, but I had to admit that didn't exclude her; murderesses had put on acts before this. "If it isn't Ada, then it'll be some man or a grudge——"

Some man might be Pete Fenrood. Or Clint Boyce. Or perhaps some conquest of whom I'd never heard. But the grudge—that would be Mother or me. Mrs. Gamble didn't know about the check yet either. I could imagine what was being said. Nothing open—just a careful, oblique "Funny the way it happened, wasn't it? Catherine Kingman going up there the first time in her life. And when Rose told her mother, she fainted. That's what Rose said. Fainted right dead away——"

It's a queer feeling, knowing that people you've regarded as friends can be thinking you over, wondering if they should fit you into a place in a jigsaw puzzle that would make you a murderer.

Waslewski's last words to me had been that he'd want to see Mother, but the day wore on and he didn't appear. That too was a strange feeling—to know so many activities must be going on in connection with Sylvia's death, to be almost fiercely impelled to know what those activities might be uncovering, yet to be cut off, abandoned to nothing but unquiet, knowing that more would come. Torn between us and her telephone, Rose Gamble after a while decided the latter might be more productive and hustled off home again; in an effort to make life at least on its surface be normal Mother and I tried to take up a Saturday routine. I went to get groceries, one of the inevitabilities if you're to eat on Sunday, walking to the grocery store to see window curtains pressed closer to the glass as I passed, to have teenagers fall electrically silent against their bicycles, to have the grocer greet me with hushed sympathy, "That was a terrible thing you got into this morning, Miss Kingman," while his eyes held the same reserve as Mrs. Gamble's.

Back at home I did housework; Doris Orfelt called, her voice too sounding cautious. There was a time, in midafternoon, when the temptation to call Russ grew almost overpowering; if anyone would know what was going on, he would. But I had never in my life let myself call him; I couldn't begin now. Once, with the idea of calling Pete Fenrood, I got as far as lifting the receiver from the hook, but then I turned from that too; Pete's position was similar to mine, and I wasn't in the habit of calling him either.

Toward suppertime two men appeared on the front porch—reporters, it turned out, from Twin City papers. Shortly after they'd left Emil Hasko and another man drove up, but they had neither information nor questions to offer; they had come to look over our woodshed and garage, and they insisted on doing so without comment. It wasn't until after eight that the phone rang, and the voice said Sheriff Waslewski would like to see me again, please. I was to be at Gainer House at nine in the morning, and I should bring my mother.

CHAPTER SEVEN

IF BEING PULLED in two ways is my natural state, then when I got the car out next morning I should have been at the top of my bent, hardly able to wait for the meeting ahead because through it, somehow, we must find out more than we knew; shrinking from it not only as a guessed ordeal but because of fears that I couldn't let formulate.

Mother and I, as we soon found, weren't the only ones summoned; when I turned into the Gainer driveway the Boyces' station wagon swung in just after me, and Pete Fenrood's green convertible was already parked in the graveled area behind the house. In the much too clear morning, with the fog of a sleepless night heavy around us, it was good to seek company; Mother and I waited, beside our car, for the Boyces to alight from theirs; the four of us, almost huddling, walked around to the front of the house.

Clint Boyce—or so I had been led to believe—had a good deal of money; he owned an auto-parts factory somewhere in New Jersey. Mostly I'd seen him as just another resorter, someone to be neither liked nor disliked—a chunky man somewhere in his forties, given a little loudly to sports, drinking, and women, minus much hair but grimly determined to be young, the deep upper lids of his eyes giving him a hooded, slightly predatory look. The first time I'd met him, at a pavilion dance to which I'd gone with Pete, he'd invited me out to his car for a drink, but when I'd said no, thanks, he apparently hadn't been bothered; he'd said, oh well, someone else would. Someone else, according to Long Meadow report, usually did.

What Nila Boyce felt toward these philanderings was something

65

that not even Long Meadow knew; she wasn't the type to give away much. Seen from the back, in her tailored clothes and with her really lovely red-gold hair flowing, she looks twenty-two; it's only when you notice the slightly hardened planes of her well-dieted face, the slightly darkened tone of her skin, the slightly tired look of her long-lashed green eyes, that you begin guessing she may be twice that.

"Church—or a wake," she murmured as we met, but no flippancy was able to make the occasion flippant. As her glance first rested on me there was a glint of—was it curiosity or something else? The glint quickly faded; the eyes remained merely covert and a little insolent.

"Can't get over it." What Clint had to offer was no more than the heavy and inevitable. Sunday or not, murder at hand or not, he was gotten up as usual in the green and red plaid shirt. It was he who opened the door for us, without ringing, as if through this last of its deaths Gainer House had grown public.

And it was public. It was, as Nila had said, something like church, or a wake. Together with Florence Squires and Pete Fenrood, Russ and Ada sat in their own living room as if they like the rest of us had been summoned there, which I suppose they had. When Russ rose at once to come toward us, it was more as an usher than as a host.

He was quiet and strong as he always is. "I'm glad you're here; now there's only Lucy to come. Waslewski's over in the other part of the house, but he should be back soon. Someone's in the dining room taking fingerprints; you're supposed to go there first."

Under his quiet he was, I could see, inexpressibly weary, more so even than we; lines bit into his fair skin between nose and mouth, shadows underhung his eyes. As he turned toward me at least some of that tiredness smoothed away, and I wondered again what I would have given to be able to return to him, openly, what his eyes asked of me. At the same time the irrepressible question spurted from my tongue:

"Do they know any more yet? Have they found——"

Weariness lowered once more over his face.

"Very little. They're not being informative. We've been told we can have the funeral, probably on Tuesday. There'll have to be an inquest first. They must know now about what time it happened; Dr. Diebuhr did the autopsy yesterday afternoon. Probably that's why we're asked here this morning."

I managed only a feeble "Oh." A funeral—of course there must be one, even after murder. An inquest—I should have guessed that. The autopsy—"probably that's why we're asked here this morning."

Still hope and still dread, then, the two fusing and mixed. Only, as we went on into the dining room, where for the first time—at any rate for the first time in my life or in Mother's—our fingers were expertly rolled on an inked pad and then pressed on paper, it was somehow hard not to have hope recede and dread grow.

Together with the others I returned to the living room, and there too was no leavening. Pete sat silent and stretched in his chair, lifting his head for a brief nod of recognition but then returning to a scowling perusal of his shoes. Florence Squires, arms crossed high on her bosom, grimly held down a further chair. Ada, taking no notice whatever of anyone, sat taut, jerking and feverish, now supporting her head on one palm, now tearing at a handkerchief. Nila Boyce drifted over to rest a hand on her shoulder—"Ada, you should be in bed," but Ada did no more than twitch in answer, and Nila moved on to a corner of her own.

After the small rustle of our arrival there must have been at least twenty minutes in which both sound and motion might have been absent if, in the middle of it, Lucy Hague hadn't eased himself in, gracefully silent of foot, highly vocal of tongue.

"Barbaric; the whole thing is barbaric; Ada, you poor girl, if Dr. Diebuhr knew you were down here he'd be simply raving; he'd be stark, staring mad." The exaggerated scolding, in Lucy's clear piercing tenor, penetrated all corners. To people who don't know him, and who hear him referred to only by his nickname, Lucy must sound like a woman, but he isn't, or at least he almost isn't. His christened name, as he reminds people sometimes, is Lucien—an unfortunate choice, or maybe his mother had foresight. Not that there's anything objectionable about Lucy; he sings and teaches singing; no woman's club meeting or church program in Long Meadow is complete unless he appears at it. He's small and neat and plumply turned, with a small dark mustache and big, begging spaniel eyes. Any other man in town, forever hanging around a married woman the way Lucy has for years hung around Ada, would have rocked the place with scandal; it's typical of Lucy that the most I've ever heard said, on this particular subject, is "Goodness, the way Ada pets him."

For him, Ada even now roused enough to walk to the dining room; the two of them came back together. After that the previous waiting would have resumed unabated if Lucy's voice hadn't poured forth unstoppered.

"I'd have been here at seven if it would have done the least good, you know that; I stayed down here last night until almost midnight; it was hours yesterday before that stupid dolt at the door——"

In my place beside Mother on the long semicircular couch I detached my ears; no one ever—or hardly ever—got anywhere by listening to Lucy. Instead, of their own undirected accord, my eyes began moving with a different and growing focus about the room and the people in it. Ada and Russ, they of course. Florence Squires, who worked here. Pete, who had been with Sylvia the night she died. The Boyces and Lucy who, according to Pete, had been here too, in this living room with Ada. Mother. Me. Nine of us. Did Waslewski believe now, did those other men believe, that someone now here in this room . . .

On its second round my glance flew. Russ. Oh, surely not Russ. Anyone else, but not Russ. Mother. Me. I could know we weren't guilty. That left only six. Pete—Pete had been in the Army; for men in the Army killing could be different—but it couldn't be Pete. Florence—it would

take a cataclysm to shake Florence to so much as anger. Lucy Hague—
it seemed incredible that mincing Lucy could be a strangler. Poison, yes,
or a gun. Never a rope. That left Ada, the Boyces. Ada, who sat there
pent in her fever, as if she were tranced. Clint Boyce, who stood near the
hallway with Russ, smoking, his hooded glance crossing mine, then sliding quickly away. Nila, aloof in her corner . . .

Mother and I, waiting for company near our car, might very well
have waited the company of murder.

When Waslewski did tramp in, Lieutenant Kopp still at his heels,
it came almost as discord, I was so rapt in my weeding. Any guesswork
of mine, though, could yield itself quickly; what Waslewski produced
must be more factual. Lieutenant Kopp, shaved, trim, fresh-faced as
before, stopped near Russ at the entrance, but Waslewski advanced to
the center of the room, taking over. He might, this morning, look heavy
and sagging, but his central doggedness remained untouched.

His first remark came almost at a tangent.

He said, "I've seen murders got done by strangers—two men
quarreling in a beer joint, say—maybe they don't hardly know each
other. This murder we had here in this house don't look to me like that
kind of murder."

It was harsh, aggressive, decided; the words seemed to charge at
us. I thought, "I was right, then; he thinks it's somebody here." Lucy at
last had stopped chattering; when Waslewski's voice fell the room once
more sat in quiet. Sun streamed in from the room-wide plate-glass windows which Ada too had had set into the east wall; the long, corniced,
salmon, green, and gray draperies hung flawlessly at the ends of the
room; the rest of the place too—the huge curved sofa on which I was sitting with Mother, the gray mahogany tables, the salmon lampshades,
the gray rugs, the gray flagstone wall—again like Sylvia's—that surrounded the fireplace, the two huge paintings, also carefully salmon,
green, and gray, on the north wall—it all might have come from some

decorator's magazine, it was all quiet, unworn, unused. The nine of us facing Nick Waslewski might have been quiet too, but that didn't mean we were; behind our faces—behind at least one of the faces—there was something unquiet and moving, because that was what could be felt.

Waslewski went deliberately on.

"As far as we can find out, nothing of Miss Gainer's was stolen. This is a good-built house, but if Sylvia Gainer screamed over there— she had a window half open—it seems funny nobody heard it. Besides, she'd hardly have somebody upstairs in her bedroom unless it was somebody she knew."

Again he paused to let his words take effect. A little ripple of motion, this time, went over the room; feet and hands stirred; one of Pete's long legs shifted upward to rest ankle over knee; Lucy Hague bent forward and his mouth popped open as if he were about to start talking again, though he didn't; Russ stepped sideward to sit at the distant end of my sofa.

Waslewski pursued his logic. "Mostly these last years Sylvia Gainer's been gone, only coming here summers. If you start thinking, there aren't so many people she still was close friends with, not such close friends she'd invite them up to her bedroom at nine in the evening. There's maybe a dozen men she went with a little, in school or later. Most of 'em are married, though—some moved away—can you think of any she still had much to do with?" The pause here was infinitesimal. "Can you think of anybody not here that she was such close friends with they might have a reason for killing her?"

It came with his eyes narrowed and hunting, and the impact was inescapable, even to me, who had more or less had that idea already. What my mind fled to was a conception of Sylvia's life quite different from any I'd had before. In New York, of course, Sylvia had many friends; Pete had said so, and so, by report, did the mailman. I'd thought of her, though, even here in Long Meadow, as being glamorously gay and surrounded. People gave parties for Sylvia, Ada and Russ gave parties, Sylvia herself gave parties, she was continuously around town in her car, and never alone. But who gave the parties, who went to them, who rode in her car? Who were the people I'd thought of as Sylvia's crowd? Girls she'd known in school, girls who had married, girls in whose lives she no longer had any place except as a brief cause of flurry. Resorters she met and then, after one summer, probably never saw again. Men—this summer it had been Pete. And of course the Boyces. Last summer it had been a bachelor resorter from Chicago. Before that another resorter. Before that boys who, as Waslewski said, had moved, married, dropped out . . .

Nine of us. The room we sat in had been big and open, but now for the rest of the people in it, as well as for me, it had grown peculiarly hemming and close.

A murmur or two arose, of names contributed. Lucy Hague produced quite a few. But the narrowness stayed.

Waslewski said, "We won't be giving it up; if there's anybody else she had much of any dealings with around here, we'll find out. Right now there's just one other person I wish I had my hands on. Since I don't, though——"

Lucy asked sharply, "Who's that?" but Waslewski ignored him. "Since I don't, I'm going ahead with what I got all you people together for. First about that check we found on Miss Gainer's desk. Your story the same as your daughter's, Mrs. Kingman?"

I don't know what I had expected; certainly I had known he would take up the check with Mother sometime; I had waited for it half of yesterday. I had also thought he would be alone with her when he did so; having it brought out before all these people made it humiliatingly open. Heat began creeping up my cheeks to my forehead, at the same time I wanted to reach out protectingly to Mother. Mother, though, sat entirely cool and at ease.

She said levelly, "If Catherine's story is that neither one of us had any idea Sylvia was making out such a check, and that neither of us knows why she did so, then that's entirely correct. The only reason we can think of is that Sylvia decided we should have a small share in the family inheritance."

"You hadn't had any such part before."

Mother again replied pleasantly, "No, we hadn't."

Waslewski made it more general. "Anyone else here know anything about why Miss Gainer would have made out a check for six thousand dollars to Mrs. Kingman?"

As if the question had been addressed only to her, Ada answered at once, harshly and surgingly. "I can't possibly imagine why Sylvia would have done any such thing; it doesn't have any sense in it whatever." She, I could see, had been told of the check before, and having it brought to her memory acted like a goad; she was sitting erect, much of her trance worn off, and the glance she edged over at us repeated more personally what had been said twice before—that if she could circumvent it the money represented by that check would never reach us.

Russ whipped a quiet phrase at her, "Ada, we talked this over," and she closed her mouth, but the sullen dark fire stayed in her eyes; she wasn't receding from the position she'd taken. Russ went on with the same quiet, "It's obvious Miss Gainer wanted the Kingmans to have this money; I'll see they do."

Mother threw back spiritedly, "That's not the least necessary; if we don't have it coming we don't want it."

It wasn't hard to see where we were getting; again, briefly, I was torn by my desperate need for that money and a pride which was equal to Mother's. Other reactions in the room seemed only what might be expected: Pete and Florence looked interested and agreeable; Lucy, chiming in with Ada, interested and indignant; the Boyces interested but otherwise indifferent.

Waslewski was reading those reactions too; when nothing else came of them he abruptly dropped the whole subject.

"So much for that, then; we'll hold it. What I'm going into now is——"

It was no time for an interruption, but we got one. There had been, some short time before, a murmur of voices at the front door; now Emil Hasko came into the room, ushering Dwight Starbird, who is Long Meadow's postmaster.

"Something here you might want to see right away, Nick," Emil offered. "Dwight just——"

"Yeah," Mr. Starbird contributed, "one of my pickup men just brought it in, turned it right over to me." Mr. Starbird is incapable of hurry, but this came almost fast. His gaze, careful and a little judging, moved over each one of us in the room, resting a little longer, I thought, on Russ. Then it went back to Waslewski. "Called up and found out where you were; dropped right over."

The object he held toward Waslewski was a gray, letter-size piece of cardboard, a piece that looked as if it might perhaps have been the back of a cheap tablet. Pasted on each side of it were what, at my distance, looked like irregular oblongs of newsprint, some one size, some another, some headline type, some small. Waslewski gazed down at it, first one side, then the other; over his face, as he looked, moved varying expressions of intentness and surmise. When he lifted his eyes again it was to meet those of Dwight Starbird and Emil Hasko; his eyebrows rose high, but otherwise, by that time, he'd put on a poker face.

He asked, "Like to see this, Kopp?" and the state patrolman moved forward to look at the cardboard back and front as Waslewski had; he too exchanged glances with the sheriff before he nodded, scarcely perceptibly, and stepped back.

No breath stirred in the room when Waslewski then spoke. He

said, "You'll all want to know what I've got here. It's a note. Looks like it's made up out of cut-out letters and words from newspapers. One side addressed to me at the courthouse. The other side says, 'What was car B7000 doing outside Gainer House 8:40 Friday.'"

CHAPTER EIGHT

BLANK AND UTTER BEWILDERMENT isn't an expression that can often have crossed Russ Bennert's confident and authoritative face, but it crossed his face then. He repeated, "B7000—but that's my car. My license. What was my car——"

He stood up, reaching for the cardboard in Waslewski's hand; he turned it first one side, then the other. He went on, "No name, naturally." A flush of color began rising under his fair skin, but when his face lifted it was no more than scornful.

He said, "I don't know what ill-feeling lies behind this, but I'm sure nothing else does. Eight-forty Friday, I suppose, means Friday evening. I spent Friday evening at the hospital, as I've been spending a good many of my evenings; I had my car parked there, and the keys in my pocket. Not knowing I was going to need proof, I don't suppose I have any, but I'd like to see someone start proving I left there and came back here until close to midnight."

It was decided but with no other emphasis; he couldn't let himself be angered by this anonymous attack, but I could be angered for him, at the same time I felt a kind of sickness. "Isn't that like Long Meadow?" I thought. "Russ has position in town, and so someone has waited this first chance to smear him. I could imagine what went with it, too, the slimy, "Nice for Russ Bennert, his wife getting all of that dough; it won't be the state legislature he'll run for next time." That, though, wasn't entirely what made me feel sick—it was that I too, with Russ right there in front of me, transparently straightforward, transparently clean, must be swept by a horrible moment of doubt, a moment in which I thought, "Suppose it's true, suppose Russ wants money that much"— it was something that could last only a second, but that didn't alleviate my shame in thinking it.

Poker-faced as before, Waslewski reclaimed the cardboard.

"We'll be checking." His answer was inflectionless. "And we'll see what we can do about tracing this thing. Kopp—you too, Emil——" He beckoned the two men with him; all three men, with Dwight Starbird trailing, moved out to the hall, where their voices could be heard in murmured consultation. The nine of us in the living room also broke into speech, most of it consternation. "Can you imagine a thing like that . . . somebody trying to rouse up . . ." Most of the eyes, though, stayed away from Russ.

When Waslewski returned to the room he let ejaculation run awhile; he stood, in fact, listening. Only when comment broke down of its own accord did he go on.

He said softly, for him, "There's one thing about that note none of you seem to be bringing up. Maybe because you don't have the angle. We know just about the time, now, that Sylvia Gainer got strangled. Doc Diebuhr says there ain't any doubt it was sometime between eight-thirty and nine-thirty on that Friday night, and he'd put it early in the hour rather than later." Deliberately he allowed time for the swift inrushing of surmise.

"Whoever sent that note seems to've had awfully close information."

I've been out in duckblinds when a whole flight has risen; I've stood feeling the press and beat of the hundred wings right over my head and around me, so close I could almost have reached out my hands against the feathers that covered the warm living breasts. What went on in that room, then, was something like that—I felt the beating of a force near at hand and in motion—a force of fury and movement, a murderer, active, defending a life that was forfeit, triumphing and falling, but not too far, swiftly planning what else must be done now that this note against Russ had done no more than hit glancingly before it recoiled on the sender.

With new horror I made the round of the faces. Ada—could Ada be guilty of such an act against her own husband? Clint and Nila Boyce, Lucy Hague—sending an anonymous note, yes, that was one thing of which I could believe Lucy capable—Pete, Florence Squires. Each face— so much I got in a glance—was apparently doing exactly as I was, gazing about in abhorring and aroused conjecture.

Waslewski was in no hurry; he left plenty of time for this too.

From the place he had retaken at the end of the sofa Russ spoke. "If that's true, then of course." His eyes looked as sick as mine felt.

When no one else ventured anything, Waslewski went grimly on. "Anything that note has to tell us, in the way of fingerprints or anything else, we'll soon have. In the meantime I'll go into what each of you was doing in that hour I'm interested in—that hour between eight-thirty and nine-thirty on Friday evening."

It took adjustment to make the switch, a reorienting in which most of the others too—all of the others, perhaps, except one—brought their minds back from a horrified outreaching to concentrate on self-defense. Maybe it's some sort of commentary on human nature that this adjustment was made so rapidly; I know that one second I was still staring straightforward at Ada, and the next—without even thinking of Mother—I was swiftly sorting through my own evenings just past. Between eight-thirty and nine—evenings at the hospital were so much of a pattern. Night nurses coming on at seven, day nurses leaving. Admissions—not so many on a Friday, because Saturday was seldom an operating day. Visitors coming in. Flowers. Visitors leaving, and the stir through the building of patients being settled for the night. Then more and more quiet, only a quiet that never entirely was still, as if the whole hospital were corporate and in its one entity breathed with some difficulty, slept only uneasily, suffered some pain. The hospital books—bills, charges, checks, memos—and when I could get my chance, the quick trip out for coffee. No one night any different, except in details too minor to grasp.

Then, gradually, a little sifting. Friday was only the day before yesterday, the last night I'd worked. The day I'd gotten the phone call from Sylvia . . .

Waslewski had proceeded, "Mr. Bennert, I guess I've got yours. Mrs. Bennert, I'll take you next, please, since you were here in this room, you say, with Mr. and Mrs. Boyce and Mr. Hague."

I returned at that to not being alone. What I had just been going over was no more than self-defensive, and however important that might be to myself as a person, there was something else more important. Sylvia's murderer, in the questioning now to be done, might somehow slip. I didn't expect it to be simple—not after what had just transpired. But I could listen.

Ada, in the voice that was at once so feverish and so muffled, began an irritated and complaining reply. "You've heard it all. I had the Boyces and Mr. Hague here for dinner and bridge. Mr. Bennert was here for dinner, but left to go to the hospital. By eight o'clock we'd begun playing. We had the bridge table right there"—she pointed—"in front of the fireplace. If anyone went out of the room it was only to go down the hall to the washroom, or to the kitchen for fresh drinks. No one of us could possibly——"

She not only looked ill, as she spoke, she looked ravaged. One concession had to be made for her—if she had guilt to conceal, she was doing it under difficulties; I guessed she had been dosed with sedatives that hadn't entirely worn off. But then, as I was touched by all the animosities I hold against her, I took concession away; Ada was hard, Ada was hard all the way through, with that most unpleasant of all kinds of hardness—the kind that's soft and yielding toward itself while it is indurate toward others. Ada could be keyed to a pitch where she could defend herself even under drugs.

Nick went on, "There's that door over there by the fireplace, cuts through to your sister's apartment. Say when somebody was dummy— it wouldn't have taken more than five minutes, maybe six, for someone to slip through there——"

"We'd have noticed. I'd have noticed the minute anyone went toward that door."

"Or someone could have gone out to the porch, and around to the side door——"

"I'm telling you, nobody did." Increasingly the answers were cross, as if she found being questioned intolerable.

I was disappointed when Waslewski left her to go on to Lucy Hague; if anyone was ever to get anywhere with Ada, the idea was to press and press again.

"Mr. Hague, would you say this was true——"

"Oh, absolutely; it would have been absolutely impossible . . ." Lucy, at length, corroborated every word Ada had said. Yet curiously, as he spoke, I thought I detected evasion; the very rush of his repeated assertions carried a lack of conviction. At one point he almost made an admission: "Yes, I did go down the hall once—no, not to the porch. Oh yes, all four of us in the room all evening, except, as Mrs. Bennert says, for trips to the washroom or kitchen——"

He was the weakest link in that particular chain; Clint Boyce spoke strongly and decisively; Nila stayed cool, detached, but equally assertive. Yet I wondered if they too couldn't be covering up doubt or worse; behind Clint's hooded bold stare, behind Nila's calculated detachment, there was something slippery. Their drinking—this too was a guess—hadn't been on the light side; it was almost impossible that they could be as certain as they said they were; they were simply standing cohesively together.

From them, no point made and no conclusion drawn, Waslewski passed to Florence Squires.

"Remember how much of that hour you were in the kitchen?"

"Most of it, I reckon." Florence's arms remained stiffly crossed on her bosom; only her eyes got around.

"Leave it at all?"

"Went to bed, soon's I had the dishes done."

"For any reason whatever, did you go into Miss Gainer's apartment that evening?"

A crackle of the black eyes. "Told you that already. Nope."

"See any of the others go in?"

"Wouldn't've known it if they did. But Sylvia had a bolt on that door, her side; she didn't like nobody popping in on her when she didn't know they was coming."

A pregnant quick silence caught up this last. Did I imagine it, or was there again a flutter in the room? If there was, it went as evanescently as it came.

Florence could remember the sound of a car when Sylvia came home with Pete, and the sound of Pete's car leaving. Neither she nor Ada nor Lucy nor Clint nor Nila could remember any sound from Sylvia's apartment after that. No new car arriving or leaving.

"Though it's perfectly possible," Nila put in here, "for a car to have stopped down on the Shore Road, and for someone to have walked up and gone in at Sylvia's without our knowing. If you look at Sylvia's place—it's awfully well designed, isn't it, for someone to come and go without being caught?" She said this as coolly as she had made all her other remarks but the long-lashed green eyes—for a moment as they moved about the room they weren't cool.

That time I was certain about the flutter. Only it too was brief; Ada uttered a wordless protest and Russ said, "You might remember Sylvia's dead."

Nila answered, untouched, "I am remembering Sylvia's dead. Someone got in and out of her place unseen." She leaned forward to open a cigarette box on the table before her and proceeded, as if idly, to light one.

Together with others in the room, I took a deep breath, glancing toward Waslewski to see his eyes tight.

"Go on," he said, "that's what I want. Nobody has to tell me there's been things going on around here I don't know about." When no one proffered anything more, though, he went on to Pete.

"I guess I got yours. Maybe you'll be interested to know, though, that we found a fingerprint of yours on the back of a mirror on Miss Gainer's dressing table. Miss Squires says she cleaned up that place Friday morning. You anything to say about that?"

Pete squirmed, but his wary eyes were steady. "I picked that mirror up, going by to the bathroom. It was a fancy thing, crystal. I'd been wondering what I'd get Miss Gainer for her birthday next month; I decided then it wouldn't be a dresser set." The wry grin came briefly on. "I thought I'd better make it bourbon."

"Anything new to say about what you did after you left here?"

"Same as before. Drove up and down a bit, sore. Then the water show."

Without comment on the indefiniteness of this, Waslewski turned to Mother.

"Mrs. Kingman?"

Mother said crisply, "I stayed home absolutely alone all evening," and dropped it there.

I forgot about listening. "If you can think for one instant that Mother, with her hands——"

"Please, Miss Kingman." Waslewski held a restraining hand against me. "Mrs. Kingman, you might have had a phone call perhaps— anything that would place you at home?"

"Not a thing." It was as crisp and defined as before.

No hand could stop me. "Mother's lived in Long Meadow a good long time. If you——"

"She can make people very uncomfortable," Waslewski returned, and for a second I almost thought he was going to smile. "All right, Miss Kingman, if you want to talk."

I had been so upset over Mother it took me awhile to get back to myself.

"I was at the hospital. The only time I ever leave, in the evening, is to go out for coffee."

"Proof?"

"How could I have? I'm alone there——"

Russ spoke up—coals of fire, if he'd known it, for the suspicion I hadn't been able to keep myself from having about him. "I believe I can give some support to Miss Kingman's whereabouts. As I remember, I went out to the lobby about eight-thirty that night, to ask Miss Kingman if she'd bring coffee for me if she got any for Dr. Diebuhr; I was planning to work right through. Then about nine or so I went back to see if she'd returned; she was gone from the desk, but the coffee was there for me in a wax container; I was sitting on the edge of her desk drinking it when she came in—she'd been in Dr. Diebuhr's office. I'd say it was impossible for Miss Kingman to have left there after eight-thirty, to have gotten the coffee and been back there by nine, and also have gotten across town to—have any quarrel with Sylvia."

Through my new shame at his support of me, I began remembering too.

"That's right. And later on—Mr. Bennert went into Dr. Diebuhr's office, and some ten minutes afterward they both came back past the lobby toward the common room; they were both there when I left at ten. That would split both half hours in the middle—you can check with Mrs. Haushofer when I got the coffee——"

Waslewski grunted, "If she remembers. Three miles across town—five minutes each way—would've been a tight squeeze, but maybe . . ."

When neither Russ nor I could narrow the time further, he left it there, hanging.

In fact he left the whole thing hanging. After he turned from me he walked slowly up and down in the center of the room for three turns, pulling, ruminatively and savagely, at his lower lip. I could share his disappointment; of the answers to which I had listened so intently there were many in which I'd glimpsed loopholes, but none that had made me pounce.

He said, "I guess I'm letting you go for a while, unless there's anyone here knows anything to the contrary of what's been said."

When no reply arose to that he tried another cast.

"Unless there's anyone here has anything new to say, or has any new ideas on why Miss Gainer was killed."

No response to that either.

"All right, you can go. No, one thing more—any of you remember old Hector LeClerque around town these last couple of days?"

Up to then the nine of us had been separate; at the mention of old Hector's name, though, something took place that was like a rush toward cohesion.

Someone—I think Nila Boyce—asked, "Who's that?" and then several voices sounded at once. "That old lumberjack—Hector, did anyone—you mean he's missing, cleared out? Anything definite, Nick?"

Relief, willingness—they were both tumultuously there; almost every face in the room, right then, might have been saying, "Of course, Hector. Thank goodness, just Hector."

But after that first interjection and easing, a pause ensued, in which I heard myself speaking slowly.

"I don't believe it. Hector's been in and out of this town since I can remember. Some of the time, especially since he got too old to work much, he may have been almost a bum. But I've never known him to hurt so much as a grasshopper. All he does, when he feels injured, is droop. He saved Grandfather Gainer's life, once——"

Impatience replaced me, from Mother. "That's every word true, and we all know it. He's come to my kitchen for a plate of food any number of times. There's not a scrap of viciousness in Hector. I don't say he has morals; I just say he hasn't any strength. Not enough of any kind of strength to do murder."

While we were talking some of the light died out of the faces, but not all of it.

Russ put in more equably, "It's only something to be looked into, with the rest. I don't know where he'd go—usually he makes the rounds of the sawmills, since there aren't many camps any more. If he's really in hiding . . ."

Waslewski took it all laconically. "We got him being looked for. All right, you can go. Remember you're all to turn up at the inquest, nine sharp tomorrow morning, Judge Haessley's court. There'll be notices sent."

That ended it; we all, even Russ and Ada, stood up to go. Around the front door a half dozen photographers and reporters had gathered; I recognized the two who had been at our house. They insisted on pictures of Pete and of me, but they rather soon let us go.

As Mother and I drove home all I could feel, along with that cankering certainty of more-to-come, was exhaustion and letdown; out of the whole morning, it seemed to me, very little had issued, except the new unpleasantness of the pasted-up note.

I asked Mother, "That session this morning, did you get much out of it?"

Mother too looked tired and drawn, and her reply came slowly, for her.

84

"Yes. That feeling of something secret and struggling. That note, whatever it's going to turn out to mean. And then, of course, who felt a need for an alibi, and who didn't."

"M-m." That last was a little startling. I'd felt a need to have that hour in my life taken care of. So had everyone else. Except Mother.

It was nice, for a change, to be up against something human and funny.

"Too bad you don't go in for crime, Mother," I said. "You're the one with the head for it."

Three minutes after we reached home Rose Gamble, naturally, was with us too, and the inevitable ensued. Rose, though, once more had astonishingly little of her own to impart; either Waslewski wasn't making much progress or else he was playing his cards very closely.

There were two or three hours that Sunday afternoon—until I put my hand in my coat pocket, that is—when I thought I was working around to a little perspective. I thought, "There Sylvia's death is, and here I am; I'm involved in it; Mother and I are general suspects, as are quite a few other people; I've someway got to find out what happened; whoever's a murderer isn't going to get away with it. But I'm really outside it, and so is Mother."

In that frame of mind, evanescent and unfounded as it was, I got meat loaf and a buttercup squash in the oven, I peeled potatoes and mixed a Roquefort dressing. The table got set and the three of us, talking mostly about Sylvia, of course, ate. Around two o'clock Agatha Pence came in to begin an account of what life had been like, during the twenty-four hours just past, on the Long Meadow *Record*. At twenty minutes to three, allowing plenty of time, I got ready to leave for the hospital, slipping my pink coat over the suit I'd worn that morning, because it would be chilly by the time I got home.

I have a habit of storing things in my coat pockets, especially handkerchiefs. Just as a matter of course, when the coat was on, I shoved my hands in to see what was there. What my right hand encountered wasn't any wad of fabric but just one small object. Something smooth, made of cardboard.

It was a good thing I stood there alone in the hall; a good thing Mother was with Rose and Agatha in the kitchen. Or maybe it wasn't. I think I stayed transfixed for several seconds. Slowly, then, my fingers closed again on the thing they had found and drew it forth.

A matchbook. A matchbook with a line of blue paper matches, green-tipped, still in it. The outside cover was almost entirely plain—dark red with a border of russet. Plain except for two lines of diagonal gold-script lettering—"Wernick's Catering, Madison at 53rd."

I don't smoke. I don't carry matches. Wernick's Catering. Madison at Fifty-third. That was where Pete Fenrood had worked in New York.

Where had I gotten this? Where had I picked it up?

My mind couldn't tell me, but my body could. Remembered in my body was the act of reaching out to touch Sylvia's hair, reaching out to touch Sylvia's arm. And of then bending farther to pick something up from the floor.

I HAD TO SAY GOOD-BY to Mother and Rose and Agatha. I had to get the car out. I had to drive. But my stomach was a tight, repulsing knot, shrunk into a tiny core in the middle of the space it was supposed to occupy. Why had I let myself in for anything like this? How could I have loaded myself with any such responsibility? Right under Sylvia's hand was where this matchbook had lain, as if Sylvia had held it and then, when her fingers relaxed, it had fallen to the floor. Why had I picked it up? In all earth and heaven there wasn't any answer. I had seen something on the floor, and because things were supposed to be picked up from floors—"Cathy, pick up your blocks," "Pick up your crayons now, Cathy"—maybe it went as far back as that. I'd picked it up.

Now I had to take it to Waslewski. If I didn't I'd be concealing evidence. If I did, then Pete . . .

That note this morning had rebounded from Russ to reflect on the sender. This note . . .

Waslewski wouldn't like my having picked it up. He might disbelieve me, he might think I was trying to crawl out of a hole of my own by throwing suspicion on Pete. I could have gotten that matchbook from anywhere, almost. I'd be harried, pressed, questioned again and again— already, anticipatorily, I could feel moisture at my forehead, at my waist. That, though, could make no difference. I'd still have to do it. They'd believe me somewhat; at least they'd have to consider it. And Pete already was suspect; next to Ada he probably was more heavily under question than anyone else. Pete was the one who admittedly had seen Sylvia last. He'd been quarreling with Sylvia; he'd said so himself;

there'd been a kind of wariness over him all during the questionings yesterday and this morning.

I didn't need to anticipate sweating; I was already sweating. I slipped the Pontiac in just beyond Dr. Diebuhr's Studebaker without bumping any fenders, but it wasn't until I was out of the car and slamming the door that I realized I'd reached the hospital. What was in my mind then was swift rejection—no matter what the matchbook might seem to say, it too, like the anonymous note, must be false evidence. Sylvia could have picked it up around Pete's place herself. Or someone else, evilly, could have saved it for the purpose for which it was used. The same someone whose felt but invisible force—devious and fulminant and tricky—I had sensed this morning in the Gainer living room.

Any thinking such as this, though, wasn't for me; it was for Waslewski and Lieutenant Kopp. The only thing I could do was take this new evidence to them, immediately. But I pulled open the hospital door and walked on down the corridor toward my desk. The matchbook stayed behind my driver's license in my billfold, where I'd put it.

Perhaps if Doris Orfelt had met me as usual I couldn't have temporized; perhaps I'd have said, "There's an errand I've got to run, Doris; I'll come earlier tomorrow if you'll wait until I get back."

But Doris didn't meet me as usual; Doris, as I was aware while I was still only halfway across the lobby, was quivering and transported; I let myself be taken up by what poured from her.

"You should have seen what was in here this afternoon." She opened up while I was still beyond the counter. "Straight off the most super dream boat that ever sailed. Lieutenant Kopp. Lieutenant Harry Kopp." Her voice lingered over the syllables and her big dark eyes, more extravagantly wide than ever were off on a dreamboat of their own. "Couldn't somebody of told me a guy like that had reached town? The minute I saw him I knew it—he sends me."

"I must say he hasn't sent me. Not the way I met him." So far I had surfaced only partially from my own preoccupation. My hands were still clammy, and the matchbook, as I couldn't forget, was right there in my handbag.

"He does me. Those round innocent eyes—Cathy, did you ever see anything like 'em? If he doesn't get back here to see me——"

By that time I had realized what Lieutenant Kopp must have been doing there in the hospital, and that was something I needed to know too.

"I suppose he was here on business."

"I don't care what he was here for," Doris tossed from her dream, then, closer to earth, "I'm sorry, Cathy, what it means to you and all—I guess he was checking. Anyway that's what he said, and I don't think he could just of seen me around town. He asked about you, some—it's too bad I didn't run in to go out with you that Friday night, only you know I had that date with Buddy Upsher, maybe likely the last date I'll ever have with Bud, probably. I hope. You know, Cathy, I never was you could say crazy about Bud, not the way I could be about Harry. That's his name, Harry. Harry Kopp." Again the dream almost mired her, but she got back on track. "Of course, Cathy, I told him you'd never think of a thing like that; I told him you're absolutely one of the nicest girls in Long Meadow. I said——"

"Thanks." It was dry. "Anything else?"

"And about Mr. Bennert. He got that all fixed up. I remembered something. Laura Firbeck—you know, night nurse on second—stopped by at the desk yesterday morning on her way out and she had a streak of black on the back of her uniform. I told her about it and she said she knew—she'd got it leaning against Russ Bennert's car. So I told Lieutenant Kopp—Harry Kopp—and he called her to come over. She said she came downstairs that Friday evening and went out for a ciga-rette the way she often does with that diabetic patient on her floor. She said it must of been after eight-thirty, because all the visitors were gone, but she hadn't put her patients to bed yet and you weren't at your desk—it must of been while you were out for coffee. Anyway she went out the side entrance, and Mr. Bennert's car was right there, parked where he always parks it if Dr. Diebuhr doesn't beat him to it. She sort of stood there leaning against it, and she was mad when she noticed the streak on her dress—that was what made her remember the license, and it was that B7000 all right, the number Mr. Bennert always has. I'm sort of glad of that, aren't you? I mean Mr. Bennert—if I'd been grown up when he was around loose——"

I had known Russ must be cleared, and yet it was relieving to have it happen; I could breathe on it deeply, not realizing, until I did so, how corruptingly that doubt had stayed with me. Doris still chattered; I lost a few sentences, but caught on again.

". . . fingerprints. He said they found quite a few of yours around Sylvia Gainer's apartment, but none where you hadn't said you'd gone. Mostly doors and things. A lot of Sylvia's, of course, and quite a few of Ada's and Florence Squires. Just one print of Pete's. Isn't that funny? Just that one, upstairs. Then he said it was a secret and I mustn't tell a soul, so for heaven's sake, Cathy, don't forget and give me away. They even found some of old Hector LeClerque's prints, right upstairs in Sylvia's room, too. That's why they're trying so hard to find him. He says it looks bad for Hector. He says they've picked up loads of things—ropes and stuff—that they've sent in to their central laboratories; he says they don't have any way of knowing, really, but they may have the murder weapon already. He was just simply too dreamy, Cathy, so if he calls here and asks for me—you know my home number, but I've got it written out here on the pad too; for goodness' sake make sure he gets the right one."

Lengthily she drew her recital to a close, lengthily relinquished the desk, coming back several times because the phone rang, and she wanted to make sure it wasn't for her. What occupied me most, during all this, was the one thing in Doris' story that was something to seize on—that Hector's fingerprints had actually been found upstairs in Sylvia's room.

When Hector's name had first come up that morning the idea of his being Sylvia's murderer seemed so impossible that I had been sure, with every bone of my body, he couldn't be. Hearing about the fingerprints shook me. Suppose I'd been wrong. Suppose Mother was wrong. The fact that we'd known Hector most of our lives didn't mean that he couldn't do murder. Suppose, under his mild exterior, some violence finally had fired. Sylvia, especially in the mood Pete had said she was in on that Friday night, might have been derisive and cruel, she might have managed to touch the one spot which, in almost all of us, can't tolerably be touched.

If that was so, if Hector was guilty, then the matchbook meant nothing. If they caught Hector and it was proved he killed Sylvia, then not telling about the matchbook would make no difference.

It wasn't a kind of thinking to bring peace. The hospital, that afternoon, was rather quiet—maybe most people were staying home to talk over developments. Still my thoughts were broken by incomers and outgoers. "You'd like to see Mrs. Pugnacci? You'll find her in 63. Good-by, Mrs. Halstead, I hope you found Mr. Halstead much better." Ordinarily people stopped for a little more than that, but the reserve I had noticed yesterday in Long Meadow was apparent here too, not in anything said, but in sidelong glances, in a lack—or an excess—of heartiness. Evening brought more of a rush, but that too ended; as the lobby cleared of its last visitors and the time approached when I usually took my ten minutes off I found myself dawdling over first one little job and then another, wishing Doris would come back, wondering if perhaps Laura Firbeck might run down. Russ hadn't come in; he naturally wouldn't, not on Sunday, and when Ada must want him. Just after six-thirty Dr. Diebuhr had stamped his testy small self past my desk, barking, "All damn foolishness," for no connected reason; there'd be no coffee to bring in for him.

Restlessly I wanted someone to talk to. The only people to whom I could talk about the matchbook would be Mother or Russ, but Russ wasn't available and I somehow shrank even from telling Mother; both, undoubtedly, would simply say I ought to go to Waslewski. If I went to the Kitchen it was possible Pete might be there. In a way that might help me; maybe, in seeing him again, in talking with him, I might get some clue or some indication. And then again I might just get more uncertain and mixed.

When I eventually got into my coat and walked down the side corridor it wasn't because I had made my mind up, just that I couldn't decide to the contrary. With both Dr. Diebuhr and Russ away, no car was parked that night with its nose to the side door; distant rain hinted its coming; since three o'clock the leafy smell of September had turned cooler and more moist. I followed along the sidewalk to the Kitchen.

The first thing I saw, as I opened the door, was that Pete was there. Pete and, of all people, Lucy Hague. The two of them sat, side by side, at the long counter, a plate, an empty coffee cup, and an assortment of crumbs at each place. Both turned at my entry—Lucy with a glance that somehow was secretively expectant, Pete rather morosely.

"Coffee on the house," he told Mrs. Haushofer, at the stove. Then elaborately, to me, "Dull night tonight, Miss Kingman; I wondered if you'd drop in. The population of Long Meadow—except for Mr. Hague, here—isn't running its chances of poison. Aren't you venturing?"

It was more than glum, it was bitter; the pointed brows rose to a central peak almost of pain, and the eyes, too, were reckless and angry.

"I'm a strychnine fiend," I threw back as lightly as possible. "Haven't you heard? That's why I stay on at the hospital, to be near the drug supply." I couldn't entirely be light, though, not while I hugged against my side the handbag that held the matchbook.

Certainly I found no favor with Lucy Hague, who slipped from his stool while I still advanced toward the counter, his wide spaniel eyes deeply offended.

"You people may joke," he indignantly scolded, "but I must say I see nothing funny in any of this anywhere, nothing funny at all. I can't say I was a great friend of Sylvia's, not a great friend, but I feel her loss deeply. And the whole thing is simply devastating for Ada; I don't think any of you realize what a *sensitive* person Mrs. Bennert is." Nervously, as he pointed this out, his own sensitive fingers adjusted the gray silk scarf he wore folded about his throat in what, he had once told a woman's club audience, was permanent Hollywood fashion. "I don't think you any of you realize," he went on in equal heat and equal fervor, "just what murder can do to you; I don't think you know how you'll suffer; I'm sure no one knows how Ada is suffering, or how I'm suffering for her, *intensely*."

His feet hadn't seemed to move, actually, but the last of this was delivered with his hand against the doorjamb, which he abruptly rounded, letting the door slam behind him.

"Well," I said. Tenuously I was aware that I hadn't been the person Lucy had expected, or that something about me had been disappointing. There was nothing, though, firm enough to catch. All I could do was make it a question: "What does that mean, do you think?"

"Lucy ever mean anything?" Pete stayed stuck in his glumness. "Sometimes I wonder," he went on, as Mrs. Haushofer set the fresh cups of coffee before us and he shoved the sugar container along to me, "if anything means anything. I get in a deal like this, and I'd like to know what in heck a guy like me can do. I've never had any experience collecting evidence. Probably I wouldn't know a piece of evidence if it crowded up and bit me. I don't know anything about psychology. I can't take fingerprints and I haven't got a lab. If I did try anything, Waslewski and Kopp would be down on my neck harder than they are now, probably. How're you making out, Cathy?"

"About the same," I told him, and for the moment at least it was true; I knew clearly, right then, why I'd come and that I'd been right in coming; as I sat beside him I thought with a kind of sinking, "I can't tell about the matchbook, of course I can't." His hair had been roughened a little; the side of his mouth that was toward me looked surprised and hurt. Yet with the same sinking I realized I couldn't entirely be sure of his innocence either; I could only once more feel guilty of my suspicions, miserable at being so torn.

Since any silence between us was also impossible, I fell hastily into repeating the gossip I'd just had from Doris, as well as some that had come through Mrs. Gamble.

"Of course Ada inherits." Comments he made remained gloom-sunk. "I can see Ada wanting Sylvia dead—Ada's a kiln-dried bitch for my money if there ever was one. But I can't see her getting away with that strangling—not Ada to Sylvia. Sylvia was three inches taller. I'd bank on Sylvia's killer being a man. And that's good, coming from me, isn't it? Nobody has to tell me I'm the favorite. Old Hector—maybe his fingerprints were there in Sylvia's bedroom; he was always around her for money, but I can't see him the killer either. He's another little squirt—Sylvia could have banged him on the head with—well, with that mirror I picked up, and that would have been that. Who else is there? That pip-squeak who was just in here? A swell guy like Russ Bennert? That's what's eating me. I can't——"

I said, "There's Clint Boyce."

He stood up on that, to prowl the linoleum between counter and door. "I know. Clint Boyce. If I thought he'd actually got anywhere with Sylvia it would be different. But I don't. I——"

"That could be why."

"Not with Clint. No one woman means enough to Clint."

I strained against it. "But it's got to be someone."

He answered, "Yeh, it's got to be someone. If I could just get an idea. If I could get myself started——"

There was a pushing and driving insistence about this last; he had turned a little toward me, not to look at me, but enough so I saw more of his face. The blue eyes, already narrow, had narrowed further, the peaked brows had flattened, the nostrils widened. His face, right then, was a hunter's face, waiting and wanting to pounce.

I thought, "If he did know, if he once got on the trail . . ."

But then my heart turned again. Suppose that wasn't the kind of hunter he was. Suppose this was performance for my sake, suppose the matchbook told the truth. Suppose he had found out something about Sylvia that angered him and pierced his vanity; suppose, for instance, there was another man. Suppose, right now, I told him about the match-book—what look would spring then to his face?

He walked back to the hospital with me; insisted on it. We had gotten, by that time, around to talking over the anonymous note. I happened to notice, as we reached the sidewalk, that Lucy Hague's tan Chevrolet was still parked under the maples across the street, and commented on it to Pete, but he shrugged it off. "Lucy probably warms up, a night like this, fifteen minutes before he starts wearing his motor."

Outside of that, nothing happened; I just walked back to the hospital beside him, holding the handbag tight to my side. That same hand-bag was once more tight to my side when I drove home at ten through the slight mist just beginning to fall; it was tight at my side while I parked the car in the dark garage and walked from the garage toward the kitchen door, slipping a little on the damp grass. It was still against my side when the slight dark figure stepped from behind a bush near the porch and, after a moment, whispered, "M'selle Cathy?"

CHAPTER TEN

WHAT MY MIND somehow accepted, when the intruder appeared and before he spoke, was that he was Lucy Hague—Lucy who had been so histrionic at the Kitchen, Lucy whose car had been parked too long under the maples. I'd never again—this was the first coherent thought I had—dismiss Lucy as negligible, because what filled me when I thought him lurking there to confront me was blind, freezing, reasonless panic; I could have done nothing but stand, turned to a pillar of ice or a pillar of salt. Only when I grasped the fact that it wasn't Lucy, but Hector, could I begin melting. A few hours before I had been trying to persuade myself that Hector might be a killer; no sooner was he there before me than that idea had to be ridiculous again. I couldn't stay frightened of Hector.

In the backwash of panic, though, I was irritated.

"Do you know there are at least three dozen men out hunting you?" I asked sharply. "Where have you been?"

There in the darkness, in the mist that clung rather than fell, he stood limply in what seemed nothing but dejection, his shadowed thin cheeks, his black French-Canadian eyes, his black mustache, his thin shoulders, all sagging.

"Please, M'selle Cathy," he whispered back at me, "these two days I am in the woods. But in the woods these days—nowhere is there cover. Nowhere is there food."

He swayed slightly. Not toward me, away from me.

"Oh, for heaven's sake," I scolded, and what I felt, right then, was mostly a despairing crossness. He would come to me. Turning old Hector in—was this something I'd have to do too? "Let's get in the kitchen; I'll find you something to eat. I'll wake Mother. But you'll have to realize, Hector—you can't hope, not possibly, to keep away from the men looking for you; you can't hide out much longer. You haven't even a car. You can't take a train or a bus——"

He meekly accepted it. "Yes, m'selle, I am aware."

Even outdoors he was fragrant; the kitchen, as soon as he came into it, became permeated with the scents of damp wool and infrequent bathing. While he sank his dejection into a chair I drew the shades— "Noticed you had the shades down and a light on, last night," Mrs. Gamble would tell us in the morning—and woke Mother. The two of us filled up the coffee percolator, sliced cold meat loaf and fried potatoes; as soon as anything reached the table the old man fell on it ravenously.

"Even on Friday I eat but little." It was not so much apology as explanation. For all Hector's limpness, for all his hunger, he retained dignity. In the security of the kitchen he no longer whispered; he sat by the table in his rubber-soled felt boots, his thick shapeless and colorless trousers, his plaid jacket; his aroma wasn't lessening. But he was a guest in our kitchen, his cap was off, and he had risen to rinse his hands and wipe over his mouth at the sink before he tremblingly snatched the first slice of bread from the plate.

After a while he said simply, "To the sheriff—I can see it is a necessity I must go. But I will not go hungry. And first I see friends. Around the Kitchen of Pete there is too much light; I come here."

"Well," Mother said. "It's something that you know you'll have to go to Waslewski." She had been entirely asleep when I went into her room, but she waked quickly; it hadn't taken her more than a minute to realize how things were. It was cool in the kitchen; as soon as Hector had slowed to the place where I could supply him alone she sat down opposite him, running her tortured hands for warmth up the opposite sleeves of her blue flannel bathrobe. "You know what's happened, don't you, Hector? You know Sylvia Gainer is dead?"

"Ah, *oui*, that I know. That I saw."

Mother's eyes, as they met mine, were quick; she waited an instant before she repeated carefully, "You saw it?" Then, more swiftly, "Why is it you want to see friends?"

Hector had reached a point where eating, too, could be done with more dignity; he took in a last bite of apple pie, wiped his mustaches delicately with the napkin, and took a long drag on the scalding coffee.

"When a man has a story to be told," he said then, "it is best he first tell it to friends." His two hands rested flat on the table beside his pie plate and coffee cup; his attitude was still one of dejection, but he no longer drooped quite so much. Deliberately the black eyes moved from Mother to me. "Friday, that is the day of Miss Gainer's death. On Friday, in the morning, I go about town, I visit here and there, I see friends. On Friday afternoon I go back to my house, my small house which looks on the lake. Under my coffee cup which I have leave that morning on my table there is money, five dollars. Imagine it—never such a thing has happen before. While I am gone money comes to sit under my cup. I take up the money. I look at it. It is good money."

Once more the black eyes moved from Mother to me, waiting comment.

I began, "You mean you actually found——"

He nodded. "Under the coffee cup I have leave that morning on the table. I think fine. I think among my friends there is one who have come to surprise. I go out to celebrate. When such a thing happen, should I not celebrate? I celebrate all over town, a long time."

"Hm," Mother said. Celebrating, for Hector, takes just one form.

"With all the world I am pleasant. The world grows dark. It is night. I have use up the money. But I think, 'Tonight I will see M'selle Gainer. The world is good, of M'selle Gainer I have save the life of her *gran'pere* who leave her much money. In a world of such good M'selle

98

Gainer will give me a little of that which she had from her *gran'pere*, I will celebrate a little more.'"

The black eyes asked if this was not, indeed, reasonable reasoning. Mother and I, intent, both nodded.

"I go to the house of M'selle Gainer. All is quiet. I ring the bell. All remains quiet, but the door she is not catch. I push a little and go in. There is light, but no M'selle Gainer." He paused, infinitesimally.

"You understand, I have celebrate. I go upstairs, where she maybe is. There is M'selle Gainer, but she will not give me of that which she got from her *gran'pere*. She is dead. I see it at once. She is dead."

The eyes, asking for belief, managed to widen enough to include both Mother and me at the same time.

I asked as slowly as he had spoken, and with plenty of time to go on, "Do you have any idea at all what the time was?"

The hopeful head shook. "It is dark. It has been dark for some time. Maybe it is nine, maybe ten, maybe eleven. I do not look. I am not afraid, but I do not wish to stay there. I think, 'There are those quick to think evil, and if it is known Hector LeClerque is here, it may be thought Hector LeClerque has done this thing.' I go from there. Many times I have go to the woods; I go to the woods then. Only this time I cannot appear at the camps, I cannot stop with the farmers. This time I grow hungry."

Again slowly I asked, "When you saw her, how was she lying?"

"She is on the bed, but the wrong way. Her head hangs down, and one arm."

The same, then, as when I found her. His story, at least as far as his discovery of Sylvia was concerned, was substantially the same as mine. I began "Mother, do you——"

Mother had come to the same conclusion. She said stoutly, "I think it's every word true; I think he should get to Waslewski right away. What I don't like—that money under his coffee cup, that's what hits me most. I don't see how it could be imagined. And if it isn't——"

She didn't need to finish; I could feel what she meant. Most people in Long Meadow knew what Hector did when he got money, and just how much it took. Two dollars, for instance, would hardly dent him; five was just enough to make him do what he did when he got really sunny—he'd think the world had relented and go to Sylvia. There'd been times when Russ had had to pry him loose from Sylvia's dark doorstep by main force, and drive him home to his tarpaper shack. If the money under his cup wasn't imagined, then it meant more of the same devious kind of action behind that anonymous note, and more than that, too—since it had been done before the murder, it meant a terrible premeditation.

Getting Hector drunk so he would blunder into Sylvia's at a time the murderer wanted him to. Who, in Long Meadow, could be as artful as that? Once again, irresistibly, it was Lucy Hague to whom my thoughts flew; I could imagine how sinuously he could have slid into old Hector's shack, just as I could imagine him almost happily snipping and pasting at that anonymous note. He'd be the one—even if he never had expressed any such emotion—who might feel inimical toward Russ.

Only, how pin it on him? Once again I felt the cold finger tips of panic. That much craft on the loose . . .

That, though, was nothing to bring into the open, not then; Mother was capable of her own surmises. We both thought that Hector had finished his story; he stood up to go; it was agreed I should run him to the courthouse. In a ritual of farewell, he held out his hand first to Mother, then to me. After that he once more sat down.

This time even some of his dignity left him. Not all of it, but some. He pulled off his cap, held it by both hands, and directed his eyes toward that.

He said, "All these years, thirty-two years, I have tell a lie. I do not save the life of John Gainer. Me, I am little man; John Gainer is big, he does not need me to save the life. John Gainer is friends to me because he have kill a man, and I see him."

Mother's exclamation got out first. Yet we needn't have been startled; the explanation, when it came, was simple enough. John Gainer, in the days when he was a young lumberjack, long before he made his fortune, had gotten into a fight with a quarrelsome foreman; the foreman had gone into a log-boiling river, and John Gainer had turned coolly to the only onlooker. "Keep your mouth shut, Hector, or in you go too." That was why, from his later superfluity, he had granted Hector so many alms.

It was only a small revelation. Mother said grimly, "I should have known it was something like that, to make Father hand out good money." There was nothing, however, that seemed applicable to Sylvia; that quarrelsome foreman was thirty years dead.

And after he had finished this second tale Hector seemed to realize it; he once more stood reluctantly up to repeat his ceremony of leave-taking. That over, I drove him, as planned, to the courthouse, where he passed very quickly into the keeping of Emil Hasko. Not my decision; he walked up the courthouse steps his own man—not with any happy anticipations, naturally, but willingly enough.

Just the same, it wasn't an act that improved my spirits. As I came down the steps, once more alone, I found myself looking sharply about for a tan Chevrolet. The fact that I saw none didn't ease me either. What crowded my mind was a very usual, rueful, and painful hodgepodge, only the elements now were different. From where I stood it looked as if Sylvia's murderer might artfully elude pursuit forever. Sylvia had left us that check, but without helping us any; it looked as if I was as stuck in Long Meadow as I'd ever been, with suspicion of murder now added to the odds against me. No one knew what would happen next, except that there'd be an inquest in the morning and a funeral on Tuesday. And I had driven poor old Hector to the courthouse, but the matchbook was still in my billfold.

If any residents of Long Meadow County hadn't already determined to be on hand for the inquest, the wildfire news about Hector must have finished the job. When Mother and I tried reaching our new white cement, tan granite, glass, and chromium courthouse next morning, the streets were blocked with cars, the two town cops struggled hopelessly with a traffic jam that looked as if it would take two weeks to untangle; we had to park six blocks away and walk over. Two thousand people, at least, packed the lawn between the courthouse and the old red brick shoebox of the jail that flanks it; only up a path plowed for us, football fashion, by two deputies, did we finally get to the doors, and inside it was worse. Not until we reached places in the second of the two front benches saved for witnesses in Judge Haessley's courtroom was there space even for breathing.

Yet as I looked about at the faces, as I caught the atmosphere of tight, savoring expectancy that pervaded the room, I thought it was not because of a hope to learn anything new that the people had come; by the unfailing Long Meadow grapevine they already knew what was known; most of them, already, probably knew Hector's story, as repeated to Hasko and Waslewski, in just as much detail as Mother and I did, who had heard it first. It was on another and greater necessity that the faces were intent—here, at the inquest, they had drama, here they could see with their own eyes, hear with their own ears, those of their members on whom the violet light of their own avid interest had turned. By coming here they too became part of Sylvia's death; they could tell of it afterward—"That's right, I was there at the inquest; heard it plain as day. Right then I said to myself . . ." They were laying the grounds of that superior wisdom they would swiftly produce whenever—or if ever—someone among us was proved to be walking with a false face of innocence.

My own first necessity—even before I sought for Russ—was to

hunt out Lucy Hague. He was there already, third in the row ahead of me, sitting between Ada and Florence Squires, with Russ on the other side of Ada, and Hector with a deputy directly in front of me. From time to time Lucy turned as he fussed over Ada; I got the wide back of his head, and then his profile, assiduous and solicitous. I thought, "He can't mean that, either—or can he?" Once more I pictured him snipping and pasting, pictured him slipping into Hector's shack, and once more I could produce that much clearly: the brown spaniel eyes could be pleasantly absorbed over the note, as over a puzzle, the too graceful figure could be entirely at ease about an entry into Hector's shack, ready with an "Oh, there You are, Hector, I was looking for you," and an excuse. It wasn't too hard either to imagine Lucy slipping with that quiet of his around to Sylvia's door; I could imagine his moving closer to her so imperceptibly she wasn't aware of it herself, imagine him slipping the gray scarf from his throat . . .

There, though, the picture broke. Sylvia hadn't been in bed asleep when that attack was made; she'd been up and dressed. She must have faced her attacker. She might have had her back to him at the beginning, but she wouldn't have stayed that way; Sylvia played tennis and went skiing; she was as swift and as strong as a whip; Sylvia would have turned on Lucy, furious and fighting; it was impossible that he could have strangled her and emerged with face unraked, clothes untorn. Clothes could be burned, but the face—Lucy's face presented itself to me first one side, then the other, and on its velvety olive surface was no mark of any kind.

No one else in the two rows showed any scratches either. I took every face as it came, omitting no one—Russ, Ada, Lucy again, Florence, Hector; then, in the row I occupied, Pete, Clint, Nila. I couldn't suspect my own mother, but I found myself furtively glancing even at her. Yet it had to be one of us; Waslewski had argued that out, and I had agreed with him.

So far I hadn't expected much of the inquest; I too, like the rest of Long Meadow, probably knew everything that would be produced here. As I once more beat my head against the wall of unanswerable questions around me, however, I couldn't hold down a surge of desire for the unforeseen to happen.

Proceedings, as they began, seemed almost excruciatingly pedestrian, but I set myself to listening. Under the droning directions of old Dr. Manion, the coroner, the jury box lingeringly filled, only to empty itself immediately as the men filed out to view the deceased—to satisfy themselves by personal perusal, apparently, that Sylvia was as dead as it was claimed she was. On their return Waslewski told of being called, and of his arrival at Gainer House. Dr. Manion, as coroner, related how Sylvia had lain when he saw her, and gave his decision that Sylvia at that time too was no longer living. Dr. Diebuhr, testy as ever, read his autopsy report—death by strangulation, probably occurring, if evidence given him concerning time of the deceased's last meal was correct, somewhere between eight-thirty and nine-thirty on the evening of Friday, September third, and more likely early in that hour rather than late. Photographs taken on the scene were sent up to the jury, and also fingerprint photographs brought in by a member of the state police, in evidence that persons named Sylvia Gainer, Florence Squires, Ada Bennert, Hector LeClerque, Peter Fenrood, and Catherine Kingman had at some time or other touched objects in Sylvia Gainer's place of residence.

Routine. Objective. Yet even in my place among the witnesses I could feel, as these proceedings continued, that I wasn't the only one absorbed in listening; tightness in the room increased rather than diminished, and when, first of the non-official witnesses, I was called to the stand, I had a chance to realize how really focused that interest was. From the golden oak witness chair on a stand beside Coroner Manion's high desk there was nowhere to look but forward into the ranks of grave faces, all the eyes turned on me intently, hunting me out—if my skin had been transparent I couldn't have felt more surely that my last secret was exposed. With a gesture that was beginning to be compulsive, I found myself clutching my handbag to my midriff; it took effort to relax that hold. To avoid all the other eyes, I fixed my own on those of Nick Waslewski, who stood up to question me; no matter how cold or how searching any one pair of eyes might be, they were something to fly to as refuge away from that other battery.

"Miss Kingman, I wish you would please tell the jury what happened on the morning of September third when you went to see Sylvia Gainer."

Waslewski was dressed up, this morning, in a tight navy-blue suit, but the face was the large, small-mouthed face, the eyes presented the shellac-bright aquamarine surface that I so well knew. In answer I gave what I had given before, talking in a quiet in which words seemed snatched from my mouth before they were said. It was as dryly factual a recital as I could make it; when I got to the place where Florence and I had Ada back at Gainer House and the bakery man ran off to phone, I thought I was done; Waslewski nodded at me shortly, turning to whisper to Lieutenant Kopp at the table from which he'd risen. But as I half rose he turned back to me.

"Miss Kingman, you had two previous contacts with Miss Gainer this summer."

So I had to go on, telling of Sylvia's unintelligible visit to me, of her equally enigmatic phone call with its reference to a railroad ticket, and of something that Sylvia wanted to tell me. Gradually then, as I talked, I sensed something going on. Not just the somehow once more made manifest presence of that active, writhing, fighting force I had sensed yesterday in the Gainer living room, though I again felt that presence too. But something beyond that, something different. I couldn't, right away, sense what that difference was, but then I did. The person in whom that dark and moving force existed hadn't known, before, about

Sylvia's visit to me, or at least hadn't known as much as I was telling now. That person hadn't known, at least not in such detail, about Sylvia's call to me, and how close Sylvia had come to revealing some secret.

That person perhaps wondered if I might be concealing more than I told.

I had a minute or two when I actually felt that force moving against me, like a draft of chill air wafting up to me from the packed, overheated crowd. Even while that draft blew freshly on me, my eyes, with a kind of desperate necessity, hurried once more from face to face along the two vital rows. Russ, Ada, Lucy, Florence, Hector, Pete, Clint, Nila, and Mother. Nowhere was there a flicker; each face might have been a mask.

From whom that draft came, that was impossible to determine. But of what that person was guilty, and how he—or she—now felt toward me, that wasn't so hard to guess.

CHAPTER ELEVEN

WHEN WASLEWSKI at last nodded to me in dismissal I was trembling; I had to catch at the chair arm to steady myself as I rose. If I could have fled through the judge's anteroom I'd have done so gladly. Instead I had to walk with what strength I could muster back toward the source of that chill. Yet there was nothing now, nothing at all—Lucy's eyes met mine blandly; the other faces, too, were if anything sympathetic, each girded, apparently, only against its own coming ordeal. Even that impression of invisible force had receded. Mother unobtrusively squeezed my hand; all I could feel was an empty exhaustion.

It wasn't until somewhat later that I roused myself to new interest in what was going on. After me, Pete Fenrood testified, once again flatly repeating the story he had told before, his eyes under the peaked brows inscrutable, almost invisible, his long body well encased in protective armor. I wondered what form that face and that body might take if I stood up now to produce the matchbook, but the same indefinable unwillingness weighed down my voice and my limbs. After Pete, Ada was called, then Lucy Hague—carefully noncommittal, as he could be counted on to be. Waslewski, obviously, wasn't considering him seriously; most of the questions for him were merely in corroboration of Ada.

It was while the Boyces were testifying that I caught a point that made thought once more start churning. Not that Waslewski stressed this point either. Nila, in reply to a query, answered, "Oh yes, I'm sure there were lights on in Sylvia's apartment when we left, about eleven." After her, Clint gave the same evidence, and Florence Squires, in turn, testified to the same fact.

Lights, then, long after Sylvia was dead. Hector too—hadn't he said, last night, that he found Sylvia's place lighted? That meant, then, that Sylvia's murderer must have returned, sometime in the night, to turn those lights off. Certainly they had been off when I arrived in the morning, and no one else had spoken of turning them off.

I was so busy thinking through the possibilities in this that I only half listened from then on, even when Russ testified, when Mother followed him, and Hector, after her, mournfully repeated his tale. Nothing, I did notice, was said of the check, although everyone in the audience and the jury certainly knew of it by this time; nothing, either, was said of the anonymous note. The audience began growing restless, some onlookers squeezing out and others squeezing in even before the jury briefly retired and then returned with its verdict—"Willful murder by a person or persons unknown."

Only a part of my mind dwelt on this termination, actually. When Mother rose I rose with her; we began an inching exodus. Why had the murderer stayed on there in Sylvia's apartment long after she was dead? Or why—and this was more likely—had he returned there? Merely to get the lights off at a normal hour? Or was there some other reason?

By the time we were freed from the inquest it was already well past two; I had to grab a bite in a hurry. But even the break to normality, even being back at the hospital, couldn't keep me from the plaguing new puzzle. Recurrently, too, I was visited by freshets of the queer fear that had touched me as I sat in the witness chair. All I had to do was think back to that moment to have my hands grow icy.

If I had been able to think up any plausible excuse for doing so, I think I'd have asked Doris to work a double shift. "We've got to hurry," I could tell Waslewski. "At least I feel I've got to hurry. A murderer like this—he's too cool and too daring. I'll take notes, I can do

108

some typing; you can send me out on any job you can think of—just let's get it finished."

I had no need to be told, though, that Waslewski simply would stare at me and then send me away; he had no need for notes, or if he did he made his own: he had his own arrangements about typing; he couldn't use me for hunting out evidence while I was still one of the suspects.

Doris, of course, knew what had gone on at the inquest; knew its outcome.

"I guess they haven't really got one thing so far out of that anonymous note." Doris once more also had information of her own to impart, but it too was on the negative side. "Harry says it's awfully hard. Fingerprints on that cardboard don't show up. Charley Reed on the *Record* says he thinks the word 'Friday' must of been cut off the date line in last Friday's *Record*, because there's a little piece broken off the bottom of the F that got broken off only that day. Harry says that means whoever sent that note must of pasted it up either Friday night or Saturday or Saturday night. The whole note is *Record* type. But Harry says that tells them just hardly nothing, because of course everyone in town gets the *Record*, and it's no use going around looking for snips of paper when everyone has a furnace or a stove or anyway a—well, a bathroom. It was mailed in that big pickup box down near the station. I wouldn't of known, would you, that police work could be so discouraging?"

Her dreamboat evidently now scudded along under slightly less breeze than at first; difficulty for Lieutenant Kopp had become difficulty for Doris. After she'd gone I found myself beset by a restlessness which seemed less a personal than a community matter. Dr. Diebuhr stamped out to bark at me over a small mistake in addition, Doris had left an inch-wide ink splatter in the drug ledger, night nurses, coming on, paused only to say, "I suppose you'll be at the funeral tomorrow"—an oblique question that somehow seemed intolerably inquisitive. All I could do, though, was stand it and wait. Wait as the rest of Long

Meadow waited, for the next link in the chain, the next piece in the puzzle, hoping that, when it came, it would be more intelligible.

When it did come, though, it wasn't. Because what came next was that Hector LeClerque, sometime before ten that evening, managed to slip jail.

I heard it from Mother, at home.

My seven long hours had ended, finally; I had slammed the books shut, switched off the office lights, set the night latches. Outside the night had been clear and cool—moist from the rain that had fallen the night before, moist from the leaves that clung sodden and tramped to the walks and sent up their decadent, nostalgic fragrance of fall, moist from the tangled and stiffened grasses that filled vacant lots.

Long Meadow has never been dangerous, not in the way a city is dangerous; all my life I've come and gone through it, daytime or evening, without any least sense of fear. This night, though, after the inquest, after the evening I'd just spent, I found myself listening on the hospital steps, hunting out the dark corners of the side parking area, before I ventured out. Once in the old Pontiac and moving, I felt safer, but even then I watched narrowly, along both sides of the street into which I emerged, for anything that might look like a tan Chevrolet; I maintained that same watchfulness along all the blocks I passed. I hardly knew, at first, when I actually saw such a car, whether it stood where I thought it stood or whether I was projecting it there—dark and empty, again under trees, only these trees were elms. The elms bordering the Methodist church from which, in the morning, Sylvia was to be buried.

Cars don't have individualities, or so I told myself. I didn't know Lucy Hague's license number—he has never bothered, the way Russ has, to secure a special number each year. Just the same, as soon as I glimpsed that tan sedan so inconspicuously sitting there, I was bitten by a certainty it was Lucy's. If Lucy were to sing in the morning—that might be irony, a murderer singing at his victim's funeral—then he could have a reason for parking there; he could be in the church practicing. The church, though, stood as dark, as ostensibly uninhabited, as the car.

I drove around the block twice. Each time I came around the car stood as deserted as before. So did the church. What—if this was Lucy's car—would he be doing around here? He'd never park here to walk all the way to Ada's. His own rooms were at least six blocks north. Of all the people concerned in Sylvia's murder, Mother and I were the only ones living in this part of town.

Light from our kitchen window was a good deal more than a light of home that night; if the house had been dark when I drew up to it I scarcely know what I'd have done. As it was, the car didn't get to its garage; the spot I parked in was smack alongside the back porch. My dash from there to the kitchen must have broken all records, at least for me. Mother and I aren't in the habit of locking doors, but that time I turned the key and stood breathing hard, listening and waiting for I didn't know what—maybe a light rush of feet you'd never see moving, but that supplied very swift motion nevertheless.

Only when I'd stood there at least two minutes did my heart begin easing its thud. I told myself, "I'm getting terrible. There's nothing out there. There wasn't anything at the inquest. I'm running from nothing . . ."

Sometime around then I noticed that Mother was at the wall phone, just hanging up the receiver.

"That was Rose." As she turned to me Mother too was caught up by something, so caught up she missed the signs of my panic. "I suppose you've heard already—heard about Hector's getting out."

I asked hollowly, "Heard what?" Car at the church, irrational flight—now this about Hector. Jumping from stone to stone isn't one of the things I do best.

Mother came slowly forward. "Oh, then you haven't heard. It must just have happened; Rose called only this minute." The outside of

Mother's face wore the blank expression that means activity of thought inside. "If there were only some sense to it. Hector went into custody willingly enough last night; at least that's what I thought, didn't you? He talked as if——"

My knees were still weak from the other. I sat down.

"Hector." I repeated. "You mean he's escaped? How could he? That's a perfectly good jail, a strong one. The commissioner's report said so, when the new courthouse was built."

"He's gone, though. Emil Hasko says Hector didn't feel well all day; that must have been our fault, Cathy, giving him all that food on an empty stomach; we should have had more sense. Emil says Hector asked to see Dr. Diebuhr tonight, and Waslewski said it was all right. So Emil put him in what they call their sickroom, and I guess that's not as tight. They don't seem to have been particularly worried about Hector anyway—after they heard his story they only held him as a material witness; he'd walked in of his own accord, and they must have believed him, just as we did. When Emil walked in with Dr. Diebuhr, though, he was gone."

"Well." My thoughts still weren't functioning with any speed; they went through the process of getting my body back on its feet, but my body stayed put. "You mean Hector walked out of there, in a town this size, as early in the evening as this . . ."

Mother soberly nodded. "And they haven't found him yet. At least that's what Rose says. I can understand that much—Hector's had years of experience in sliding quietly around. People don't notice him much. What I can't see is why he'd want to break away. It isn't as if it's the first time he'd been in either."

To us it couldn't make sense, but apparently—if briefly—it did to the rest of Long Meadow. Later that night Rose Gamble called excitedly to ask if we'd locked our doors; everyone else in town, she said, was. In the morning, on our way to the funeral, we noticed that the sidewalks were almost bare of small children, wagons, and tricycles. Hector, all of a sudden, had become a fire-breathing dragon.

Yet for all the ostensible fright caused by Hector's jail break, there was also, perceptibly, an easing of tension. There was also a lessening of the reserve toward Mother and me. Rose Gamble's first morning call included a wonder as to whether she could ride with us to church. On the walk outside the church other people stopped for greetings too.

"You can't tell me," comments now ran, "he bust out of jail unless he had good reason. More in Hector than we ever saw, I guess."

We moved on into the quiet of Sylvia's funeral—a packed funeral, as packed as the inquest had been, with people soberly and somberly paying respect, as they always do at funerals, not just to the dead, but to that other death which is also inevitable, their own. Again one of my first concerns was to look about for Lucy Hague; I caught sight of his meticulously combed brown head—so meticulously and damply combed, as usual, that the marks of the comb's teeth still showed—ahead in one of the forward pews; I knew then he wouldn't be singing. If that had been his car near this church last night, it was just one more riddle, but one temporarily to be shoved aside. Pete, the Boyces, Florence Squires—they too were present; Ada and Russ of course were in the minister's parlor at the side; I didn't see them—Ada in black and leaning heavily on Russ—until we went to the graveside.

The minister spoke feelingly and tolerantly; Sylvia as she had been while living, ruthless and generous and highhanded and arrogant, was forgotten in favor of the Sylvia who had met so untimely and horrible a death. A great many people cried. My grief for Sylvia seemed casketed; instead my fingernails bit into my palms with an urgency all too familiar—not this easily, my thoughts said, not to be dismissed this easily. Not Sylvia. Not death. Not continuing menace.

After the funeral, in the relieved way also common to funerals, people returned to their talk of Hector. "I hear they got men out looking again. He won't stay gone forever."

Talk about Hector, though, didn't go on forever either. Something else very quickly superseded it.

Mother and I were still at lunch in the kitchen when Rose Gamble rushed back after being no more than twenty minutes gone. She sank, wheezing loudly, into a chair, one aimless and undirected hand waving back and forth as if it were a fan, before her face and ample bosom. Color had faded from her cheeks so thoroughly that only the dusky dregs of the wine red remained.

Defensively half rising, I asked sharply, "Now what?" and Mother too rose, gripping the table edge.

Rose Gamble said, "They've found out who did it. It wasn't old Hector at all. It was that young man went around with Cathy awhile, that Pete Fenrood. They found what he did it with. A piece of his fishing tackle. A stringer—that piece of thin rope you use to keep the fish on. They got it right out of his tackle box in the trunk of his car."

CHAPTER TWELVE

AT LEAST, NOT RUSS. That, ridiculously, was the first thing I thought. Waslewski and Lieutenant Kopp pouncing, and not, thank heaven, on Russ. Just the same, after Mrs. Gamble had exploded her bomb, I sat with fingers chilling and stiffening in my lap, while the kitchen stove, when I looked at it, swayed slightly and tilted upward, reservoir end first. *Why couldn't it have been Lucy Hague?* That, I think, was the second thing I thought. During the two days just past, as I now recognized, my own suspicions had tended increasingly toward Lucy. I didn't want it to be Pete. Maybe my feelings toward him had been wayward and inconstant, maybe I'd recognized in him a tendency toward sometimes being harsh and moody, maybe he'd shown no ambition beyond an easy income and plenty of time for fun, but still I'd thought him nice in many ways; he'd been exciting.

Over the three of us in the kitchen rested a silence that went on long enough for me to remember the movies I'd been to with Pete, the dances, the rides in his car. It was Mother who spoke first, asking thinly, "He's admitted it? They've proved it for sure?"

"I don't know yet. I guess so. Anyway he's been arrested. I got it straight from Agatha, and she had it straight from Lil Olson at the phone exchange. The sheriff's been waiting for a report on a lot of ropes and things that were sent in to the state laboratories. He just got his report. It says there were flakes of skin, human skin, in the stringer that was marked as coming from Pete Fenrood's car. Agatha says Waslewski went right out and got Pete—he was there in his Kitchen. She says the *Record* is putting out an extra. She says reporters have got the long-distance lines all tied up——"

Mother said lengthily, "I can't believe it." She got to her feet, which I'm not at all sure I could have done; she began walking up and down, kneading her knuckles, as if by quickening that familiar pain she could inject reality into what she was hearing. "Whatever people may say about Pete, I've liked him. I've liked it when he's come here—maybe he does get in a fight once in a while, maybe he once or twice has had too much to drink—he's wild and hard the way young men are for a little while—the way they're supposed to be for a little while. Under that I've thought he was all right. Cathy's father—before we were married some people called him wild too."

Her glance, as she turned herself about, just cleared my head. Of the few people who have guessed at my hidden emotions, Mother of course is one; she's too intuitive. What she's guessed has caused her dismay and a long relentless drive to shake me out of it—not that she has anything against Russ, but she can't believe me so foolish as to keep centered on him, now he's married, the affections I formed as a child. It's a subject on which I've wretchedly agreed with her; the only thing I haven't been able to do is change.

She went on, lips firm, "I've liked it when Cathy's gone out with Pete. I'm not going to believe he murdered Sylvia until he says so himself. A part of his fishing tackle out of a tackle box in the back of his car—if he's like everyone else in Long Meadow that tackle box was unlocked, and the trunk too. Anyone could have gotten at that stringer, both to take it and put it back. I can't imagine Pete sending anonymous notes. I can't imagine him sneaking around to leave money in Hector's shack. Until he admits it . . ."

Mother could be belligerent. But as she talked my own misery increased rather than diminished.

Mother didn't know about the matchbook.

If keeping knowledge of the matchbook from Waslewski had

been reprehensible before, it was twice that now. I knew it. Knew I couldn't delay longer.

That I did nothing was a decision my body seemed to come to at the expense of my mind; I suffered for it. If, within the next hours, I opened my billfold once to look at the object within it I did so a hundred times. The matchbook quit looking like a matchbook and began looking like the scarlet flat head of a snake.

Yet the day wore on and I still kept it secret. More news seeped in—Pete still was denying his guilt; Pete doggedly was holding to his story. Witnesses came forward who had seen him Friday night at the water show, but since he could have killed Sylvia before then, that didn't help.

If speculation about Hector—now half forgotten though still hunted—had in its inception raged over Long Meadow like fire, argument about Pete billowed and eddied in ocean currents. He had, it appeared, friends. For every person who said, "You take a guy like that, now, coming in here, no more background than a hamburger," or "That guy's a scrapper, he just got something too much to take, that's all," there were others who took the opposite view: "Right to me he says, 'Any time you want a good cook and good cooking,' he says, 'you go hunt up a good German or Norwegian woman that's lived on a farm, raised a big family. That's what I want for my Kitchen,' he says. You take a young fellow smart enough to know that much, and he's too smart to take his own stringer out of his own tackle box and choke a girl to death, no matter how mad he gets."

"Besides, he's cute." Among his adherents was Doris. "You were the one he had time for, but I liked him." Both indignation and exasperation colored her attitude toward me. "If you'd been the way any right-minded girl should have been about Pete," she might have said, "none of this would have happened." Apparently she had even gone so far as to disagree with Lieutenant Kopp. "I know Harry thinks it's all Pete now; he as much as said so. I still don't believe it. I said so right to him. I said I didn't care what proof he got, I still didn't believe it. Not a cute guy like Pete, with the way he can look at you so you know he's lying but you like it anyway."

This last didn't help either; Doris' reasons for not wanting Pete to turn out a murderer had too much kinship with my own, and, put in her words, I had to see how insubstantial they were. The kind of work I did that afternoon, I'd have been a luxury for the hospital at half what they paid me. And after managing to get myself safely home at ten—this time without so much as a glimpse of Lucy Hague or any tan Chevrolet—I wasn't of any more use to myself in my bed; certainly I didn't sleep in it. At nine in the morning, after having been unpardonably bearish with Mother at breakfast, I got myself into the car and drove toward the courthouse.

Only it still—and despairingly—wasn't Nick Waslewski for whom I headed, it was Pete. Seeing him again couldn't get me anywhere; I'd tried that. That, though, was what I wanted to do. Sometime I would have to come up against something I could recognize as final.

I knew being inside a jail couldn't be a pleasant experience, and it wasn't. From the moment I got face to face with Floyd Tripp, the jailer, I began wishing I hadn't surrendered to this particular compulsion. "You ain't no relative," Floyd insisted on repeating, suspiciously, and even after he'd called for permission from Waslewski he remained reluctant, grumbling as he rose from his desk, grumbling again as he drew a bunch of huge keys from his pocket, stalking ungraciously toward an inner door.

He asked, "You ever been in a jail before? All right, all I say is, don't start yelling. Every time I get a woman in here, almost, what she does is yell."

I could understand that. Advancing with Floyd Tripp into the tunnellike gray cement corridor beyond the door he unlocked, I saw what a jail was like, smelling of dust and Lysol, cold with a damp cold far beyond the chill of the fresh September morning outside, lighted by ceiling bulbs in wire cages, broken at the sides by grilled iron doors through which, as we walked past, I caught glimpses of high narrow windows, cots that were simply shelves let down from the wall. In each of the two first cells a man, disconsolate and solitary, looked out at us. Whether I wanted to or not, I couldn't help feeling what it was like to be enclosed here; pressed and confined within the small cut-off closeness. I had to breathe rapidly because there was so little air. "A jail," I thought, "is a mausoleum, these cells at the sides are vaults, this is a place where people are brought to be buried, not dead but alive."

And when I saw Pete I thought, "That's what he feels too."

He was in the third of the cells on the right-hand side, sitting on the edge of his narrow shelf, smoking, entirely rapt and quiet, his one hand holding the cigarette, his other hand cupped under a cardboard saucer, plum-stained and crowded with stubs. Behind the exterior emptiness of his face was a look of tense and active anger, as if he might be engaged, in some distant place, in fighting a distant battle. When Floyd jingled his keys at the door and stood aside for me to step in, Pete didn't even look up; his eyes remained intent on their rebellious activity.

"Company, Pete," Floyd tossed in laconically and inflectionlessly. "Thirty minutes."

I wasn't aware, actually, of moving past Floyd and into the cell; I only knew I was inside it. There was a small push at my back, the keys again jangled, and then the tramping footsteps receded back down the corridor.

It was so quiet the two of us in the small space might have been the only living beings around.

I began shakily, "Hello, Pete." I was aware of a good deal of heat—or chill—at my diaphragm. Another of the things I hadn't foreseen was that I would have to think up something to say.

119

He asked, "Interesting sight, Cathy? I didn't know you went in for staring at animals in zoos."

I said, "I don't."

He said, "I can't think up any other reason why you'd come." He remained sitting, his gaze still toward his hands, his face on the defensive, not just against me, but against everything. His hair had been combed neatly and smoothly into the one deep wave it makes on the right side of his head, but under his too bright eyes were creased folds I'd never seen there before, and a dark stubble of beard clouded his indented cheeks.

I replied swiftly, although this too wasn't anything I'd planned, "I could get things for you. Clothes you'll need, and your razor. I could——"

"Thanks," he declined. "I was at the Kitchen when they picked me up, and I told Mrs. Haushofer to send over what I'd need. Should be coming through pretty soon."

"Magazines. You can't just——"

"Thanks. Cigarettes, though." This time, at least, he wasn't entirely declining. "No magazines. I'm—I'm indulging in a unaccustomed exercise. Thinking."

Of itself, because since I had come in he hadn't lifted it to his lips, his cigarette had now burned to a short stub; he held it until the longer ash tipped and fell off, then ground it in among the other stubs before setting the cardboard ash tray on the ledge of his shelf.

He said then, carefully and still remotely, "I was beginning to worry about cigarettes. Nice offer, Cathy. You should try a jail sometime. Surprising. I find myself looking at people in a clear cold light. Even you, Cathy. On the outside—you know this, don't you?—you just look like an armful. A warm, soft nice armful. Nice light brown hair, waving a little, and falling and turning under. Nice brown eyes. Your mouth's soft. But you aren't soft inside, are you, Cathy? If you were, you wouldn't have stood me off the way you have. Or maybe you are, and you're try-ing to hide it. It's hard to tell, isn't it? Everybody wears a face, outside, and inside that face he can be almost anything. What're you, Cathy, inside?"

He stood up to stare at me speculatively, the harsh line of bitter-ness growing around his mouth.

"Should I apologize for wondering if you killed Sylvia? That's what I've been doing, and I don't have to apologize because haven't you wondered about me? Two days ago I wouldn't have done it, but I do now; I wonder about you and about all the others. Ada first, maybe—once I said I couldn't see Ada killing Sylvia, but I've made myself see it. Ada Bennert—she's a shrew, isn't she? She probably makes life a holy hell for Russ. Probably she hated Sylvia. No one else has a motive to compare with Ada's, not that we know about yet. Or Russ Bennert's. Have you let yourself think of that, Cathy? Oh, I know it's unlikely; I know the mur-derer's first try was to weasel the murder on Russ, but just the same, Russ has motive. If Ada inherits, so does he; Ada may be a shrew, she may be addicted to prairie violets like Lucy Hague, but Russ has a chance to be big stuff, and as long as he does Ada will be sticking to him."

A sound began forming itself in my throat, but he had no time for me, pacing the three steps that his long legs made of the distance from door to window.

"Clint Boyce. What do I know about Clint? He's solid at poker. He handles a glass with the best. If a lake has a fish in it he finds it. He's hell on wheels with women and Sylvia was a woman he was hot after. Only that's still not enough, not for Clint."

Again I might have made comment, but he disallowed it.

"Nila. Sharp and hard and plays 'em close to her chest. Nila could get one affair too many from Clint. Maybe, for Sylvia, Clint would have ditched Nila, and Nila wouldn't have liked that. Then there's you.

I don't have to think it up. You and your mother. You had plenty to hold against John Gainer; you had plenty to hold against Sylvia—there isn't anything festers like one of these family carbuncles, I've seen 'em before."

Again he left me no space for reply.

"Lucy Hague. And that's something, isn't it? Ada's lap dog. A lap dog for any woman, maybe, who'd have good scotch and fancy dinners to hand out for free—and who'd want him around. For my money, though, Sylvia didn't. I never saw him in Sylvia's part of the house unless Ada was there too. Maybe that was the trouble; maybe he wanted to cut in and Sylvia wouldn't play. In that case I'd have expected it would be Ada who'd have killed Lucy. Lucy's right in there, but I still don't see it. Old Hector—the same to him. Florence Squires—just a servant. Sylvia could be damn highhanded, she could make promises and not keep them . . ."

The pause, when he at last came to it, was entirely of his own making. He stood in front of the foot-square window, the window making a frame for his face, which momentarily looked empty and drained. When he next went on it was more slowly.

"I don't know enough about Sylvia. That's the trouble. I don't really know what she was. I played around with her, I took her on faith, pretty much. Just the way I took you—I'd have married you any time you said, Cathy. On faith."

He hadn't invited me to sit on his shelf; he hadn't invited me to anything at all. But I sat on his shelf.

He said, "Funny, isn't it? Maybe we're finding out about faith. Maybe we're due to find out how different people can be inside from what they are outside. Sylvia and other people too. It's not doing me any good to say it, but I wasn't the one who put that stringer around Sylvia's neck. I hadn't used my tackle for a week. My car stands there, alongside the Kitchen . . ."

At last he was getting to it, the same defense Mother had made for him. And while he was making it I believed in it, strongly—that and the honesty of every word he had been speaking since I came. I believed that the matchbook too meant nothing.

I began swiftly, words tumbling, "Mother said the same thing; lots of other people are too. You needn't believe, just because you're shut off in here, that you don't have friends. Almost everyone you know is——"

He broke in on it. "That's good to hear, Cathy." His voice, then, had dropped, but his intentness hadn't. In a little wait he reached for the package in his pocket, squeezing it to make certain it held what he wanted, before he shook out a cigarette. The movement he made then, from the window to the shelf beside me, was very swift; just one moment he wasn't there, the next he was.

He said, "Because there's someone around who's no friend of mine. I suppose that's what gets my goat worst—the try for Russ failed, because be had an alibi. So now I'm the fall guy.

I could see it coming, and I've got to see it better now. Russ first, because he was right there in the house. If it hadn't been for an accident letting him out, we'd have been getting plants against him, just the way we are against me. Me second, Hector third. Somebody wasn't running any chance of running out.

Sylvia was seeing someone that night; I was sure of it then and I'd swear to it now. Don't you see, Cathy, that five-dollar bill under Hector's coffee cup, that was playing it safe in case I slid out too. In case you think I killed Sylvia, then where does that five-dollar bill——"

He broke it himself, he said, "Uh," as if the syllable were jolted from him, then he wiped his right hand slowly and lonesomely over the dark stubble of his face.

He went on, "You know, when I thought that up, I thought I was being quite fancy. I thought the murderer was making a mistake, maybe, allowing for so many suspects. But he wasn't, was he? For any other killer, it would look better and work better to have just one suspect, me. But if I killed Sylvia, if I'd sent that anonymous note and put the money under Hector's cup—I'm the one who might think it would obscure things to get Russ and Hector messed into it too."

CHAPTER THIRTEEN

HE SAID ALMOST NOTHING more, but sat as if appalled by the logic he himself had evoked. After a while he got around to lighting his cigarette; he sat with the cigarette in one hand and the ash tray in the other, just as he had when I came in, distant and unapproachable.

I was shaken too. I said miserably, defying my reason for being there, "More evidence will come out; no one could possibly prove you did anything you didn't do. You haven't much motive; not motive for premeditated murder; everyone knows that; everyone's talking of that. You've got so many people who like you; I like you; I really do like you, Pete; if I can do anything . . ."

He wasn't even listening. When Floyd Tripp very shortly appeared to tell me the half hour was over, he roused enough to say, "Good-by, Cathy," but it was from a long way off. As if his forehead were open I could feel the pulse of his thinking, fast and hot, slow and cold.

The door closed with a metallic clunk, the keys jangled, my feet and Floyd Tripp's feet struck harshly against the cold cement of the corridor floor. I was being let out. But Pete . . .

For a half second something went on inside me that I didn't recognize at all. It was almost as if I could have caught Floyd Tripp in the stomach with my elbow and snatched his keys; it was almost as if I could have hit at him to beat him down.

When Floyd Tripp relievedly let me out at the side steps I was still breathing a little hard. Already denying, with horror, that I could possibly have had any such impulses as I seemed to have had, but still having trouble getting enough breath. All I was doing, actually, was hold more tightly than ever the handbag that held the matchbook.

If I once more apprehensively wondered, as I made my way to the cigarette counter at the drugstore two blocks down, what the next move in this chess game might be, I didn't have to wonder long. When I got home Ada Bennert was waiting to see me; she must, indeed, have been waiting for me then. On opening the kitchen door I heard the voices, and when I walked through to the living room there they were, Mother stiffly and defensively erect in the platform rocker, her cheeks marked, by two high, bright spots of color, her gnarled hands swiftly knitting in the awkward way they still can knit. Across from her, in the walnut armchair we covered last year with needlepoint, sat an equally stiff Ada.

If it hadn't been for that mutual stiffness, the scene might nearly have been cozy. Mother greeted me with a bright upward smile. "There you are, dear. Too bad you were so long; Ada's been here almost twenty minutes."

The white lace curtains—we're one of the Long Meadow families that cling to them—billowed freshly and starchily in the still chill sunlight at the three windows, the marble-top table and the red glass lamp were the table and lamp Mother and Father picked up at a farm auction when I was six, the much too big square Steinway with the cracked sounding board was the one that had been bought at another auction when I was eight, so I could begin piano lessons. During the last ten years there's been no money in our family for furniture.

Then Ada said tautly, "I had to see you," and any illusion of coziness vanished. In an expensive black suit and an equally expensive black hat with a single, lovely, upcurling feather, she exuded nothing but fever and strain. The eyes that pressed from their deep pits might not have known sleep for weeks, tiny indentations seemed to play under the dark skin stretched so tightly over the thin cheeks,

126

her hands fiddled continuously with the bag and gloves in her lap, even her feet, in beautiful small black suede platform pumps, seemed to twitch.

I could be sorry for Ada; if it turned out she had nothing to do with Sylvia's death I could be very sorry for her. But I could never, under any circumstances, feel cordial toward her, and certainly I didn't feel so now. If it had been unprecedented for Sylvia to come to our house, it was ten times that for Ada to do so; caution told me to look out.

Offering a third stiffness to the varieties already on display, I said, "Of course you're free to come here."

She seemed able to approach her purpose only obliquely and jerkily. "I know it—looks queer, my being here. I know we've never been—friendly. But I——"

She might have been trying frantically, and contrary to anything she has ever wanted from us before, to force us into an attitude that would be more gracious. As she realized the impossibility of this effort hysteria crept into her voice.

"Everyone's against me. That's true, isn't it? Lucy Hague's almost the only person that comes around to talk to me any more. I get the money—all Sylvia's money. That's what everyone's saying, isn't it? Pete Fenrood's in jail, but that doesn't make the least difference. How nice for me—that's what everyone's saying—that I've finally gotten my money."

The handbag in her lap was a good one, but it wasn't going to last long with the treatment she was giving it.

I replied as quietly as possible, "You're not the only one beside Pete who's still under suspicion."

Her mouth wobbled, but when she spoke again she was more controlled.

"I didn't come here to—talk. I came here because of what you—said at the inquest. You said Sylvia was here. Just a week before she died. You said she phoned you that Friday. I didn't know about that, before. I——"

"No, you didn't know about that," I thought, and whether it was memory, or whether I was feeling it again, I once more sensed an echo of that chill I had recognized while I was testifying. Was it from Ada that chill emanated—was it coming from her now? Again I tried reaching out for it, but once more, as soon as I did so it vanished.

"Sylvia never did things without reasons." Ada continued her jerking, anxious speech. "Not anything as out of the ordinary as that. And there's something else. Ever since Sylvia—died, I've felt someone was—hunting. Not the police, I mean, someone else. I've felt someone is—hunting for something, and not finding it. I've thought about that visit of Sylvia's, and that check——" Once more she paused, and what followed was direct and blurted, an accusation thrown at us like a slap: "Sylvia came here to give you something. To keep for her. That's what she was here for, isn't it? That's what she was paying you for. And now you aren't giving it up to me. You're keeping it——"

Little of that was enough. "Something so valuable," I erupted. "That six thousand is nothing. Something we're holding onto—another star sapphire maybe—until her death has blown over and we can skip. Something we thought it was worth killing Sylvia for. Of all the——"

Long before I was in any condition for listening, Ada was beginning some sort of denial, pushing forward in her chair, defensive but not giving way. "Wait. Wait. I didn't say that. You may have some reason for keeping it——"

Blood sizzled in my ears. "Can you tell me just what this something we're keeping is supposed to be?"

Mother, by that time, was trying to get her oar in too. "If both of you would——" But Ada ignored her.

"I don't *know* what it is. And I've got to know. I can't keep on this way. It could be anything. A note on a small piece of paper——"

"Sylvia hadn't seen me for ages. She must have had a deposit box at the bank. If you can tell me one single reason——"

128

"I did tell you. Sylvia'd never have come here without any purpose. She told you nothing important—you said so yourself. She had to have——"

That time Mother's oar did cut in, sharply. "You say somebody's hunting through Sylvia's things—what makes you think so?"

The fever now burned toward Mother. "The sheriff asked me to look through Sylvia's jewelry. So I did. That was Sunday. Afterward—Monday—I went back. The pieces were almost in the same places, but not quite. I remember things like that. Somebody had pulled the velvet bottoms out of the trays—I'm sure of it. I——"

"Naturally you've gone through her deposit box."

A swift nod. "Yesterday, after the funeral. There wasn't anything except the things supposed to be there—deeds and stocks and certificates. But yesterday Florence used the vacuum all over Sylvia's part of the house—Waslewski said we could clean up. And this morning there was paper lint under the desk. Don't you see? *After* the deposit box was opened. It's got to be—something that hasn't turned up yet. Her house has been gone through—I've gone through it myself. You're the only other place. You're the people she went to. But you've no right to keep it. If it's the six thousand you want—all right, you can have it. Just let me get what she brought here. I don't care what it is; I don't care if it isn't valuable. *I've got to know what it is.* Can't you see that?"

She sat in her chair, beating down on her handbag with one fist, now, with an automatic, tom-tom beat; her head, too, turned in a kind of rhythm, from me to Mother, from Mother to me. She had a suit on, a hat. But behind the desperation of her eyes she was naked—naked in the way that counts, indecently, letting us see a necessity that had much more behind it than anything she was saying, a necessity outside any proportion or reason.

"Sylvia brought nothing here." Against that disproportion and unreason nothing sounded decisive, but I could try. "I don't know how

129

to prove it——"

She gave way not at all. "It's no use your saying that. You've got it here. If you didn't, you'd let me look. You both know you've got it here, hidden. You——"

What she now said was entirely uncontrolled, spilling from her in a spurting, vitriolic flood. Mother, somewhere along in it, rose to stand beside me; anger once more began boiling but then very quickly subsided; anger, against anyone as out of her senses as Ada, just didn't seem to apply. Mother's eyes met mine, and in them I met a decision I was helplessly willing to echo.

Mother said, in great quiet, "If nothing else will convince you, Ada, you're welcome to look."

Ada's spate stopped. And for a moment then, just for a moment, she looked uncertain and weakened, as if she felt the force of her own logic—if we let her look, then we didn't have what she looked for. But then swiftly, galvanically, she brushed aside that uncertainty, getting to her feet as she did so. She said with a stony sort of satisfaction, "That's better," and made for Grandfather's old desk in the corner. "You probably think you've got it put away so neatly I can't find it, but you'll find yourselves mistaken." With a queer, methodical facility, as if this were an activity practiced for years, she pulled down the desk lid and began going through the desk, emptying each pigeonhole in turn, taking each letter from its envelope, glancing at it front and back, returning it to its envelope, laying it on an accumulating pile of other old letters, old receipts, old canceled checks, each one thoroughly scrutinized, each returned with its mates to the proper pigeonhole before she went on.

Near the doorway where we were left standing, Mother and I stood looking on. Gaping, I have no doubt, in what was more an appalled disbelief than anything else—disbelief that this could actually be going on, and that we were letting it go on. At any other time Ada's rummaging through our possessions would have been unthinkable;

now, so overwrought was her state, it seemed almost the least we could do. Unable to leave her—the idea that she might have some quite contrary purpose in being here did hit me—unable to help her, since we knew how fruitless her search must be, Mother and I could only hang about at the outskirts of her activity, awkward, useless, and for the most part speechless.

It was an activity which, as it continued, grew only more intent and absorbed. The desk finished, Ada went on, no words spoken and no gestures made, to shake out each of the magazines on the lamp table. She lifted the lamp to peer through its flower-frosted red globular base, turned the lamp table upside down, apparently to make sure nothing had been pasted under its top, moved on to the bookcase.

By two-thirty, when I pulled myself away to get ready for work, she had not only gone painstakingly through every book in the bookcase, she had also probed the insides of the radio, probed all the chair cushions, prodded along the edges of the piano keys and baseboards with a nail file, and looked under the rugs; in the kitchen, refusing lunch, she spooned through the flour, tipped coffee from one can to another, poked through baking powder—and she still had the dining room, Mother's room, the bathroom, the hall, my room upstairs, and the woodshed, to go.

Not until almost seven o'clock that evening, actually, did that search end. It was seven when Mother called me, just after I had come up from supper in the employees' dining room.

"Finally she had to give up." Over the wire Mother sounded pinched and subdued, as if she too, like her house, had been ransacked. "Not ashamed at all, either. She just muttered, 'I can't be mistaken. I can't be. I just can't find it.' And then she went home."

I had known what the result must be, and Ada's attitude toward that result couldn't be a surprise either. But there were other questions. I began, "Mother——"

"I know," Mother said. "Why is she so worked up? She's hunting something—no doubt about that. But whether there's anyone else——"

Questions she, nor more than I, could answer.

For a couple of hours, that afternoon, I had tried to wrench Ada and Sylvia and everything else but work out of my mind, but after I had hung up, as if in revenge for that temporary expulsion, the whole indecipherable puzzle wound itself around me more stranglingly than ever. "But Sylvia *must* have had some reason for coming here," Ada had said, and that much had to be true, even if that reason weren't the one Ada's fevered unreason had supplied. I knew a different sequence. Mother had asked Sylvia a question on the afternoon of that visit— "You couldn't be in danger, could you?"—and it was after that question that Sylvia had come straight to me.

Suppose Ada wasn't as entirely wrong as I thought her; suppose Ada, at least partially, was right. Suppose Sylvia had had something she had recognized it was dangerous for her to keep—no use asking now what that something could be; just suppose. Suppose—impossible, but still suppose—that for some reason Sylvia had come to me, intending to ask me to keep this something, but changing her mind. Who then would she have gone to? Russ? Pete? If Russ, wouldn't he long before this have brought out anything he had? Pete—would Pete be withholding evidence even in jail? And it hadn't been about any *object* that Sylvia had hinted; she had hinted only at telling me something. The only actual *thing* she had mentioned had been a railroad ticket. Was it that railroad ticket that Ada—and perhaps someone else—now so avidly hunted?

When Sylvia first spoke of that ticket I had immediately jumped to the idea it might be for me; it might be my way out of Long Meadow. Suppose, though, that was wrong; suppose it was Sylvia to whom that ticket had reference, suppose it was the danger. Only, how could a ticket be dangerous? A ticket could be used to hint that someone wanted you out of town. Sylvia usually left Long Meadow right after Labor Day anyway—could hurrying her a few days have been so important? Had she, because of Pete, decided to stay on through the fall and winter—was that why someone had hinted she go? To whose advantage was it that she be out of town?

All I got in answer to any of my questions was a headache. Toward eight I acquired new questions—Waslewski called with a brief command: "Miss Kingman, we'd like you at the courthouse, nine in the morning." Just that, no explanation. Now what did he want of me? Could it be because I'd been to see Pete? Had he heard about Ada's hunt? Could he have guessed, somehow, about the matchbook?

Only there wasn't too terribly much of that either, not that night. That was the night when my return home began like any night's return home—night latches set, pause at the hospital's side entrance while I sought out the shadows in the side area, quick dash to my car, relief when I had the motor running, watchful scrutiny along the streets I passed. As I came even with the Methodist church I was penetrated, once more, by an icicle stab that left a lastingly chilly wake—the tan car was there again under the elms, dark as before, beside a dark church. Yet nothing had come of that car's presence in that particular spot on Monday night; at least nothing I knew of; that was the night Hector slipped out of jail, and surely Lucy Hague's car being parked near the church could have had nothing to do with that.

Home, when I rounded the corner, looked very good—narrow and white, porched across its front, cut in to hold the kitchen porch at the back; not much architecturally, but a whole lot in terms of safety. No light tonight from the kitchen, but a dim glow through the dining-room windows meant Mother still wasn't asleep. Tired out, undoubtedly, after the session with Ada, probably in bed, but keeping herself awake and her light on because she knew what a light and somebody waiting had now come to mean.

For the third time in a row, abandoning order in favor of safety,

I ran the car in along the kitchen porch, making certain, before I turned off the ignition, that no possible shadow lurked behind any of the snow-balls or lilacs, looking back toward the garage to make sure it was closed as I'd left it, and that no one could be hiding there. From car to kitchen door took me, as before, three jumps, and then I was safe—or I thought I was safe—back to door, key turning under my hand.

I called, "Home, Mother."

She didn't answer. I thought, "She's dropped off with the light on. I'll tiptoe in and—no, I'll have to wake her; she'll want to know I'm home."

I walked forward, in my security, to do just that. All day long, outside, it had been getting colder; the hospital had had heat on, but the ride home had been chilly; the sting of the weather had added to the sting of my tensions to wind me up tight. Now, however, I began unwinding. Mother must have had a fire in the kitchen range all evening; the kitchen was warm and relaxing. Maybe I'd sleep tonight . . .

Just before I stepped through to the dining room I almost had a warning; something welled up through the center of my body that bubbled, a geyser. I almost got sniveled around. But not quite.

CHAPTER FOURTEEN

I LAY BETWEEN TWO CLOUDS. The one underneath me was thick, pressing against my back, giving way, sometimes, to swallow me softly, then gathering substance and density to propel me upward, in a rhythm that was like breath, now up, now down, now up, now down. It wasn't the cloud underneath, though, that bothered me, it was the cloud on top, the one that was smothering, pressing suffocatingly close to my mouth, to my nose, to my whole face and my body, lifting a little, but then once more lowering, it too in a rhythm like breath, a rhythm that increasingly grew more cloying, more insistent, harder to shake off.

What brought me toward consciousness didn't seem to be so much the struggle with the clouds, although that too was active; what seemed to stir and rouse me was my heart beat, which at first went on so far away that I heard it as a distantly thunderous clanging, but which then grew centered inside me, so that my whole body shook with the insistent and warning drum—wake, wake, wake. Yet that life was the only life I seemed to contain; around me was darkness; I stifled in a darkness of no sight, no sound, no smell, no taste, no touch other than that of the cottony thick pressing clouds. Movement was something of which I was incapable; the struggle against the clouds was one of will, my heart's beating was done by will too, calling wake, wake, wake again, although my body was too inert to wake; it lay heavy and turgid upon its thick cloud, composed of stuff that never had and never could know motion.

Then, while the clouds still pressed, my hands came alive. I had been only a rolled bundle between the two clouds, but then I had hands, pressed flat, out and away from me, against the bottom cloud, sentient, feeling it, recognizing it as something they knew. Not cloud stuff, but sheets, not a cloud, under those sheets, but a mattress. I was in a bed, a familiar bed, maybe my bed. Above me, though, that other cloud still pressed, a cloud that, as my consciousness struggled upward, ceased in no way to be noxious, smothering. My hands lifted, after a while, to push up at it, but it pressed only closer. In addition to stifling me the cloud also was hot, terribly hot; I tried to roll; if I could roll, even a little, then maybe I could be away from that down-pressing cotton, maybe I could find coolness and strength. When I did roll, the cotton followed, but something else hit me—nausea, waves of it, rolling up from abdomen, leaving me laved in a sticky wet coolness. I opened my eyes, and there, right in front of me, was light from a window, my window, white curtains mistily looped at its sides. In the clear space left by the curtains there was moonlight, equally misty and equally pale, but clear for all that.

I wanted that moonlight. Not air—I didn't think of myself as needing air, though the over cloud still pressed. It was the light I wanted. Distance from my bed to the window was incalculable, tremendous, but distance made no difference; I wanted the moonlight, and I seemed, abruptly, to be filled by cunning and craft. Strength to rise from the bed was something of which my body could not so much as conceive, but I could fall from it; I couldn't walk to the window but I could—maybe— roll toward it.

I fell from the bed—that much came almost swiftly. The bump shook the house and almost sent me back into a final oblivion. But there was a difference on the floor; the cloud still pressed, struggling to bind me with a hundred octopus arms, but it was my body it held more than my face. I let the underneath cloud take me a little, not much; I let myself fall into it, gathering strength before I began struggling upward again. I knew after a minute or two—or maybe five minutes or maybe an hour, because I had no way of knowing—that I wasn't going to be able to roll toward that window, that I had exhausted and broken myself in the fall from the bed. Yet I moved; my will that had fought against the clouds could also drag my body quarter inch by quarter inch along the floor, now helped by hands that pulled forward swimmingly and graspingly, now helped by feet that kicked, now giving up to fall face forward into the bottom mattress, now eeling forward again . . .

The time came when I had groped past the iron girders that were the legs of the sewing machine, to touch a wall. I'd reached the window. Only, now I was only beneath it; I could no longer even see it. In all heaven and earth there wasn't strength to lift me to that window; there couldn't anywhere be strength to lift a body as heavy as mine, yet that was what I began doing, drawing my knees up, rolling so they were beneath me, using them as a lever to shove me upward, lying with my face against the iron lacework frame at the side of the sewing machine, clawing at that, worming my way up the frame of the sewing machine the same way I had wormed it across the floor. I lay with my face on the window sill, after a while, the rest of me wedged someway between sewing machine and wall; I lay there looking out at a moonlight that seemed to be wavering, lying so purely on the shadowed shapes of trees and houses, on lawns and sidewalk, on fence and porch; it too swam in the rhythm that invested everything, now lighter, now darker, now lighter, now swimmingly darker . . .

It would have been so easy to let go. All I had to do, now, was let go once more, and that would be all. No more fighting, no more struggling, no more worming across floors, no more doing of the impossible, no more debts, no more Russ, no more nightmare such as the one I'd been having—when was it?—of running headlong in some labyrinth, dashing myself at hedges, running forever in alleys already explored that I knew led nowhere . . .

All I had to do was relax here, swimming a little with the moonlight, swinging darker with the moonlight . . .

Maybe at the bottom I knew what it meant. Maybe at the bottom there was only one thing to push me to movement again—a final unwill-ingness. One moment I was swimming away, easily away, the cloud once more pressing. Then I was groping behind me, groping for some-thing, groping for anything. And the next I was smashing at the window with the object I'd gotten in my hand.

It wasn't the fight I had wanted, it was air—I found that out. As soon as I had my first mouthful I was gasping for it, thrusting my face forward, feeling the jagged edges of glass tear against my skin, but not caring. No pain hurt, nothing could hurt in comparison with the excru-ciating bliss of getting that air. I hung out the window, gasping it in, being sick, gasping some more, gasping again, seeing the world outside the window take on a stark and almost frightening clarity—moonlight harsh, flat, white, on the too stark shapes of trees and houses, shadows lying too starkly, bushes and gardens and sidewalks and fences emerg-ing sharp and hard instead of misty and swimming.

I had a minute—maybe a long time—of hanging there motion-less, my head through the hole, maybe my shoulders too; I had a minute—maybe a long time—of recollecting what the world was like. And then, swiftly, there was more. Someone had been waiting for me, pressed flat, back to the dining-room wall just inside the door, when I'd come home. I'd been hit. The house was full of terror—a killing terror. Mother. Down there. With it . . .

I ran. I couldn't run, any more than I could do any of the other things I'd done. But I ran. My door stuck. Something seemed to catch and hold it on the inside, my side; I couldn't pull it open, but I could get it wide enough to squeeze through. On the other side of that door bil-lows of heat and billows of something else, too, seemed to sweep at me; the clouds I had so recently cast off threatened to engulf me again; I stag-gered instinctively back to my window, drew in two big lungfuls of the clean air, and then with one hand clamped over mouth and nose, the other waving in front of me like a tentacle, seeking and warding, I ran

138

downstairs.

Territory I ran in was as familiar as my feet, otherwise I'd never have made it; the rooms downstairs held their night look, but the shades were up; I could see the shapes of Mother's room too was dark, but I knew her bed and the roll in it; I grasped the still shoulder and began shaking it. "Moth——" before coughing stopped me. Then I was at her window too, beating at it with something I caught up from the dresser as I passed, hearing the sharp shattering of glass as it broke, feeling the inrush of purifying air. Mother weighed nothing; I got a chair under the window and her in the chair; her head lolled, lifeless and relaxed, her body slumped, that too lifeless; I ran to shut the door to the dining room, smashed out the upper sash, rubbed her hands, called to her, shook her. Queerly I remembered Ada shaking Sylvia. I suppose I did a hundred things that were senseless and that I don't even recall. I don't seem to have had a thought that the person who had struck me down and somehow filled the house with a smothering death could still be around, or if I did it didn't matter. At some time I must have run around the house throwing all the doors open and breaking most of the other windows, because that's how they were later, at some time I must have left Mother long enough to jerk the receiver from its hook, because that's how it hung later; I must have poured most of a quart of water over Mother because her nightgown was drenched to the waist later, and at some time, finally, I must have had sense enough to jerk all the lights on, because that was what finally brought help—a voice beside me saying, "What's wrong, Cathy, what's wrong? I got up to go to the bathroom, I noticed——"

I shook hair back from my eyes. There at the door of Mother's room stood Rose Gamble, clutching the throat of her blue chenille bathrobe tight around her neck. It must have been because of the dining-room light behind her, it must have been because I was crying, but I saw a halo around Rose Gamble's head, and before I even said, "Get Dr.

Diebuhr," or maybe while I was saying it, I thought, "I'm never going to think mean things about Rose Gamble again." I had Mother back on the bed by that time, and was trying to give her artificial respiration; there wasn't any life under my fingers at all, but that didn't mean Mother did-n't have to keep living; I was making her live.

How long it took other people to get there, that's something I'll never know either, not that it's important; just one minute I was still kneeling over Mother, doing what I'd been doing for an eternity, and the next I was shoved aside. "Here, I'll take over." I think it was Lieutenant Kopp. Somebody ran in the house, somebody barked orders, and then I was out again.

When I once more began waking I was on the dining-room couch, and Dr. Diebuhr bent over me. There was a sting in my nose, stings all over my face, and another in my arm. That time I struggled upward with just one idea. "Mother. Is Mother——"

Dr. Diebuhr answered, "We think she's making it," before he vanished, but I wanted to see for myself; I staggered to my feet, managing, after a while, to get as far as the door of Mother's room. Mother still lay with her eyes closed, but as I got nearer her lips moved, as if she might be trying to whisper something. Dr. Diebuhr stepped back, to let me drop to the bedside; I found Mother's hand. This time it had life in it, firmness and being; I sat there holding it, and of course I cried again, cried for relief, cried because I was so spent, cried because what else could I do? Dr. Diebuhr and Rose Gamble came and went a good deal, to and from the kitchen; Dr. Diebuhr every once in a while took the hand I was holding, to get its pulse. One time he did so he told me, "Responding nicely now Catherine; she should be all right." It was rather shortly after that—or at least it seemed shortly after—when feet tramped in the dining room, and a loud voice spoke disgustedly.

". . . kind of thing you expect, couple of fool women trying to run a stove. Women never did have any sense about stoves. Why, I recall once——"

That was where I started waking the rest of the way. I got on my feet; the effort it took to get from Mother's bed to the door was a good deal less than it had taken to get the other way. In the dining room were three men—Waslewski, Lieutenant Kopp, a stranger; it was the stranger who still was speaking, hat far to the rear of his head, hands thrust aggressively in his pockets, legs wide in a stance of masculine arrogance.

". . . shouldn't be allowed to happen. You take a couple of women like this, now, they ought to live in an apartment or something, got a man janitor. At least they could put in an oil burner, get a man to check it. Why, I——"

Indignation is a good, healthy emotion; as its iron began invigorating me I found I could stand upright, almost without holding the doorframe. I quit crying too, very abruptly, even if my face still felt stiff and damp and caught in places.

"Or of course," I said, "women who don't have some man to look out for them could just quietly and neatly be killed off, as we nearly were. Would you mind repeating what you said just a minute ago—that part about women not knowing how to run stoves?"

He was a heavy man, middle-aged; he swung about belligerently.

"You know what you almost did to yourselves, don't you? Just about wiped yourselves out. Go to bed the way you did—big coal fire, drafts all open, damper shut so the coal gas can't get up the chimney, what you expect to happen? I been in the stove business, right here in Long Meadow, for——"

I looked from face to face wonderingly, understanding a little, from the words so far spoken, of what had been done—seeing the simplicity and the art. But not understanding the rest.

"Do you mean to tell me," I asked, "that you three people think Mother and I are responsible for what went on here tonight? If the damper was shut and the drafts open we didn't leave them that way; we've been running that stove a good eight years. Mother's expert with the stove. She never forgets it. She——"

I had recognized the third man by this time; he was a Mr. Salvail, a plumber, but not our plumber. He began replying, but Waslewski stepped in front of him.

"Wait a minute, Miss Kingman. Now you look up to it we'd like to ask you a couple of questions. We been over the house and we don't see much wrong with it, except the windows all smashed. We figured maybe you did that, getting air in. That right?"

"Of course I did that. But——"

"You check on the stove before you went up to bed?"

Indignation still burned. "I had no chance to check anything. Somebody hit me on the back of the head. Somebody was standing right there against that wall just inside the door. I hadn't any more——"

"Wait a minute. Here. This is something we'll have to go into. You don't look too strong yet, Miss Kingman, maybe you better get on the couch. All right now . . ."

Indignation or not, I was glad to get to the couch. I sat on it and told my story. Waslewski pulled a dining-room chair around to sit facing me; Lieutenant Kopp pulled another around to sit side saddle, arms over the back. Mr. Salvail stayed standing, disbelief in every fat line of his body—I could see where he was; he'd taken the position that Mother and I had been careless, and he was holding to it. Waslewski and Kopp were more receptive, but I could also see the weighing that went on in their minds.

"Let's go over this again, Miss Kingman." Waslewski was patient and careful. "You say you got into the kitchen, noticing nothing wrong. Kitchen warm or cold?"

"Warm. Mother had a fire, all right. But she never——"

"You didn't look."

"I told you. I didn't have time."

"Go slow here, Miss Kingman. Any idea at all who it could have been here waiting for you?"

He didn't have to tell me to go slow; the importance of that one question didn't have to be pointed out to me. If I could answer that, if I could dredge up one telltale fact to tell him, there'd soon be no more danger, no more waiting around doors, no other questions. I tried my best, thinking back to it, trying to get the signal which had started turning me around, trying to evoke a scent, a sound, a movement, anything that could be informative. And I wasn't entirely unsuccessful—certainly there had been a scent, animal and warm; certainly there had been a brush of cloth, certainly there had been a movement. The trouble was, none of these were really telling—anyone, standing there, would have exuded that scent that was no more than human scent, anyone who struck me must have raised and lowered an arm.

I tried to get at it negatively. "It must have been a man. There wasn't any fragrance—not of powder or lipstick or face cream—it seems to me I should have caught something like that from a woman. And the movement was quick. Terribly quick. It must have been someone who——"

Like lightning, then, a connection. That car near the church. Last night, too.

Waslewski rapped at me quickly, "What is it, Miss Kingman? Don't think twice, out with it."

He was leaning forward, poised and intent; a warding doubt began holding me back, but then I let him have it.

"I think it was Lucy Hague. Lucien Hague."

The aquamarine eyes were gimlets, holding mine. Swiftly he glanced over at Lieutenant Kopp, almost breaking the connection, but before he could really lose me he had me again.

"What makes you say that?"

"His car. Last night—I think I saw it again, on my way home. Parked near the Methodist church."

"That seems very little to go on. Any other reasons?"

Bit by bit, then, I told him what else I'd noticed. As I did so, I couldn't help being aware of how vaporous were the facts on which I'd reasoned—just that Lucy had turned up for supper at Pete's when he seldom did so, just that his car had still been across the street fifteen minutes after he'd left, just that I'd thought I'd seen his car twice near the church, just that when Hector turned up behind a bush I'd somehow expected it to be Lucy. As I talked, Waslewski grew more and more restless; the next glance he threw Lieutenant Kopp was one of huge dissatisfaction.

"You've got to see yourself, Miss Kingman, you're giving us very little. We'll check on that car near the church, of course; find out where Hague was tonight. We've picked up what look like four sets of fingerprints around here, but they all look like women's. If you'd said you thought this assailant of yours was a woman we'd have been a lot more interested. There hasn't been——"

Four sets of fingerprints, all of them women's. Mother's and mine. Rose Gamble's. The others would be Ada's.

I'd forgotten Ada, forgotten the hunt.

Ada. Could that have been Ada there, waiting? Washing before she came, so she'd give off no scent. Schooling herself to stand quiet—frantic still, hungry still, driven again, still believing . . .

Promising us six thousand dollars if she got what she wanted. Would Ada kill two people—or be willing to—in order to save herself six thousand dollars?

Not possibly true. I'd been sorry for Ada that afternoon; I thought I could never again dislike her in quite the same way I had before. Yet . . .

I began for Waslewski, "One set of prints. They're certain to be Ada Bennert's——"

He was much sharper to it than to anything I'd said of Lucy Hague; twice he went over Ada's ostensible reason for hunting, the search she'd made, breaking it only to rise.

"Doc, just a minute here." This was for Dr. Diebuhr, emerging just then from the bedroom.

"Okay for me to run along now, I hope?" Dr. Diebuhr, rolling down shirt sleeves, was, for him, almost chipper, but showing a tendency to revert to normal. "Things like this go on at night, naturally; if I ever had any sleep—anybody seen my coat? I had it just——"

Waslewski went on, "Miss Kingman here says she was hit on the back of the head. I wonder if you'd——"

"What? What's that?" Recovery in Dr. Diebuhr was immediate. "You mean you think—where?" The last word of that was for me; he already had my head in his quick fingers and was turning it this side and that, running his thumbs and forefingers expertly over my scalp under my hair. I myself felt back toward the area just above the nape of my neck, at the left, where a dull soreness still responded to pressure.

"Hm. Skin unbroken. No swelling. Though that's not conclusive. Very difficult to determine, except through autopsy, whether a specific area has suffered a blow, if it isn't too heavy. You could tell, of course, by the hemorrhaging of the small blood vessels. Perfectly possible there was such a blow, don't let me give you any other idea . . ."

He stepped back to look at me, dispassionate, scientific, interested, a little as if he would have liked to do an autopsy just to find out if I were telling the truth or not. I admire Dr. Diebuhr and with every reason; he was wonderful with Father, any other doctor would have charged us four times what he did, he's a just man to work for, watching him set a leg or sew up a cut is like watching a perfect dancer—no waste motion, no least break in the sureness. But no one could call him warm-blooded.

I said, "Then Mother. Mother must have been knocked out too. I know she intended staying awake for me. She might have dozed off, but she'd have waked. She wouldn't have slept through my being knocked down——"

Followed by all of us, and by my continuing, maybe incoherent argument, Dr. Diebuhr returned to the bedroom, where he went over Mother's head with the same care he had gone over mine, lingering longest at a spot some two inches above her right temple.

"Hm," he contributed consideringly. "Hm. It's possible. But I can't say it's conclusive either. Certainly if there is swelling it's slight. Wouldn't have noticed it if I hadn't been looking for it. Of course I thought I was treating a case of coal-gas suffocation. Responded like that . . ."

He was doing the talking by that time; I'd quit. Quit because I was too choked. Being attacked in your own house, having someone deliberately try to kill you by the filthy, insidious means of crowding the stove with coal, opening the drafts and closing the damper—that's bad enough. But not being believed, having every word I said treated as if I were simply trying to crawl away from a stigma of carelessness—that was infuriating. I stood holding the foot of the bed, and I think I shook it; anyway Mother joggled.

I said, "You must be able to get at it someway. There must be some proof. Look—what time is it now?"

Three wrists lifted.

"Almost five-twenty."

"Nearly morning. If Mother and I left the stove that way when we went to bed—wouldn't we have been dead long before this? I don't know too much about coal gas, but does it take that long? Wouldn't we——"

Dr. Diebuhr, at least, was looking a little aroused.

"Something there, you know, Nick. My own knowledge of coal gas isn't——"

"Conclusive," I snapped.

146

"Conclusive. But I should say that was a point. Of course I don't know how long it might take for a charge to collect——"

"Yeah." This, loudly, from Salvail the plumber. "Those drafts could've been blown open, for all that. Or the lady could of got up three, four o'clock, thought the house was chilly, fixed it then, forgetting to open the damper. You take a——"

"I know," I interrupted, "you take a woman handling a stove— only that isn't what happened. *Someone knocked me unconscious.* Maybe I can't prove it, but what proof have you it isn't so? Can you——"

Lieutenant Kopp put in the first question he'd volunteered.

"Miss Kingman," he asked delicately, "what were you wearing when you came home from work last night?"

I'd been so occupied with Mother, so absorbed in my apparently futile efforts to convince Waslewski of what had happened that I hadn't, up to then, had any thought for myself as a person. At Lieutenant Kopp's question, though, I had to look down at myself, and what I saw really stopped me. What I had on, under a blanket I was clutching and that someone must have thrown round me, were my pink-sprigged percale butcher boy pajamas. Mother's bedroom slippers covered my feet.

There'd been other times, since Sylvia died, when the border between reality and unreality grew thin and seemed almost to dissolve; this was another of those times. Without being told, without seeing, I could guess that upstairs, probably neatly folded over a chair, would be the clothes I had worn yesterday, just as if I'd taken them off and left them there. "Maybe," I thought then, "maybe it's the plumber who's right; maybe what I think happened is nightmare; maybe this is the kind of hallucination you get when you've nearly been smothered by coal gas. Maybe I just came in here quietly last night, peeping in at Mother, seeing her sleep quietly, turning off her light. Maybe I tiptoed on upstairs without waking her, going to bed as usual; maybe it was the first whiff of the coal gas, reaching me, that made me dream I'd been knocked on the head. Maybe *Mother left the stove half tended last night, intending to finish it later, but instead she dozed off . . ."*

It was entirely credible that way, so much more reasonable—in spite of Sylvia, in spite of everything else going on. I could see it in the plumber's face, in Lieutenant Kopp's, in Waslewski's, in Dr. Diebuhr's, even in Rose Gamble's.

I lifted my hand to the back of my head. Soreness there, but I could have gotten that when I fell from the bed.

Revolt shook me. I *knew* what bad happened. I said, "Mother never, never even for two minutes would leave the damper entirely closed. She's warned me——"

I looked down again at my pajamas. I said, "Somebody undressed me and put me to bed." I was still angry, but it was new anger by that time; it was a frightened, sick anger. What had been done was the kind of thing you couldn't look at. Not really.

I don't think the other four conscious people in that room looked at it either. Not really. Maybe they did, but if so they didn't show it. They looked disturbed, they looked uncertain, they looked abrupt and harassed; they looked as if they wanted to be out and away from it.

And that's what they did—the men, anyway. They got out and away. They mumbled among themselves, something about its being nearly morning, and they could just as well get along; maybe later, when they could question Mrs. Kingman . . . Dr. Diebuhr repeated instructions about Mother to Rose Gamble, who volubly and fervently agreed to stay. He told me to go to bed.

Then they went. Just like that. In a file, Indian style. Out through the kitchen and the back door.

It was only after they'd gone and I began obeying Dr. Diebuhr's order about getting to bed that I found out about the other piece in the puzzle. My merry-go-round, part of its top crushed, and one figure from it missing.

CHAPTER FIFTEEN _____

BEFORE GOING UPSTAIRS I of course had to fiddle for a while over Mother, making certain everything Dr. Diebuhr said should be done for her was being done, checking the hotwater bottle at her back and feet, checking her pulse again, talking over with Rose Gamble what should be said when she woke, just standing to revel in the lift and fall of her breath. While I was doing that last she stirred again, seeing me, I think, smiling faintly and then rolling contentedly over to sleep on her right side. Dr. Diebuhr, I guessed, had given her a sedative; certainly her sleep now looked like normal sleep.

When I tore myself from there I delayed longer—clutching my blanket tighter against the chill that poured in from all sides—to look at the havoc I'd made of the windows. One thing you had to say about me, as I pointed out unhappily to Rose, was that when I got an idea I carried through on it. Every lower sash in the downstairs was broken. Jagged fragments of glass, glittering dully in the predawn light, littered the floors all along the outside walls, littered the plants on the dining-room sills. Why I hadn't taken the little extra time to open windows instead of breaking so many I didn't know; Mother and I could be grateful to be alive, but one of the things we'd live for, in addition to all our other debts, would be a good healthy bill from the hardware store for new windowpanes.

Upstairs in my room, too, broken glass lay around the base of the sewing machine, with my cutting scissors plump in the middle; that must have been what my hands had found, on the near ledge of the sewing machine. The job I'd done on this particular window was

150

especially thorough—three fourths of the pane was out, though long pointed splinters still protruded from the sides. Funny I hadn't . . .

Along about there I got around to looking at myself in a mirror. I had one more idea, then, why perhaps Waslewski and Kopp had found it hard to put entire credence in what I'd said. Hair every which way, eyes swollen and buried by weeping and other emotions, dried lines of glass scratches crisscrossing in all directions over my cheeks and fore-head, followed by orange-red stains of antiseptic which Dr. Diebuhr must have applied before I came to the second time. Around all the rest of me the orchid huddle of Mother's foot-of-the-bed blanket.

It's something to see yourself transformed into a witch. Before I did anything else I had to brush my hair, tie it up, and get into a bathrobe. Not until I had back that much, anyway, of a normal sem-blance, did I begin thinking again. Except for the broken window and the scattered glass, my room looked normal enough; my clothes lay, as I'd thought they would, folded neatly over a chair. Again, part way, I approached realizing what that meant, and not just my face but my whole body burned. Being lugged upstairs like a lifeless doll, being undressed and put to bed—that was intolerable in a way that was almost worse than being so nearly murdered. If I knew who . . .

Any necessity I'd felt before toward wanting to hunt out Sylvia's murderer couldn't approach the determination which began pouring into me then. This murderer hadn't only killed Sylvia, now; he was mov-ing against Mother and me; having tried once to kill us, and failed, he might all too likely try again and succeed. Why? I'd already considered the possibility that Ada might have been our assailant, and that idea seemed as impossible at second examination as it did at first. If we'd refused permission to search our house it might have been different; in her overwrought state she might have done even this to see if we had what she wanted. But we hadn't refused permission. She could have come back any time, if she wanted to, to hunt once more . . .

If not Ada, then someone else. The someone else she had said was hunting, but who didn't dare do so openly, because he hadn't any excuses; he was Sylvia's murderer. Someone who had come here not primarily to kill us but to get a chance at the house, someone who had the same idea Ada had. If I hadn't waked, Mother and I would simply have been found in the morning, dead, in a house filled by coal gas. And probably there'd have been nothing to show that a second hunt had followed Ada's . . .

Experimentally I pulled out the dresser drawer nearest me, a drawer that held ribbons, gloves, handkerchiefs, cosmetics. Undoubtedly it had been rummaged—handkerchiefs had been shoved from their pile, rolls of ribbon lay scattered, the lid was off a powder box. The lingerie drawer beneath was tumbled too. From the dresser I turned to the closet—clothes jammed together at one end of the rack, shoes and boxes jumbled on the floor. Not the way I kept it; not, I thought, the way Ada would have left it—not if Mother was along. But proof? Where could there be proof of that second hunter? I remembered how the door had stuck and whirled to that, but the object caught under the door, like a wedge, was one of my own shoes, one of the brown loafers I'd worn the day before. As I pulled it out I thought again, if additional corroboration was necessary, how evilly clever was the brain pitted against mine, against Waslewski, against Lieutenant Kopp, against the whole community that thirsted to hunt him out. This murderer wouldn't bring in any object from outside to wedge a door; no, he'd take one of my shoes, that I might have stuck there myself as an understandable safeguard.

Earlier that night, falling from the bed, I had felt in myself a kind of cunning; now I knew how far from cunning, how far from artful, I really was. Just the same, as I grimly began going over the rest of my room in that dawn light, I didn't feel exactly helpless either. If there was so much as a thread in that room which had been brought in from the outside and so could tell a tale, I would find it.

Of course I found nothing. Or at least, almost nothing. When I got to the sewing machine one of the things that had to be gone through was the red box like a hatbox, sitting on top of the Montgomery Ward catalogue and holding my merry-go-round. I took off the red lid, and the first thing I saw was that the circus-tent top had been broken. I lifted the toy out, thinking, "I must have done that; I fell against it, maybe, when I broke the window." But then I looked at the box again, and that was uncrushed. Ada. If Ada had done the breaking, yesterday, surely Mother would have said so when she phoned.

No. It was the second hunter, the night hunter, who'd broken it; I took it as certainty, without further debate. Ada's story was true, then; there had been someone else who hunted. He'd come here after Ada, thinking he must find what Ada sought and hadn't found, willing to kill Mother, willing to kill me, to get a night in the house undisturbed.

More than that, maybe. Why had he broken this merry-go-round? Was it because to him too, as to Sylvia and to me, it had carried some meaning? In some kind of anger, when he saw it, had he thrown it top down at the floor? Except for a few lost flakes of enamel, the base still was intact. The toy ponies, the toy riders, ringed the base in an unbroken circle. Only the top was damaged, the red and green striped fabric torn from center pole to edge, three of the metal ribs snapped off. Not anything that couldn't be repaired, with splints, solder, and sewing. Nothing missing . . .

Then as I turned the toy I saw that was wrong too. The little Italianate, waving small man who had balanced so debonairly, one foot to the platform, the other free—he was no longer there. Just below the broken top, on the platform edge, was a tiny, shiny, rough spot of solder to show where his foot had been fixed.

I hunted amid the broken glass. Took up the rugs and shook them. Went over the floor inch by inch for a second time. No toy man.

Nothing might have come into that room that night, but something had gone out of it.

Dr. Diebuhr had said I should go to bed. After a while I did. Any position I took, though, grew immediately uncomfortable. Out of the whirling, seesawing medley of suppositions, conjectures, tries, and failures to which I then treated myself, only one fact emerged healingly: if the intruder in our house last night had been Sylvia's murderer, then Pete Fenrood was innocent. Pete, in jail, couldn't have stood just inside our dining-room door to strike me down. That matchbook again meant nothing; I'd been entirely right in concealing it.

It was an idea so whole, so consoling that maybe, after I'd had it, I finally dozed a little; at least what went on in my head wasn't clear. What roused me was a rumble of men's voices downstairs, and as soon as I had identified them for what they were I was immediately alert again. Bathrobe belted and slippers on, I got downstairs to find two men already—Rose's doing—at work on the windows, while in Mother's room Waslewski and Lieutenant Kopp once more stood at the bedside.

Mother then was awake, not sitting up, but resting against her pillow, mouth a little sunken and cheeks colorless, but eyes open and cognizant. When I said, "Mother," and knelt to her, she smiled at me and lifted a hand to my arm.

"Not to speak until we've questioned her," Lieutenant Kopp was saying. He'd probably said more than that, but I hadn't heard it.

Rose bustled at me, "You come right out for a bite, Cathy; your mother's just fine now; Dr. Diebuhr was here again——" She was insistent and kind, but I could guess the presence of Waslewski and Kopp was her doing too; they must have asked her to call them as soon as Mother woke, and before she saw me. I could see, though, why they'd had to do that.

I nodded at her and at the two officers, to show I understood. But I couldn't leave. What Mother said could be too important.

Waslewski was being extremely cautious.

"I guess you understand, Mrs. Kingman," he began, "You were

154

a little sick in the night. Seems your stove misbehaved. When we found it the damper was shut and the drafts open—that the way you left it?"

"Damper shut?" Mother's voice was weak, the words a little thick; she brushed over her face with the hand that wasn't on my arm. "No. No. Of course not. That damper's entirely too tight. I never quite close it. I had a small fire last night——"

"Fill it up before you went to bed?"

The head on the pillow shook slightly, wonderingly. "Just a small fire. I—the forecast was colder for morning. Maybe I should have left a bigger one, but we both like to sleep cold. I was getting up early——"

Waslewski lifted a hand too, lifted it to tug quickly, angrily, at his lower lip.

"Would you tell that again, please, how you left the stove last night?"

"Certainly." The one word came much more firmly than anything that had preceded it. The hand left my sleeve to push against the bedclothes as if she wanted to hoist herself up, then as realization of her weakness hit she frowned, puzzled and for the first time alarmed. "What happened? Certainly there wasn't anything wrong with the stove last night. I checked it over before I went to bed. I always do. I had a small fire, pretty well burned out. I turned the damper to be open about half an inch, and made sure the drafts were shut. I——"

"When was this?"

"Sometime after nine. I wanted to be awake when Cathy came home, but I was tired. I came in and lay down here. I guess I dozed off. I woke, though. I heard Cathy come in. I said, 'Remember about locking the door, Cathy.' Then——"

Weak or not, she was struggling up now, and alarm was growing on her face.

"I can't remember anything after that. I can't remember Cathy answering me. I——"

Holding back any longer was impossible; I had to bend forward.

"Mother. Suppose that wasn't me that came in. Mother—you had the light on—didn't you see anything?"

She stared at me blankly and wildly, still trying to rise, though I pushed back against her.

"There was something dark. But I thought it was you. I—it was time for you. I was turning around—but that's all I remember." She fell back, both hands, this time, going upward. "My head aches. Cathy, what happened? If that wasn't you, who was it? I can't understand——"

"You will," I said tersely. I whipped about to the lieutenant and Waslewski. "There. Do you think she made that up? She was hit, just as I was. Do you think she's in any shape to be thinking up tales? Do you think she doesn't remember about that stove? I haven't talked to her— ask Mrs. Gamble. And if you want something more——"

I was past them, quickly up the stairs and back again, the merry-go-round in my hands.

"Mother, look at this," I commanded. "Look, was this broken when Ada Bennert left here yesterday afternoon?"

Mother had closed her eyes in my absence, but she opened them again.

"More," she said. "Something more again—does this mean someone broke in here last night?"

I said, "It means exactly that. My merry-go-round, Mother. Was it broken?"

"No, of course not," she said slowly. She wasn't just answering now, she was thinking. She said, "But then it couldn't have been Pete Fenrood," arriving at that guess long before I had, in my series of conclusions. That seemed to encourage her too; she went on much more strongly, "Of course it wasn't broken. Ada and I took it out and looked through it. We shook out the tissue paper in the box and examined the box—it was perfectly whole then. I put it back myself."

"See?" I held the toy out to Waslewski. "See? It's not whole now. Broken, as if someone threw it at the floor——"

Lieutenant Kopp inserted swiftly, "I'll call Mrs. Bennert." He disappeared toward the kitchen; while he was gone Waslewski took the merry-go-round over, turning it in his hands, frowning, looking more and more harried, annoyed, and cross.

"What's more," I went on, "there's a part of it missing." I described the little mustachioed man and showed where he stood; Mother couldn't actually remember seeing that one part of the toy on the day before, but that made no difference; it was easy to see where he'd been. And when Kopp came back he looked disturbed too.

He admitted, "Mrs. Bennert corroborates that entirely. She remembers the merry-go-round sharply; she couldn't imagine why her sister should ever have sent Miss Kingman any such toy. She's distinctly sure it wasn't broken when she saw it."

For quite a few minutes, after that, the two men just stood there. Mother still looked more than a little bewildered, but I suppose I showed my triumph; this much I'd accomplished anyway—I'd established this small beachhead of truth, or at least of doubt.

With a gargantuan sight Waslewski turned after a while to stump out to the dining room where, still moodily considering my merry-go-round, he sagged to the couch; Lieutenant Kopp followed him, dropping on a chair.

The shade in Mother's room had been half pulled over the already repaired window, but the dining room swam in light as well as in currents of air from the sashes on which the two hardware store men—ears almost visibly stretched—still labored.

Lieutenant Kopp said wearily, "If what you and your mother say is true, Miss Kingman, you don't know what it does to us. To our case. Everything we've done so far, everything we've found out—all blown to heck and gone."

Not only Waslewski but he too looked disheartened and discouraged; looked, in fact, almost lost. So far I'd never before seen the young state patrolman except as spruce and freshly groomed, but the stubble of his beard this morning could have vied with Waslewski's; there might almost have been wrinkles around his eyes.

He said, "Up to now most of it's worked the one way. Pete Fenrood moves into this town a year and a half ago. He starts up a business, a good enterprising business. He begins going out with you. When Sylvia Gainer comes back to town he drops you to go out with her."

I would have pushed in an objection, but he lifted his hand. "By your own evidence, Sylvia Gainer was talking of marrying him. She loans him money—not too much, but enough to show she has confidence in him. She writes your mother out a check for six thousand dollars—we've talked this over with Mr. Bennert, and Mr. Bennert says frankly the only reason he can see for that check is that Miss Gainer wanted you out of town, again because she intended marrying Mr. Fenrood."

Hot blood in my face. Of all the puzzling I—and other people—had done over that check, this was one answer that hadn't come out before, but as soon as it was given I could see the force in it; all too likely—oh, all too likely—Russ was the one who was right. Sylvia wasn't repairing any wrong with that check, she wasn't making any payment; she was just making certain she wouldn't be having any interference. "We'd make a good triangle, you, me, and Sylvia"—Pete was at least this much like me: where his affections had struck once, they had a tendency to stay.

Lieutenant Kopp was still speaking. "Sylvia Gainer gets killed. Pete Fenrood was with her that evening within the time she was killed. As far as we know she saw no one else after he left her. No one saw him leave, no one saw him until nine that night, at the water show. We find a fingerprint of his in Miss Gainer's bedroom. The rope with which she was strangled was found in his car. It's unlikely——"

158

I said swiftly, "He had no motive whatever. He——"

"Oh yes, he had motive. We've had a couple aces up our sleeves, Miss Kingman, and this is one of them."

He reached a hand toward an inner coat pocket, pausing halfway, glancing over at Waslewski as if he might object, but Waslewski, apparently almost sodden, turning my merry-go-round in his hands, made no gesture whatever. The hand then continued its way to the pocket, emerging with a small white envelope, the kind of small white envelope that commonly is enclosed with a gift or with flowers. He held it out and I took it, hesitating a little, dreading to know what it was that, until now, they had concealed as a motive for Pete's killing of Sylvia. If I was determined to help track down this murderer, though, no ignorance could help me; I slid out the card in the envelope.

Two words on it. Or, rather, one word and a signature. "Anytime, Clint." That was what the card said. "Anytime, Clint." No one needed to be told what it meant; I felt color reflooding even as I objected.

"But this——"

Eyes harsh for all their tiredness, Lieutenant Kopp nodded. "It needn't mean anything. We've questioned Clint Boyce, of course; he admits readily enough that he sent the card; sent it sometime last November, he thinks, with chrysanthemums. Clint Boyce denies that either the message or the flowers got him anywhere; Sylvia Gainer, he says, wasn't to be had, not by him. In another way, though, it does mean something. Or at least it seemed to. Where we found it."

He hesitated; if there'd been any possibility he wouldn't go on from there; I'd have asked, but I could see I wouldn't have to; he wanted to tell the rest.

Unhappily it came. "We found that card in its envelope hidden under the rubber mat in the front of Pete Fenrood's car."

Hearing it, I almost felt shaken again myself. Pete, who could get drunk, Pete who admitted a hair-trigger temper. I'd turned him down; he was being successful with Sylvia. But then suppose Clint Boyce had lied, suppose this card did mean something, and Pete had found it out. Suppose this card had been evidence for Pete. This card and . . .

With a shock that was like a hammer blow against my chest, I thought, "*This card, and maybe a railroad ticket.* 'You'll probably hear about a railroad ticket I found last night under my pillow.'" A railroad ticket could be something entirely different than I'd so far thought of it as being; the stub of a railroad ticket, or the unused half of a round-trip ticket, perhaps, could be evidence, held evidence, that Sylvia had sometime been somewhere she wasn't supposed to be, with someone she wasn't supposed to accompany. Especially if its back had a time stamp. That would explain why no such ticket had been found; Sylvia would have destroyed it. That would explain why it had been put under her pillow—as a threat. You're threatening me, that ticket could have said, don't forget I have something to threaten with too. . . .

Mounting, wild surmise, which I tried to shake off, but couldn't; that one small piece of the puzzle, at least, I thought solved; if I never heard of the ticket again I would be certain that this was its explanation. Who had put that ticket under Sylvia's pillow—that was the part not yet answered. Not Pete, though. This was no time to be having fresh suspicions of Pete, when my own experience had proved him guiltless.

I said, "Someone else stuck this card in Pete's car. Like the stringer. It was planted there——"

The lieutenant admitted it slowly. "So it would—now—seem. We can't—give up what we've gotten, but if you were attacked here by someone last evening you weren't attacked by Pete Fenrood. And of course there's the opposite side of the picture——"

Whether, right then, he would have gone on to tell me what he saw on the reverse of his canvas I don't know; Waslewski was stirring; Waslewski might, at that juncture, have intervened, thinking Kopp already had talked enough. But that point didn't come up; what came up instead was the next link in the chain.

Rose Gamble burst into the dining room, ushering two boys and a dog. The two boys, as well as the dog, were in a state of excitement bordering on transport. Both boys held soiled red hunting caps and had bedrolls strapped to their backs; they were in flannel shirts, blue jeans, and boots, so dusty they must have been tramping for hours. Rapt as I was, it was impossible not to be snatched aside, even at their moment of entry, by their visible excitement; they were sweating with it, their eyes tense and wide, their bodies electric, and under the ruddy coloring of their healthy young faces was a tinge of some paler shade that might have been green.

One of them burst into immediate speech. "We been looking for you, Sheriff—we went to the courthouse, and they said you was here. We been—I guess we been playing hooky. We found old Hector. We went on this hike last night, see; we got late waking up. We were coming back, though, we were coming back past that old cemetery up by Dickinson's woods, the one they don't use any more. There's a great big pile of brush, see, kind of alongside a pond, and my dog, that's my dog Lazy, here, he sort of went whining around in it——"

THEY HAD FOUND HECTOR and Hector was dead. That was what the boys had to say. For two days and three nights, now, as a background activity to everything else that had gone on, a quiet but undeviating search for the old man had continued, bus drivers and train conductors had been told to keep their eyes open, highways had been watched, men at work in the woods had been questioned, men in cars had stopped in at lumber camps and farmhouses—"Seen anything since Monday of Hector LeClerque?" That much could end now; Hector too, like Sylvia— and so nearly like Mother and like me—was dead.

At first there seemed little reaction in Kopp or Waslewski; the two faces betrayed, if anything, only arrest. When Waslewski did speak he was kindly and leisurely.

"Well. Sounds as if you two boys really ran into something. Found me right away, too. Stop anywhere else except at the court- house? That's fine. All right, let's get this straight. You say out by that old cemetery——"

"Yessir." It came as a chorus. So far the shorter boy had done all the talking, the taller merely nodding his head in quick confirmatory jerks. Now he added eagerly, "Right there off the highway. There's this kind of open place next the cemetery—pond in the middle, mostly dried up but still some scummy spots and a lot of cattails. This pile of brush——"

"Uh. Body pretty well covered, or out in the open?"

The two young faces had been regaining color, but at this ques- tion the greenish tinge once more made itself manifest.

"Pretty well covered. We wouldn't of seen it at all, I guess, only

Lazy——"

"Okay. You kids can take us——"

Action, then. Both men rising. Lieutenant Kopp neatly nipped Clint Boyce's card and the envelope from my fingers and disappeared once more in the direction of the kitchen phone. Waslewski handed me the merry-go-round as if it never had counted for much.

Important and shattering as this new development was, it also seemed wrong that the experiences in which I was immersed should be even temporarily shelved, wrong that I should again be shoved from the main current of what was going on. I heard myself asking loudly and flatly, "Can't I go too?" and it was only when Waslewski turned to give me one of his measured, calculating, and much more normal glances, answering, "Do you think you should, Miss Kingman?" that I recollected the state I was in, and how impossible it was that I be one of the party. A minute or two later the official car shot off, Waslewski driving, heavy body forward over the wheel, Lieutenant Kopp beside him, unshaven still but once more firmly erect, the two boys in back, their dog jumping and yapping at a side window. Justice on its way.

Or was it? Was that justice whose muddy fenders disappeared around the corner as I watched from another of the repaired windows, or was it simply more of the error, more of the blind groping, that we'd been having already? Merry-go-round still under my arm, I bent until my forehead was against the cool glass. Of course it was ridiculous to have wanted to accompany them—what could I have learned, what deductions could I have drawn, from seeing what they must see—the body of a tired old man, flung like refuse under a pile of brush? I had to do something—but what? I couldn't just go on as I was—forever watching, collecting, noticing, puzzling, but not *doing* anything.

And then that too left me; all I wanted, temporarily at least, was rest. Too much had hit me in too short a time; as I stood looking down the empty street I realized how desperately I was in need of sleep, how desperately I would have liked to shove the whole black enigma out of mind. Mother too would be needing me, she'd have a hundred questions, she'd be heartsick about Hector . . .

Only that wasn't what was going to go on immediately, either. At the previously empty street corner appeared Mrs. Upsher and Mrs. Meerus, the grocer's wife. Both had dishtowel-covered plates in hand, both were talking animatedly, and I knew without being told where they were bound. In addition to her other duties Rose Gamble, that morning, had put in a stint at the telephone.

In this guess, at least, I was entirely right; we might not have been inundated by friends from then on, but we had a steady trickle. On entering, mostly, they palpitated—"You poor, poor things, when I think what nearly happened"—only to be met, necessarily, by the later news about Hector, and so to be swept into a maelstrom of horror, surmise, what-is-the-world-coming-to, and I-can't-really-believe-this-is-Long-Meadow. Toward us their attitudes once more had changed; there was some severity mixed with their sympathy—only bad taste on our part could have let us in for such a horrendous experience. The snap telephone verdict, though, had apparently been that if Mother and I hadn't really been attacked, then we had at least almost suffered a terrible accident, and as such we were worthy of fuss and condolence.

As I might have expected, it wasn't only women who came, not only Doris Orfelt who called; Russ came too—slamming his red Studebaker to an abrupt stop at the gate, advancing grimly and purposefully up the front walk. Still in bathrobe and slippers because I hadn't had time to change, I went to let him in.

"What's this about what went on here last night?" he wanted to know. Then, at my face, "Good Lord, Cathy."

Mother had insisted on getting into a robe and walking out to the front room when visitors turned up; that bedroom of hers is a hole. From not more than five feet away, therefore, four pairs of ears were interested participants in anything said; I drew a rueful hand over my face, managing a laugh.

"Awful, isn't it? Just glass cuts, though; they'll soon heal. Mother's fine too. I'll be going to work in a minute——"

"You'll do nothing of the kind." Russ too could guess at the near-by ears. He listened without comment to my recital, but when I was done he wasn't less roused and angry, he was more so.

"Look here, Mrs. Kingman." He stalked past me to throw short, brusque phrases at Mother. "You can't afford to have this kind of thing happen twice. You and Cathy can't stay here alone. If our house—if Sylvia's apartment was any safer, I'd ask you up there. Since it obvious-ly isn't, I hope you'll let me advise you either to get some man in here nights—I could send one of my workmen—or else spend your nights at the Admiral. I'll make arrangements about the bill. You must see for yourself——"

It took discussion, of course; having a man stay at the house meant he'd have to sleep on the dining-room couch, which would be about the same as asking him to sleep on spikes; our bathroom, besides, is off the kitchen in what once was the pantry; the house isn't arranged for anything but a family. Going to the hotel meant an expense we could-n't possibly let Russ take over for us; that, though, was what we decid-ed on; we too could see what being in the house alone at night must be like, after this.

"It can't be for long, though; this can't go on forever." Mother rather forlornly voiced the hope that seemed, right then, to be all that held us together. "I never thought I'd see the time when I'd be afraid in my own house, when I'd let myself be chased from it."

Before leaving, Russ made the arrangements, calling the Admiral, calling the hospital too, to say I'd need a substitute that day. After that he took time to go over the house, scowling at our antiquated locks—"Skeleton keys like those? Anyone who wanted to could get in here any time"—scowling more blackly when I showed him how the stove had been. For once I had someone who believed me entirely; I might have relaxed in it if he, as we proceeded, hadn't done just the opposite.

"It's intolerable," he exploded, while he still glared at the stove. "Hector, now, too. Hector, that poor defenseless and harmless old bum. I suppose all we'll get is more questioning, more poking around that gets nowhere—there must be some other approach that would be more productive. I believe in every man to his job, but if this thing doesn't end soon . . ."

He thrust with his foot at the leg of the stove, and then stood grimly silent; as he did so, for the first time since Sylvia's death, I felt the tingling of a hope that wasn't in the least forlorn. Beat my head at the puzzles around me as I would, I couldn't believe—not really—that I'd get far by myself. Waslewski might be dogged and stubborn, but before be got to be sheriff he had been a farm implement dealer. Lieutenant Kopp might be shrewd and incisive, but for all his incisiveness he could run a wrong track, no one knew that better than I. Pete might look like a hunter, sometimes, but apparently it had gotten him nowhere, and besides what could he do, in jail? Russ, though, if Russ once got started . . .

There wasn't much time for it, not then; two more women arrived, and Russ had to get back to the grain elevator he was building. During the next hours, however, in the intervals of saying, "Yes, it really was terrible," and "No, not even a glimpse," every once in a while the spark of that hope relighted; just having Russ come in, protective and masculine, liking me even when my face was as scratched and crisscrossed as a chicken yard, knowing what had to be done and firmly seeing that it got done, was blissfully comforting.

All this, naturally, was subordinate; what held the floor was conjecture, wonder, horror about what had happened in our house in the night, and also, gatheringly and increasingly, more conjecture, horror,

166

and waiting for news about Hector. Rose persevered at the phone, women coming in brought what they had, but it wasn't until toward suppertime that reports trickled in, and then not too much. Hector, one of these reports—or rumors—ran, probably hadn't been killed at the spot where he was found; broken grass stems and streaks of earth on his clothing suggested he had been dragged. Like Sylvia, he too almost certainly had been strangled. In the coroner's opinion he had been dead over forty-eight hours, which would put his death back to the Monday night before Sylvia's funeral the same night he slipped jail. Dr. Diebuhr, again, was to do an autopsy. Nothing about the body, nothing about the clothing—or at least nothing Waslewski was giving out—suggested who had done the killing, or why.

"Another riddle. Another of these hornet-sting, cankering riddles." Mother, that afternoon, was almost entirely overcome and mournful. "Poor old Hector. We helped him, didn't we? Fed him so much he got sick, took him to Waslewski just to have this happen."

"What else could we have done?" I asked. "We couldn't have told him to go on hiding; it wouldn't have worked if we had. He realized himself he'd have to go——"

Mother, though, wouldn't be solaced. "We believed what he told us; we could have made more of a point of it."

Not anything we would have expected to feel in addition to everything else, this shamed kind of sorrow, but neither of us could escape it. The old lumberjack hadn't had much of a place in our lives; too often he was simply a nuisance. But he had been a person too, he'd been a relic of the town's colorful past; he'd been old and we somehow had failed him—it was this last that edged our emotions.

Not that we had much time for that either. Lieutenant Kopp, just after supper, reappeared at the kitchen door. Waslewski, he said, was asking Miss Kingman to come to his office.

A summons different from any I'd had before—it didn't take long to know that. Only last evening—forgotten until now—Waslewski also had asked to see me; that had been an ordinary request, apparently forgotten in what ensued. The difference in this brusque and terse order lay not just in the lieutenant's coming for me, which might have been done because, after my night's ordeal, I could use an escort. What made up the difference was in Lieutenant Kopp—a sort of harsh wonderment that seemed to exist in his round, almost innocent eyes when I opened the door for him, the way those eyes then slid away from me is if they scarcely could bear to rest on me, the coldness and the harshness of his voice as he delivered the order, the coldness and the harshness of his haggard, still unshaven face. He asked Rose to help me dress; from my room upstairs I could hear the crackle of his voice as he talked with Mother; even with Rose's help it was hard to get clothes on; it took effort to remember how a brassiére hooked and how garters worked. "What now?" I asked. "What possible accusation can they have against me now?" When Waslewski and Kopp had left the house in the morning they had seemed almost won over to the idea that my account of last night was a true one; at least any bent to the contrary had been badly dented. Now, if perception could be relied on at all, they must have swerved again.

"Cathy, catch hold of yourself, you can't shake that way," Rose told me. She, for the moment anyway, was almost wholly sympathetic and indignant. "It's enough to get anybody unsettled," she muttered, "I've got to say that; first you almost get killed in the night, and then they come ordering you—that Waslewski had better know what he's doing, or he won't get many votes around here next election."

That peculiar and distant threat was the comfort I had to stay me as I said good-by to Mother—several voices chorusing that they'd be with her until I got back, of course they would, at the same time they echoed a wonder as to whether I'd be back at all—and got myself away with Lieutenant Kopp. In the car he drove silently. I tried questioning him—"What's up now, Did you find anything much about Hector?"—but he still was abrupt and remote, "I think we'll leave that for Waslewski." In the courthouse he ushered me into what obviously was an anteroom, bare except for a golden oak settee against each side wall, sat me down beside an unhappy-looking farm couple who were the room's only occupants, snapped, "Wait there," disappeared beyond the inner door that had "Sheriff Waslewski" lettered in black on its frosted glass window, and almost immediately returned to snap again, "All right, come along in."

The room I then entered was also bare—bare, that is, of material furnishings. Within its small square space it held only one window, one varnished oak desk, one green metal filing cabinet, and three varnished oak chairs. It wasn't, however, bare of men; in addition to Waslewski there were five others, in uniform and out, standing with a foot in a chair, leaning against the window sill or half seated on the desk. Six men, all of them immediately staring at me, tearing at the essence of what I was.

I gasped, going into that room. Quickly, glad of any support, I sank into the chair Lieutenant Kopp shoved toward me. Light in the room came from the one big west-facing window to shine directly upon me; the men for the most part were between me and that window, looming dark, heavy, solid. Long ago, long long ago, in the Gainer living room, I had faintly rebelled because that seemed a wrong setting for interrogation. I could never quarrel with the official tone of this room.

In the car Kopp had said he'd leave questions to Waslewski. But as soon as he'd gotten me seated it was he who began speaking.

"Miss Kingman, when I talked with you this morning I went rather thoroughly into our reasons for holding Pete Fenrood. I went over some of the evidence that gives Pete Fenrood opportunity, motive, and means, as far as Sylvia Gainer's death is concerned. Opportunity because he admits being in her home within a few minutes of her death, motive because he apparently had—and knew he had—reason for jealousy, means because it was with his stringer she was strangled."

He paused, leaning against the desk, arms folded, as if he waited for comment. That morning I'd had comments—objections in plenty. Now, against this battery, all I could do was nod.

"I also said this morning that there was an opposite side to this picture. It didn't seem helpful, right then, to go into what that opposite picture might be. Now it does. You see, it's this way, isn't it? Either Pete Fenrood is guilty or else someone is going to a good deal of trouble to make it look as if he is. He's being framed. He——"

I could do at least a little more than nod, there. "I'm sure of it."

"Interesting, Miss Kingman. Just after Miss Gainer's death, Miss Kingman, Sheriff Waslewski argued out for you our belief that Miss Gainer was killed by one of ten people—Pete Fenrood, Ada Bennert, Mr. Bennert, Lucien Hague, Mr. and Mrs. Boyce, Florence Squires, Hector LeClerque, you or your mother. Hector is now dead, himself murdered. If Pete Fenrood is being framed, then that framing is most likely being done by one of the remaining eight. We can't think of any reason, beyond picking a likely scapegoat, why Ada Bennert should have picked Pete, or why Mr. Bennert or Lucien Hague or any of the others should. When we come to you, though, Miss Kingman, that's not how it is. Before Miss Gainer came to town this summer you were being quite a friend of Pete Fenrood's. You——"

He didn't have to go further; I had it. Up to then I might have been trembling; after that I wasn't. I thought, "If that's all they have against me . . ." and then I was talking, almost calmly.

"Sylvia was taking my boy friend away from me—that's what you're getting at, isn't it? That would be my reason for killing Sylvia, that would be my reason for having it in for Pete. Here I am, twenty-five years old, Pete may have been my last chance——" My hand went up to my face as I remembered the scratches and the orange-red stains of Phemoral Topical, which I had tried to scrub away but which hadn't entirely come off. Unattractive as I was, a couple of the men, including Waslewski, had the grace to look embarrassed. Not Kopp, though.

I went on, heat rushing against my diaphragm in a wave.

"It's ridiculous. I'm not in love with Pete Fenrood. I never was. I like him. I like him very much. I like lots of people. I liked Sylvia—I told you that before. Pete and I had broken up long before Sylvia got back; you can ask Long Meadow. You——"

"You might suddenly have found you were very mistaken, Miss Kingman, just about the time Miss Gainer offered you six thousand dollars to get out of town. You might, very suddenly, have found you didn't want to sell Pete Fenrood at that price."

"That particular explanation for that check is someone else's idea, not mine. I hadn't heard of that check until you told me about it after Sylvia was dead."

"That's the truth?"

"That's the truth." I made it flat, I made it decisive.

"But you see where it gets us. Right back to the theory that Pete Fenrood is responsible for the killings."

"You haven't ruled out the possibility that some one of the others picked Pete just because he was handiest."

"True. You're a reasonably good debater, Miss Kingman. We have, however, a little something else to go on. Something that's come up, not in connection with Sylvia Gainer's death, but with Hector LeClerque's."

He paused there, glancing over at Waslewski as if he were offering the older man a chance to take over. From his place against the filing cabinet, however, Waslewski signaled him on, with an almost imperceptible jerk of the head. Instead of immediately doing so the lieutenant very deliberately took out a cigarette and lit it; as he did so there was a small interval in which nothing was said. In that interval I sensed tension gathering—this that was coming now, not what had gone before, was their reason for getting me here. My trembling began again.

"Miss Kingman."

"Yes."

"Miss Kingman, when Hector LeClerque came to this office last Sunday night it was you who brought him here."

He waited confirmation.

I nodded, lips too dry for speech.

"Why?"

"He'd—he'd——" It took time to get to the place where words could emerge. "He'd come to our house. Coming on here was his own idea; he knew he had to."

"Why did he go to your house?"

"He said he was hungry. We fed him."

"No other reason?"

Speech continued to be difficult, against all those leaching faces. I moistened my lips again, but at the same time a small anger began forming. I'd done nothing wrong; if no one else knew that, I did. Russ had used the right word—it was intolerable to be so used. Yet I returned the straight answer.

"He said he wanted to see friends first."

"You considered him a friend of yours?"

"I'd known him around town since I was a child. The way everyone else has."

"Ever come to your house before?"

"Once in a while, for handouts. I've seen him more often around saloons and hamburger shops." Because of the anger my voice was strengthening a little.

"Um. Then why your house Sunday night, out of all the houses in town?"

What was he getting at? "I don't know. He said he——" I got that far before I bit words back. What had I been about to say? "*Around the Kitchen of Pete there is too much light.*" It was to Pete's Hector had gone first; Mother and I were the alternate. But I couldn't say that, not to these faces. Not after what had gone before.

"He said what?" Quick and insistent, trying to prevent second thoughts.

"He seemed to think of us as—part of the Gainers." Not a lie, actually, since Hector had done that too.

"Miss Kingman, when Hector broke out of jail Monday night, didn't he again come to your house?"

I thought, "I should have expected that; this is what I've got to hold myself steady for." I answered, "No, he didn't. Why should he?"

"It was to you he went before."

I said, "That's a rather silly argument; we hadn't done any too much for him before; it would seem much more reasonable for him to try someone else."

Once more, then, a pause. And when Lieutenant Kopp went on he did so almost softly.

"I said before that you were quite a debater, Miss Kingman; I'll say so again. We have one small piece of proof, though, to suggest it wasn't to anyone else that Hector LeClerque went on that Monday night. We have this."

I hadn't seen him put his hand in his pocket, except when he reached for his cigarettes and matches. But when he held out his hand to me and opened it something lay across the palm.

The little toy man from my merry-go-round.

THE LITTLE TIN MAN from my merry-go-round.

He lay there all out of place in Lieutenant Kopp's palm, in his painted red coat and his painted red pants, posturing and waving, idiotically grinning out at nothing.

Even that. Even that. I thought, "I should have known it would boomerang somehow."

Dully I asked the necessary question.

"Where was it?"

"Hector LeClerque's coat pocket."

"Oh." There didn't seem much more to say. Instead of trying speech I looked from face to face, sectioning together what was being thought. They had found Hector with this broken-off piece from my merry-go-round in his pocket. They believed it was to our house he had come on Monday night. That somehow he had picked up the toy man there, that perhaps there'd been a quarrel . . .

Nothing to tremble for any more, nothing to expect. I said, "And I suppose you think all that business last night—I suppose now you think that was staged too. To throw you off the scent, probably. We——"

"You must have known, when you found part of that toy missing, Miss Kingman, that it might be discovered and traced back to you. You didn't dare go to where you'd left old Hector's body; you didn't quite dare to hunt through his clothes to see if he had it. Or maybe you did, and missed it. But you could put on a show that would explain its absence, and at the same time seem to put you in the clear. You——"

"You think I came home last night and struck down my own

mother. You——"

"Your mother herself said—it was almost her first testimony—that she'd thought it was you that came in."

"You think I almost killed her, almost killed myself, just to——"

"You weren't so sick, Miss Kingman. You could set the damper and wait until the first feeling of illness hit, then act fast. In fact that's a lot more reasonable than that you just accidentally happened to get conscious at the right time. Anyone will admit that the act you put on was a good one—stove still puffing gas when we got there, windows all broken, you working over your mother—most touching, most dramatic, most—almost—convincing."

I started to rise, found I couldn't, and sat down again. Somewhere in there I asked, "Why? Why is this being done against me?" But then I lost that too; I lost almost all ability to think or reason or even feel; I just sat there, numb. After a while, when I didn't speak, first Lieutenant Kopp and then Waslewski began thudding questions at me again—not new inquiries, just questions they'd gone over already, slowly at first, but increasing rapidly in tempo until the room and all the men in it seemed a whirlpool of what wasn't so much question as insistence— "you were jealous of Sylvia, you had all that stored-up festering hate against Sylvia, and then she wanted to buy your boy friend from you; you killed her in anger; you've shown you can get angry, Miss Kingman, you sent that anonymous note about Russ Bennert's car, you had the stringer out of Pete Fenrood's car and you slipped it back again at the same time you hid the card; you thought you'd be even with him too. Hector LeClerque guessed, somehow, he wanted money you didn't have, and you killed him to save yourself . . ."

I knew, after a while, why criminals break under questioning; I understood about thought projection; every mind in that room might have been willing me to say, "Yes, I did. Yes, I did." The impulsion to be obedient, to give them the answer they wanted grew so strong that even knowing I was innocent could hardly help me; they were so much stronger than I. All I could do was keep repeating the opposite of what they wanted. "No, I didn't, no, I didn't," in a dull unthinking rhythm. Later they took other tacks. Monday night, when Hector slipped jail, could I remember that? Had I left the hospital at all during working hours? Pete's Kitchen? Who was there? Time of leaving the hospital? "Who told you Hector was out of jail? So you went up to your room, didn't you, and Hector was there. He'd stolen up there, maybe had that toy of yours in his hands——"

No. No. No. I said it so often the word didn't have meaning any more. And all the time the eyes, judging.

Everything has to come to an end finally; even the interminable. When or why Kopp and Waslewski decided to let up on me I don't know; all I knew was that I sat there repeating, "No, no, no," monotonously and regularly, and that after a while I was saying it at greater intervals, and finally not at all.

I looked about then, a little, and if I was spent and haggard so were the others; so, at least, were Lieutenant Kopp and Waslewski. Waslewski pulled a handkerchief from his pocket; when it came out it was white and fairly fresh; after he'd scrubbed it over his face and neck it went back into his pocket sodden and gray.

Lieutenant Kopp said, "I'll say another thing for you, Miss Kingman, either you have strength of character or you have strength of something else." He faced about to the other men. "I don't know," he told them lengthily. "I—just—don't—know."

It wasn't any time for feeling triumph; there wasn't anything to make a triumph. But the other men, too, weren't sure; they might suspect, but they didn't know. All the way down to what pit I had sunk to, I could see it and dare a query.

"Are you—holding me?"

Silence, carefully broken by Waslewski.

"I don't think that was quite an innocent question Miss Kingman. If you were a man, there's no doubt I'd hold you. Since you aren't——"

That was what they let me go on. Just that they hated, until they were absolutely sure, to jail a woman. Waslewski looked about at the other men, either for corroboration or stiffening of will; most of the other men gave him very little back, but Lieutenant Kopp nodded, and that was that. Lieutenant Kopp took pains to add, "You understand—any time, Miss Kingman," but he needn't have bothered. I understood.

Someone let me out of there. I wasn't capable of taking in too many impressions, not clear impressions, but I did realize that the ante-room, when I emerged into it, held more people than the farm couple. Russ, for one. Ada, for another. Lucy Hague. The Boyces. Florence Squires and Emil Hasko. I managed to think of the gathering of the clan. Another murder, another questioning. They'll all have to tell where they were Monday night, since I didn't turn up pay dirt. They'll be asked for support—or the opposite—of my evidence. Ada will be shown the little tin man, and asked if she noticed it on my merry-go-round yesterday——

Russ stood up to ask angrily, "What've you been doing to Miss Kingman?" And then, after Lieutenant Kopp's answer, "She's not going home alone, I'm taking her."

Kopp, though, wasn't willing; it was Emil Hasko who drove me home, who waited until Mother got a few things together, and who then drove us to the hotel. After a second look at me, Mother forbore questions. The room we got at the hotel seemed to have little in it but twin beds; it would cost us three dollars for one night, but by the time I got to it I thought it was worth it; all I wanted was to crawl in one of those beds and leave the world well behind me, and that was what I did.

Not until noon the next day did I even begin rousing. What

seemed to pull me away from oblivion then was a touch against my cheeks and forehead; even then, though, I didn't want to wake; waiting for me, unrealized yet but overwhelmingly present for all that, was everything that was too big for me, everything against which I would have liked to do nothing but, whimper and push my face deeper into a pillow.

Then a worried voice asked, "You're all right, aren't you, Cathy? The way you've been sleeping . . ." and I had to recognize that. Slowly, flooding in to fill me, winding around me like a nest of snakes, came what the everything was. Sylvia, Pete, Hector, the tin man, the nightmare of the night before, the arrest I could any minute expect . . .

Without opening my eyes I sat up, hunching my knees, rubbing my face against the blanket over them. What had gone on in Waslewski's office hadn't been just a questioning, it had been a ransacking, a kind of violation; I was exhausted, and not only in body. It didn't seem possible, not yet, to return to my unhappy strait; not possible, yet, to begin once more beating at the problems around me, not possible even to begin waiting for what might come next.

That, though, was what had to be done, and slowly, deep somewhere, strength began re-forming. Mother, by that time, was saying, "Look, I got coffee and rolls from the coffee shop; you ate almost nothing yesterday; if you'd eat something . . ."

I lifted my head, then, and this time my eyes were open. Mother wasn't only up, she was dressed; after what she had gone through I was ashamed to have her so much ahead of me. Except for the worry in her eyes, and the deeply cut lines of strain, weakness, and sustained fatigue cut into her face, she looked almost normal; at least her movements as she fussed around the bed, tugging the undersheet smooth, patting the pillow, slipping a covering saucer from a steaming white cup and holding it temptingly under my nose, were normal enough; that was the way she fussed when I was sick.

"You don't have to say anything, Cathy," she told me as I accepted the coffee. "While I was downstairs I called up Rose Gamble——"

I put the cup down on its saucer, meeting her eyes. She'd told the truth about knowing, I saw that at once; it wasn't just night before last that had cut those lines into her face. And somehow that too was strengthening; telling her was one job I wouldn't have to do, and I had her beside me.

She said, "We can't—overemphasize this, Cathy. Even that—man from your merry-go-round. It's circumstantial only; those men—Kopp and Waslewski—can't do anything with nothing more than that to go on." Her lips trembled, her eyes were sick, but she was forcing herself to go firmly on. "What we've got to do is—think. Oh, I know" — swiftly, when I'd have interjected—"we've tried thinking before, but we've got to do a different kind of thinking now. We've got one advantage anyway over Waslewski and Lieutenant Kopp. *We know you didn't do it.* We can eliminate ourselves. Rose says Waslewski hasn't let Pete go yet; Hector was killed Monday night, while Pete was still out. But we can eliminate Pete, because he wasn't the one who attacked us. That's another advantage we have, we know that attack was a real attack. We heard Laura Firbeck ourselves at the inquest, and I'm sure she wasn't lying, so Russ Bennert must be out too. Don't you see, Cathy, that leaves only five people. Ada. Lucien Hague. The two Boyces. Florence Squires. It's an awfully small list. We should be able——"

While I slept, this was what she'd been doing; this wasn't anything she argued as she went, it was something well thumbed, spilling out. I pulled myself from the bedclothes, swinging around to dangle legs over the edge. What she said had to be true. Waslewski had shouldered aside what I'd had to say of Lucy, but that didn't mean he was right; sense and perception could count too, count as much as evidence, maybe. Lucy was sneaking. Waiting inside the dining room, shutting the stove damper, that was like Lucy. "No, she didn't, Mama," he'd whined twenty years ago, with a perfectly straight face and those brown spaniel eyes of his limpidly honest, "Sylvia didn't win my marbles, Mama, she *took* them, Mama. . . ."

Mother still was talking. " . . . Hector. Waslewski seems to have been quick enough to jump to the conclusion it was blackmail Hector got killed for, and in that much, anyway, he's probably right. I'm sure Hector didn't have any such idea while he was talking to us on Sunday, but that doesn't mean he couldn't have gotten it later. If we listened to him at that inquest he listened to us too. He'd hung around Sylvia's place a good deal; he might have seen someone go in there; he could have heard something during the inquest that made him begin putting two and two together. That could be——"

"Yes," I contributed. My mind wasn't working any too smoothly yet, but it caught this up. "That would be the reason we hunted for— the reason he broke out of jail. He'd had all that experience of blackmail with Grandfather Gainer, because that's what that amounted to. He must have thought he saw a chance to get at someone else who would give him money. Not me, someone else. Only this time——"

Mother finished it. "Only this time he came up against someone who isn't giving away anything. Except the quickest way out."

There wasn't too much we could do with it, beyond hashing and rehashing. Also the necessities of living had to be taken care of. We had to transport ourselves, minus car, from hotel to home, where Mother wanted to spend the afternoon; I had to get to work. The two rusty taxis that lounged about in front of the Admiral were outside our financial orbit; we walked the mile and a half home, through a gray, misty day. If it didn't do anything else for us, our descent to the lobby and the walk home gave us a chance to see how our social status had again reversed. As we passed the coffee shop waitress favored the desk clerk, beside whom she was gossiping, with a furtive, admonitory nudge; a sort of suspended animation fell over the salesmen and other loungers near the door; on the street we were conscious that people ran to store windows as we passed, that people in cars slowed and craned their necks, that people on the sidewalk drew back even as they stared. "Catherine Kingman." I could almost hear the words. "There. Girl in the pink coat. Do you really believe she——"

Not pleasant. Not anything you wanted to have follow you all the rest of your life, not anything you'd have had last even as long as a day, if you could help it.

At home Mother called Rose, who, also back in a state of reserve, agreed to stay until I got back; I unparked the car from the spot that was supposed to have been so safe, and went to work. Doris Orfelt—this seemed the last blow in a series of blows—scarcely glanced at me as I relieved her; only yesterday she had called excitedly, warm and moved, wanting to hear all about our intruder, but the tin man in Hector's pocket had been too much for her too.

" 'Lo, Cathy, got to rush," was what she said, and off she went.

After all the press, the exhaustion, the danger, the harrying of the hours so recently past, what I entered upon then was a peculiarly isolated and insulated afternoon. I sat at my desk with the light on, momentarily expecting that Kopp or Waslewski would turn up to take me in custody, but hour after hour went by and they didn't. Very few visitors appeared, and they soberly; if a nurse passed she did so without speaking; Dr. Diebuhr came and went by the side corridor, also without speaking; Russ hadn't been back to work over the new building plans since Sylvia died. Pete . . .

If Pete didn't know what had been happening to me the two days since I'd been to see him he would think I was neglecting him; all I had done, since then, was send him the two cartons of cigarettes.

I was so downcast I didn't even go down for supper. But then, about eight o'clock, Doris came back.

It must, by that time, have been raining a little; she was wearing a hooded white plastic raincape; just within the door she paused, shaking herself so that water flew from her the way it flies from a wet pup. She came, after that, directly toward me, and I saw immediately that it wasn't just her raincape that had been deluged. Small pink puffs underlay her dark eyes, a runnel had washed through the rouge on one cheek.

She said miserably, "I came back to say I don't believe it. I had dinner with Harry. He kept telling me all the things he thought you'd done. And I just don't believe it. I told him so, too. He was simply furious. He said I didn't have sense. He said I can't trust what I think about people. He said——"

She'd disagreed with Harry about Pete. But she'd fought with him about me.

It's not too easy for me to go overboard about a girl; liking is what I feel for a girl, ordinarily, not loving. But as Doris stood there, fumbling awkwardly with her belief in me and her handkerchief, I began loving Doris; I wanted to reach out and hug her. If I had she'd have been as embarrassed as I, but before I could get inhibitions I stood up to touch her shoulder.

"You don't know what you're doing for yourself, Doris," I told her. "When we're eighty I'll still come visiting you; I'll bring pie with my best linen napkin over it. I'll godmother all of your children——"

We both laughed a little after that, shakily. I don't smoke, and it was raining, but Doris wanted a cigarette, so we walked down the side corridor; we stood in the chilly side entrance just short of the rain and I took one of her cigarettes too; the smoke I drew into my mouth tasted acrid and bitter, but obscurely even the bitterness was something to welcome.

Bit by bit, there, she told me what else had come up that I didn't know of, most of it discouraging, but still fact that I thirsted for because, in some one bit of it, still might lurk the key piece that would give me the answer.

Lucy Hague—this was one of the more discouraging bits, as I should have expected—hadn't been caught out at anything at all. The Monday night of Hector's death he had been at Ada's until ten or so, when, or at least so he said, he had gone straight home to bed. The evening of the attack on Mother and me he had sung at a girls' club; he'd been through there at nine-thirty, but again he'd claimed a quick run home. The tan car that I'd seen parked near the church—this was worst of all—had turned out to belong to a married man who, to the entire cognizance of practically every resident around, had been calling on a widow in the block.

That one disappointment would have been enough to set me back, but it wasn't all. "Ada Bennert took a sleeping pill that night Hector was killed; you remember it was the night before Sylvia's funeral. She sleeps in a room of her own, so she could have got out, but she says she didn't. Same way with night before last, when your house was broken into. She couldn't remember anything about the little man from your merry-go-round. Her fingerprints were all over your house, but she had a reason for that."

"Such as it is."

"That's what I say too. Her husband didn't help her too much—he'd been at his office both evenings, working with Roy Engle over that addition to the schoolhouse they're going to put up. The Boyces played bridge with some people at that resort where they're staying. Florence Squires says she went to bed—Florence said she had trouble enough getting sleep, without running around murdering people."

I could hear Florence saying it.

"Dr. Diebuhr's got in his autopsy report; Hector didn't have anything more to eat after he left jail, it says, so he probably died sometime around midnight, that night. There isn't any rope burn on his neck, the way there was on Sylvia's, but there's a bruise at the back that could of come from a knot. Harry says it could have come from a kerchief" —she

183

didn't glance at me as she said it, but I could guess what had been in Lieutenant Kopp's mind—"or a scarf."

If Lieutenant Kopp had thought of me when he said "kerchief," then I again thought of Lucy Hague when Doris said "scarf." The permanent Hollywood fashion—had that been what had brought death to Hector?

Walking back up the corridor with Doris, I was let down again, somewhat. What she'd told me hadn't helped. What had come before that, though—her confidence in me—that still helped. If Doris could retain balance and judgment, then maybe other people eventually must too. No matter how obscuring what happened might be, no matter how hard the intelligence pitted against ours might fight to keep the facts obscure, maybe the truth eventually and somehow would get out.

Queerly enough, when I got home I found Mother a little invigorated too. Worry still buttonholed her eyelids and dented her forehead above the nose, but her mouth looked more relaxed. She had the house all ready to lock up; swiftly and warily—nerves jumped, now, at any slight creak or snap—we began the transfer: ourselves and Rose Gamble to the car, Rose Gamble to her house, where we waited in the car until a wave from a briefly unshaded window signaled that Rose found herself alone and reasonably secure inside. After that, as we told ourselves, we were perfectly all right; no one could get at two people in a car as long as it kept moving.

Rain had stopped falling sometime before ten, but a brisk breeze still blew damply; leaves lay thick in the wet streets and on the lawns, glistening and yellow. The rises were clear enough but here and there, in depressions, floated white night boats of fog; it was a night when it was very nice to think that just ahead of us was a well-lighted street where we could park, illegally, right in the taxi stand, and from there scoot to warm safe beds three stories up.

Mother, though, seemed less taken up by this promise of haven than she was by something else, and we hadn't gone far when she plumped with it.

"You'll find out anyway, so I might as well tell you." In addition to being faintly invigorated she was also, I sensed, faintly defensive. "I went to see Pete. In jail."

Just one single week ago the idea of Mother's going to see anyone in jail—or for that matter the idea of my going to see anyone in jail, to say nothing of being on the immediate threshold of landing there myself—would have seemed so ridiculous that I couldn't possibly have credited it. As it was I was astonished, because I hadn't expected her to do anything of the kind, but the picture evoked—Mother sitting on Pete's shelf talking as I had—wasn't too much more incredible than the picture of her talking in our own living room to Ada.

I asked, "What did you do that for?"

"I wanted to talk to him." It was still defensive, more trenchantly so. "I know what you think—you think it's somehow got to be Lucy Hague. But the more thinking I do now, the more I come back to Ada. I can't get over the way she hunted. She has a car of her own—she could have gotten around to do everything that's been done. And the money. I can't get around that either. The money, Sylvia's money, has to come into it someplace. I got thinking about Pete—jail is probably the one place in town where you don't hear what's going on. I was right, too. Oh, Pete knew about Hector; he couldn't help it; Waslewski and Kopp had been questioning him. But he didn't know about Ada's hunting our house. He didn't know about what happened that night at our house. He didn't know about the man from your merry-go-round in Hector's pocket. And he agreed with me. About the money, I mean. He says its got to count. We——"

"But, Mother," I said. I'd been over this too. "If Ada killed Sylvia she wouldn't have come openly to our house to hunt; she'd have been the one who came in the night. I can't see why she'd hunt twice."

Mother stuck to the line she was holding. "You saw her that afternoon, Cathy, saw how worked up she was. She's clever; Ada always was clever. But she never could let well enough alone. And she's unstable. If she's the murderer she'll be trying something more."

I let it take me. I couldn't go so far as to hope Ada was a murderess. For a fraction of a second, though, I let myself look at what my life might be like if she was. I turned the switch quickly, but the wires where that light had passed still glowed incandescently long after the current was off.

It was somewhere in the midst of this incandescence that Mother quit talking about Ada and began tugging my arm.

"Cathy, that couple over there," she said. "Over there by Tony Pugnacci's garage—slow down a little. There's something queer——"

That inner light of mine vanished completely. We had, I was immediately aware, reached a section of Long Meadow which definitely is one of its least attractive—a section between the railroad yards and downtown. Not squalid, exactly, just filled with warehouses, garages, hay, feed, and grain stores. At that time of night it was very quiet, very dim, very deserted.

"They look like such youngsters," Mother was saying, "but they seem to be seeing something——"

I began, "If you're going to start watching young couples——" but then I stopped too.

The two people Mother had pointed out were certainly standing still in front of Tony Pugnacci's garage, but they weren't smooching. They were peering in through the big window. Just as I looked at them the girl half turned, pulling at her companion; she pushed her face against his shoulder and rubbed it; she pulled again. The boy, however, seemed to be resisting; instead of coming with her he stepped closer to the window, and it was apparent, even in that

186

half-light, that every line of his body was watching and intent.

Mother rapped out, "Cathy, stop the car. We've got to find out what's going on there."

I could remember that presence waiting for me by the dining-room door. "Mother, we can't," I denied. "Why're we going to the hotel, except to be safe? It's not safe to stop here, Mother; we don't know what——"

Mother said, "People can be too safe, Cathy. They can think it's too important that they themselves should be safe."

That time I did as bidden. We'd gotten, by then, forty feet or so beyond the garage, but Mother was out of the car before I had the keys out of the ignition.

"Hello," she called softly, running back, "what's wrong?"

Both youngsters jumped when they heard her. Jumped and, obviously, turned to run. But then the boy, once more, held back. He was, as I saw when I too came up, even younger than I'd guessed, maybe fifteen or sixteen, so young his face still was unformed and pimply. It was also, right then, pinched by a fright in which I could readily join.

He said, "I don't know, but so many queer things going on around town now—there's somebody in there. In there in the back. You watch now. There, can't you see? That's a flashlight, back there in the workshop. There's frosted glass in the top part of the partitions in back of the counters—that's why you can see it, but blurry. It's got to be a flashlight. And I can't see why Tony would be looking around in his own closed-up garage with a flashlight. Or any of the boys either. I mean any of the boys who work here—Felix or Howie or Bud . . ."

The girl still was tugging. "I don't want to be here," she whimpered, "Let's go away from here . . ."

The boy stuck to his guns. "I guess maybe we ought to get somebody. I guess——"

Mother was sticking by her guns too.

"Yes, we should. You go. Go as quick as you can. Get anybody. Call the sheriff. We'll stay."

CHAPTER EIGHTEEN

THEY WENT. They went willingly, running. Their footfalls sounded on the sidewalk like receding rain, the gasp of the girl's quickened breathing was gone. Mother and I stood there alone, in a solitude as empty and friendless and threatened as if we'd been in an evacuated city awaiting a plunderer. At the distant corners were street lights, but no other lights showed in the block. The garage on one side had a secondhand car lot; beyond its wide driveway on the other side stretched the jungle of a vacant lot that had become a junkyard; across the street loomed the blackened brick front of what had been one of the town's earliest hotels, but which now for years had been nothing but a burned-out, gutted-out shell. Nothing near that was human except, beyond the tables of auto parts we could so dimly see in the forepart of the garage, beyond the partition that enclosed them, that other presence which so very likely might be the same one that had lurked in our house two nights before. That other presence now too engaged in only heaven knew what, again playing its flashlight somewhere behind the partition. The light showed first as a blurred, yellow-gray circle, then as a long slanting beam, then once more vanished. Whoever was in there might be about to come out. . . .

The sidewalk on which we stood lengthened and widened, as did the street; our car, forty feet farther up, receded to an almost unreachable distance. I pulled Mother's sleeve with a hand that was heavy to lift.

"Mother. We can't stay here. Not just the two of us. At least we should get in the car, have the motor running. We can't——"

Mother said, "No." In the half-light I could see the expression on her face, and it was the expression that had come on it each time, in the years past, when Father had threatened to die. She said, "We'll never get this thing solved, Cathy, unless we're willing to stand up to it. This time we won't be taken by surprise; there'll be two of us. You watch this door, Cathy, the front door. I'll move along so I can see the drive-in door at the side. If whoever it is comes out——"

I said, "At least I'm getting a wrench."

I did, running along to the car, swiftly lifting the trunk lid, grabbing whatever tools came handiest, one for Mother, another for me. That was how the two of us waited, ten feet apart, each of us gripping a piece of cold iron. Each of us thinking, anticipating . . .

A sizable chunk of eternity seemed to go by, eternity in which time dripped very slowly, in weighted, lengthening globules. Maybe it was only three minutes, or four, but it was enough for me to remember, ridiculously, that I'd stopped a run with red nail polish in the nylons I was wearing, and that that was one of the things that was going to be remembered about me, if I were found later, dead. It was long enough for some hardening of courage—"If whoever it is does come out, I've got to get in front of Mother. . . ."

That, though, wasn't what it came to. What it came to was the sound of feet, running, far away at first, but approaching rapidly. What it came to was the swish of a car approaching even more rapidly. Then we were alone no longer; the car slammed to a stop at the curb, men spilled from it, Lieutenant Kopp whipped past me, flashlight in one hand, gun in the other, Waslewski behind him. "Still in there? Good." They melted away quietly, swiftly, in the direction of the side drive-in door, but we still weren't alone; other people were there too. Men who had come running. The boy. Even the girl.

The boy gasped, "We went to Hap's beer joint. It was quickest. Somebody still in there?" Men pushed, voices around us were at once excited and smothered, faces and bodies swam up in the dim light and then away.

From the direction in which Kopp and Waslewski had vanished

there was, at first, no sound at all, then a sharp creaking, a scream, a barked order; from then on other sounds, other screams, less coherent, confused. The group around me pressed forward; whether I wanted to or not I pressed with it, finding Mother's hand, catching it, realizing how momentous this little fragment of time now might be, advancing along the driveway toward the big doors that by this time stood wide open, advancing into the oil-and iron-smelling reaches of the garage, its darkness still broken only by the erratic play of flashlights.

And in those uncertain and fading flashes we saw what there was to see. Lieutenant Kopp and Waslewski beside a collapsed huddle on the floor. A huddle that gasped, "I had a perfect right to be here; I wasn't hurting anything. I didn't take anything——"

Ada, again.

They took her to the jail, I understand, and from there, two or three hours later, to the hospital. She was at the hospital when I went to work that next day, Saturday, at three. My day off, but I had time to make up.

I had already heard about the hospital move from Rose Gamble, but if I hadn't I'd have learned it at once from Doris; it was the first thing she told me when I relieved her.

"Laura says Dr. Diebuhr gave Mrs. Bennert enough dope to put an elephant under, only she doesn't go under. Just lies there. They've got Emil sitting out front of her door, and her husband is with her. Every once in a while she starts talking. Same thing. She didn't kill Sylvia. She had a perfect right to be in that garage. She didn't take anything. Doesn't seem much like Mrs. Bennert."

Doris smiled at me, bleakly, her face still forlorn; I could guess that Harry Kopp hadn't backed down any, and she confirmed this.

"I haven't hardly seen Harry since dinner last night. He came in once this morning to go up to Mrs. Bennert's room, but he walked right past me as if he didn't know me; he didn't even say hello. A girl can't give up too much for a man, though, Cathy; a girl can't give up what she actually thinks."

I told her as staunchly as possible, "You're right, though, Doris. After all, I'm the other person who knows I haven't been going in for murder, and your Harry ought to find it out sometime, even if it takes him ten years. When he does . . ."

She mourned, "Men just hate being wrong, though, especially if a girl is right." When she trailed away she still looked woebegone.

At the desk she left I tried once more to go through those motions which, after three o'clock, I am supposed to go through. Lieutenant Kopp and Waslewski still hadn't made any new forays against me, except to ask, last night, "How'd you get into this?" That, I still realized, didn't mean anything; they were simply swiveled aside temporarily by this new business of Ada's.

While she was still in the garage, last night, they had tried questioning her, only to get the same disclaimer in reply. They had tried to make her stand, tried to make her walk; she had only sunk again to her huddle. The last I had seen of her she was being carried off bodily in Lieutenant Kopp's arms, her head bobbing limp and resistless against his shoulder.

In the still well-populated garage Mother and I had lingered a little. "We were just walking along the sidewalk outside here, see," the boy was narrating, by then, to a close group of auditors, "and we got to this window. I just looked in, kind of—you know the way you do. I could see there was this light on. I got sort of thinking——"

Nothing there to hold us; we had gone on to our car, wordlessly tossing the unused weapons we carried up on the back window ledge, starting for the hotel.

In the car Mother made her first comment.

"The garage. I was expecting Ada to break out somewhere. You know what I said. But the garage. Why she should——"

The iron determination with which she had accepted her wrench and posted herself at the garage had been gone, by then, it too cast off as useless. Instead she had sounded wrung-out and helpless.

I tried reason too. "Ada has that car of hers, but if she'd wanted anything for it she had only to go in the daytime and buy it. Unless she lost something she didn't dare let anyone know she had to replace. Unless she had Hector in her car and——"

Mother, antiphonal "A rug or a rubber mat, if he'd bled. But he didn't bleed. A tool, if he'd been killed by one, or if one had been found near him. Only none was. It was that piece from your merry-go-round that was found with him. It couldn't have been Ada who broke that little man off—no, I won't say it; I mightn't have noticed. She could have sneaked around after dark that day to stick him in Hector's pocket . . ."

I nodded slowly. "Or she could have come back to our house in the night, to do the same thing."

That was as far as we got, then, with this new piece for the puzzle. Our night at the hotel had been tossing and disturbed; it was early when we went back to the house in the morning, but there too we'd been restless, the whips of necessity once more flailing at us. When worktime approached I'd been about to call Rose Gamble, but Mother had stopped me.

"If you don't mind, I think I'll go to see Pete again; you can drop me at the courthouse."

"Again?" I'd echoed. "But you saw him just yesterday."

"I know," she'd said firmly. "I feel—well, I felt a little better, after seeing Pete yesterday. I want to tell him this new business about Ada."

"He's in jail, Mother. What possible——"

"Oh, I know," she'd answered, "but you don't mind letting me ride, do you? If you do I can walk, or maybe pick up a ride in the neighborhood, the way I did yesterday."

Nothing I'd been able to do, after that, but accede. On the way over, though, stung by little licking flicks that I neither understood nor tried to understand, frustrated by my inability to do anything or get anywhere, I found myself being unreasonably nasty.

"Maybe you should try reading Pete's palm," I suggested. "Maybe that's what this thing needs. You could look at all the hands. Not mine or your own, since we've agreed we're innocent. But all the others, just to be on the safe side. Especially Lucy Hague's. For my sake, please, Lucy Hague's. You saw a good deal in Sylvia's hand; maybe you could see as much in these others. Isn't there anything to give a murderer away?"

I'd never have said it if my nerves hadn't been stretched too far; after it Mother sat quiet, forgiving me—intolerably forgiving me since there's nothing more irksome than forgiveness. When she answered that was quiet too.

"Yes. There is something. There's a murderer's thumb. But I can't let myself look for it—it wouldn't be anything I could depend on. And if I found it—I'm not sure I could live with myself. It's a terrible idea—the idea that you could be predestined to murder by something like the shape of your thumb. I've given up palm reading. It doesn't seem possible I can play with anything like that ever again."

I'd apologized, even if I hadn't yet quite felt like it. She'd accepted apology as briefly as I'd made it. "That's all right." We'd driven the rest of the way to the jail in silence. It wasn't until I'd stopped the car to let her out that my irritation had really begun seeping away. And what I'd asked then hadn't been sensible either.

"Mother. Pete was with Sylvia that day at the bazaar. Haven't you already read his palm?"

Mother answered very evenly, "Yes, I have. I did, that day. Pete's life line has islands, some bad ones. But they're mostly up toward the top of his life line. They disappear, afterward; the rest of his hand looks all right."

194

That, then, was what I had to chew on as I sat there at the hospital desk through the hours of that Saturday afternoon and evening. Why had I asked that question about Pete's hand? No more than Mother did I believe in palm reading. Why had I let myself be cross? Wasn't it enough to be badgered by murder, wasn't it enough to expect any minute that Kopp or Waslewski might be back at me again, with what fresh and lying evidence I couldn't even imagine, without also being bothered by the aberrations and inconsistencies of my own emotions? Maybe this was what happened to people in murder. Maybe this was the way I'd continue—getting tighter and tighter, until I too, like Ada, did things as senseless as hunting through other people's houses and breaking into garages, until nothing existed between me and other human beings except fear and animosity and protect-myself-at-any-cost.

Russ, Doris had said, was upstairs with Ada. One of the things that had slipped away from me was my hard-held aloofness from him; I needed his support too much. And as this particular day wore on I reached toward him more and more. He would break the millrace I was treading; he might come down for supper. After all possibility of that had gone by, I merely postponed the waited-for good—he might go out with me for coffee. Eight o'clock came, though, and he didn't appear. Few visitors came around, either, and the nurses were as distant as the day before; by nine I had begun to think that if anyone did turn up beside my desk, especially with any expression of friendliness, I would probably scream; I was getting to the place where I understood about screaming.

When someone did turn up, though, I didn't scream. He came quietly, too—quietly and of course tiredly. Head over my books, I didn't know he was there until he spoke.

"I can just as well leave, I think. She's finally been asleep past half hour."

195

Russ at last. I looked up to have my heart melt at the hollows bitten into his face, at the droop of his shoulders, the entire dragging dejection and weariness of his big body. He ran a hand over his head, and even the brightness of his hair seemed dimmed.

He said, "I can imagine what people are saying, but it isn't Ada who killed Sylvia or Hector, any more than it's you who did it. I'd swear to that. I don't know what she's been up to, but not murder. I—well, I suppose I can just as well go get something to eat."

He was so rapt in his trouble that, except for the reference to me, he scarcely seemed aware of me. As he moved listlessly onward I half rose; there should have been some comfort to offer him. Before I was out of the chair, however, he too paused, not turning at first, just standing still, and gradually as he stood so his back stiffened. When he turned again he was still rapt, still troubled, but his relationship to that trouble was changing.

He said, "None of us can go on this way. Look, Cathy, if you and I got together on this—this last business of Ada's, at first glance it seems incomprehensible, as incomprehensible as that piece of your toy in Hector's pocket. Maybe it isn't, though. You know how Ada's been wound up in the idea that Sylvia had something someone else wants. She even went to you—to see if you had it—and you can perhaps imagine how hard it was for her to do that."

He took four paces forward, four backward, throwing himself violently about at the turn. As he did so, I caught the expression of his face, and what lit in my body was quicker than fire. Two days ago, in our kitchen, I'd glimpsed what might happen if Russ threw himself into this; if he could be roused enough to step out of place and do Waslewski's work. That was what was happening now, I could be almost sure of it; on his face, in his eyes, in his voice was the resolution of a thoroughgoing mind, made up and on its way.

He went on, "If I try pressing Ada she simply takes refuge in

196

hysteria; I can't get a sensible word from her. I can see only one reason, though, why she'd break into Tony Pugnacci's garage. Sylvia used it, we all did. Ada's so obsessed with her idea—I think now she's gotten around to thinking that if Sylvia didn't give this mysterious possession of hers to you to keep, then it must be hidden somewhere. I think she even wondered if Sylvia could have used the garage as a hiding place. Oh, I know it's impossible; I'm afraid Ada has gotten beyond knowing what's possible and what isn't. If Sylvia picked a hiding place it would-n't be Tony's garage. But let's give Ada a little something, anyway. Let's suppose Sylvia *did* have something someone else wanted—it's about as good an explanation as I can see for why she was killed. I can't really believe Pete Fenrood killed her, at least not for any reason that's come out so far. Pete's no adolescent to kill for love; Pete may be a hothead, but he's shown himself perfectly capable of making ordinary adjustments—look at the way he switched from you to Sylvia. And if there's one idea that's laughable, as I've told Waslewski, it's that you——"

He stopped, knowing it wasn't necessary to go on with it, just letting his eyes meet mine. When he went on it was more smoothly, though decision wasn't lessened.

"I know you weren't in love with Pete Fenrood. I know you did-n't kill Sylvia out of jealousy or because she was offering to buy Pete Fenrood from you, or for any other reason. I believe now that whoever killed Sylvia did so just as Ada says—because Sylvia was threatening him with something he had to get to feel safe. I'm afraid we're going to have to accept the fact that behind all this there was some kind of love affair, probably not a pleasant one; that's the only thing that will explain everything that's come up. The railroad ticket she found under her pil-low——"

My own thinking. "Yes," I said. "I figured that too. A coun-terthreat. And what she said to me about cutting her losses——"

He took it back from me. "She was planning to marry Pete.

Someone objected to that marriage, someone perhaps objected to a generous supply of money being cut off. And this is what happened."

Harsh, direct, cutting. Russ, too, had come a long way from the morning he'd said, "You might remember Sylvia's dead." I sat facing it, cringing from it, but not able to deny it. I asked, "Who then; I've been thinking of Lucy Hague . . ."

He nodded. "Unlikely. My own guess is the other man in this deal. Clint Boyce. He's being extremely quiet. So is Nila. I don't think it's particularly characteristic of either one of them to be quiet—Lucy or Clint—it's not going to matter who, but I'm going to find out. I'm going to proceed on this second idea of Ada's, that Sylvia did have something, probably some incriminating piece of evidence against someone, and that it's hidden somewhere. I don't believe it's found yet—that attack on you would tend to show the murderer's still hunting. I'm going to beat him to it. You and I, Cathy. I know the outsides of houses, you know more of their insides. I—well, Sylvia's apartment is the natural place to look first, and I suppose I have qualms about digging into Sylvia's possessions by myself. If you'll go with me . . ."

I didn't have to say anything; as I held out my hands in agreement I felt the rushing confirmation of my hope. On the surface this plan Russ had made might not have too much to offer; all we could do, actually, was hunt where others—the police, Ada, Sylvia's lawyer, the unknown murderer—had already hunted, but instinct seemed to tell me that at last I was reaching a basic activity; this was the hunt that would have to be continued until the sought-for was found.

CHAPTER NINETEEN

BY THE TIME we had our plans made it was a quarter to ten; Russ had to leave quickly if he was to catch a bite at Pete's Kitchen before we began what might be an all-night job; I had to clear my desk and get Mother to the hotel before I could meet him at Sylvia's apartment, as agreed.

Mother, when she heard what I was about to do, listened in entire quiet. She, it turned out, had spent most of the afternoon with Pete and the evening with Rose Gamble without having anything of importance develop; against what was now on foot she had the inevitable reactions—she didn't like it, she didn't like any part of it, she didn't like my working with Russ. But in the end she agreed that this too, like waiting last night at the garage, was one of the things that had to be done.

In our room at the hotel she delivered a final caution— "If you do find anything, remember someone killed Sylvia, and probably Hector, because of it. He wouldn't be apt to stop for you and Mr. Bennert."

Her reluctance, however, was something I had expected; I wasn't dismayed by it. Nothing, I thought in the rush of confidence I was then experiencing, could happen to me while I was with Russ; no murderer, possibly, could overcome the two of us. I was leaving Mother safe, too. By ten-thirty I was out of the hotel, and no more than six minutes later the Pontiac's rumpled nose once again pointed up the Gainer driveway. I was certain, right then, certain all the way down to the bottoms of my feet, that this time, at last, we were getting somewhere.

Fortunately I expected it to take time. It did take time.

Russ, as we had agreed, was at Sylvia's first. When—in the total darkness, this time, of an overcast September evening—I once more stood on Sylvia's doorstep, he immediately opened the door for me; he had the lights on and the curtains pulled. Eventualities were something not only Mother had thought of; he was taking care of them grimly.

"The first thing we're doing is see the doors are locked. I'm not just locking this one, I'm turning the night bolt. Same with the door leading over into our house—that's just too much area where someone might creep in. One thing we don't seem to have to worry about in this case, thank the Lord, is a gun; that's one thing Waslewski's checked for; guns aren't as easily come by around here as they'd be in a city."

I hadn't even thought of a gun or the possibility of one; except for deer rifles and BB guns the idea of any such weapons in civilian hands in Long Meadow had been too farfetched for imagination to bring up, but then, I realized, so was the idea of murder. Near the door, where Russ had left me, I looked about slowly. This was the room I had stood in on the Saturday morning which was only a week ago, the room which then too had been curtained and secluded, but which then had been dim. Now it stood with its contours, its furnishings, its colorings all revealed brilliantly in the blaze from the prism-hung chandelier—the chandelier which was such an anachronism and yet, in the way of some anachronisms, so peculiarly fitted. It was a room luxurious, inviting, curiously seductive, in purple-gray, dusty rose, queer dulled greens and yellows. The two huge gray and sepia finger paintings over the fireplace seemed to melt into the gray fieldstone of the wall they hung upon, the huge chairs and sofas looked as if they might melt into the purple-gray carpet; everything in the room was low—the tables, the chairs, the radio, the mushroom-topped lamps, as if the floor with its thick covering was really the living level of the room, and everything else there, including any people who entered, must ooze toward that level.

200

I hadn't, before, reacted in any way to that room, but I did then. If I had been sitting in one of the chairs I'd have wanted to do so with my back rigid. But then that chain broke too; Russ came back to me.

"That's done," he reported tersely. "No one's going to break in on us. I checked the windows before you came." He also, then, stood surveying the room, and as he did so it quit being a room, it became a job to face.

And it was a job to face. At first glance not a half dozen hiding places suggested themselves, but at second glance there were thousands. Russ said crisply, "No use being dismayed before we start; I suppose one thing we should do first is think about Sylvia and what kind of hiding place she'd choose. Not any place too difficult, such as under the middle of the carpet, because I imagine she wanted to have whatever it was handy—she might have wanted to show it to you that Saturday morning you came here, if she'd lived to do it. On that basis, where would you start?"

I hadn't anything to give him. When I once more looked about, the whole room, someway, might have been Sylvia, mocking me, saying, "Here I am, darling, you can see what I am, and you don't approve, do you? But you like me sometimes; I'm in your blood too; you could let yourself go to be this. And just as there's a little of me in you, so there's a little of you in me; I can be restrained too."

I shook myself from it, but it kept its effect over me. All I could say to Russ was, "We'll have to begin in corners, you in one, I in another, and from then on not miss anything."

That was what we did. Moving cautiously at first, in a sort of slow motion, as if we waded against opposition. "I keep feeling I'm an intruder," Russ said, and that was what I felt too. As we worked on, though, that feeling lessened a little. In my corner there was, first of all, the paneled door by which I'd entered; I felt carefully over it, looking for I didn't know what—some panel, perhaps, that might slide. I examined the chute of the mailbox beside it. I scrutinized, inch by inch, the glass frames and the decorative ironwork around the door. I ran my hands over wallpaper.

Even Sylvia's house, I discovered, had dust in it; my hands began being grimy. And as if that discovery made the whole thing more normal I could begin working as if I were merely at a routine task, inching over the carpeting, watching for loosened nails around the edge, watching for a possible break in the seaming, watching for cracks in the ivoried baseboards. Most of the chairs were upholstery and nothing else; methodically I dumped cushions, examined seams, prodded, passed on to the sofa, thinking, Ada has done this already. Ada, and whoever else . . .

At his opposite corner Russ worked with the same concentration as I; once in a while we talked, tossing desultory speculations back and forth; mostly we just worked at a pace that began increasing feverishly. When Russ rose to feel over the flagstones of the fireplace wall I was already beginning on the stack of magazines beside the sofa.

"I'm as bad at this as Ada, too," I thought then. "I'm as skilled—and as nervous—at this as she was." Looking back over the space I had covered, it was almost odd to see it looking untouched; it might have been more in accord with what was happening to look back over carpeting torn from the floor, over upholstery ripped apart and strewn. Yet there was no violence in what we did; we just moved evenly forward.

The time came when I met Russ in the middle of the floor—the two of us creeping together on hands and knees. Nothing to do after that but rise to ease our aching backs; nothing for Russ to say but "Well, not down here. I suppose the reason we started with this room is because it was the best bet, but we aren't done yet. There's still the rest of the house."

So we went on to that too. When the exhilaration and certainty with which I had begun hunting evaporated I don't know; it must just have seeped away little by little. Suddenly, upstairs in Sylvia's bedroom,

I realized it was gone entirely; all I was working on then was a kind of desperate doggedness. Over the upstairs carpeting, the pink velvet chairs, the dressers with their heaps of perfumed lingerie, girdles, nylon hose, handbags, gloves, handkerchiefs, over the bed, through the long closets with their new sliding doors and their rows of dresses, suits, jackets, slacks, coats, furs, shoes, and hats, I went with the same care I had used downstairs. Russ was doing the bathroom.

But even he, finally, had to admit defeat. Facing it without giving way to it.

"It's got to be here," he insisted, and his face then was the face of an officer who had told his men, "One month from now a hundred thousand draftees will be pouring into this camp. When those draftees get here this camp is going to be built."

"It's got to be here," he repeated. "Ada went over your house; you know nothing's there. Sylvia gave up her apartment in New York; she was moving into a hotel this fall. I called the superintendent of her old apartment house and she didn't leave a thing; everything was sent here in crates and cartons. Her deposit box has been opened. I went through her car this morning. I know Ada has fine-combed our house. It's got to be here."

But if it was, we couldn't find it. As I looked back over the room I couldn't see a single inch I hadn't gone over at least twice. I said despairingly, "It's more of the same. We must have been wrong from the beginning. All this idea that Sylvia had something hidden—that's all it was, an idea. We've been looking for something that never was anywhere."

He said savagely, "We weren't wrong from the beginning. I can't have been wrong." He had brushed his glinting fair hair back with a hand that didn't restore it to smoothness; at one side of his head strands of it arose spikily, and a streak of dust crossed his left cheek. He flung about, to pace jerkily back and forth a few steps, as he had in the hospital office, and as he did so I felt almost a little frightened; what had impressed me most about Russ, always, had been his strength; now I seemed to be glimpsing some of the sources of that strength—the fierce, engendering heat which lies behind the purposes and determinations of a strong and purposeful man. Yet when he turned around to me again he was, on the surface, almost calm; the fire within him was banked.

He said stiffly, "Temporarily I suppose we'll have to give up. I can't think of much more we can do around here." He tilted his wrist, and as he did so compunction sprang up to add another insulating layer over the coals. "Good Lord. Four o'clock. Your mother must be frantic, waiting for you in that hotel room. Get yourself washed, Cathy; I'll take you down there."

Warmth, the affectionate, light warmth I recognized, grew over his face; he reached out to pat me. Ada, though, stood as ever between us; I said, "Yes, as long as there's nothing more we can do I can just as well wash," and went into Sylvia's pink and wine bathroom to do so.

When I was done and he had replaced me I drifted downstairs, letting myself fall to a sofa. It was soft and inviting, I was almost incredibly tired, I seemed to be held by one of my usual confusions, in which what I felt and what I thought were characteristically dim. Did I feel failure and anger at failure the way Russ was feeling them? Or was it something else I was experiencing? I didn't know; I just let the sofa take me. One of Sylvia's sofas, one she must often have sat on, one on which she perhaps had been lying the night her murderer came for her.

Sylvia. In the fury of all that had happened she had slid away from me, a little, but now she came back. I could see her again, driving past in her car that August evening. She hadn't bothered even to wave. But then later she had deliberately sought me out, at my house. Just before doing so she had been at the bazaar, where Mother had read her palm. She had called from downstairs, "Cathy, you here?" and then she had risen to me up the stair well, she had sat on the bed. I had been right there with her; she certainly hadn't been trying to hide anything in my room. She'd been alone downstairs, of course, before she called to me, but our house had been hunted as thoroughly as this one—hunted twice, I was sure, once by Ada, once by the murderer. "Cathy," Sylvia had asked, "last winter, how much did you see of Pete Fenrood? . . . as your mother would so brutally say, it's time I cut such losses as I may have and settled down. Cathy, what about you?"

She had been crowding me too close, but she had dropped it. "Oh," she had admitted, "it's hard to decide. Why do I ever get serious?" Then, almost in the same way Russ had done just a moment or so ago, she had lifted her wrist to look at her watch. "Heavens," she had said, or something like that. "You'll soon have to hurry. And I'm so terribly thirsty. Herring, baked beans, and coleslaw . . ."

On Sylvia's sofa I lay resting, not feeling anything, then, not even mixed up. Not expecting anything, not waiting for anything. I looked at Sylvia's pale blue ceiling, a ceiling like a summer sky, high and cloudless.

In a minute or two Russ would be done washing; he'd be running downstairs. "It's got to be somewhere," he might say. "We'll just have to make a list of other places to look. Our old barn out in back . . ."

Only he needn't look farther. I had found what we were looking for. Or at least I knew within what small compass it must be contained.

KNOWING, I WANTED TO BE ALONE with it. I didn't want to tell Russ. I didn't want to tell Mother. Secretly and by herself Sylvia had come to find her hiding place, secretly and by myself I wanted to find what she had hidden. I was the one to whom Sylvia had said, "There's something I may want to tell you." It was to me she had considered revealing what she had, not to Russ, not to Mother. There might be a choice for me, whether I in my turn would want to reveal or keep hidden.

By the time Russ came downstairs I had gotten myself up from the sofa.

"There's no need for you to take me down to the Admiral," I told him truthfully and quietly, perhaps the one time in my life I had really wanted to go from him rather than stay. "I'm not in the least afraid; you can just see me started. I'll leave the car right in front of the lobby. It'll be terribly awkward otherwise—if you go in my car you'll have no way of getting home, and if we go in yours I'll have to come up for my car tomorrow——"

My voice speaking, my voice, entirely disconnected from my stilled thinking, but obeying orders.

He smiled at me. "Cathy, you protest too much. Of course I'm taking you. I'll drive your car down in the morning—no, better yet; we'll go in your car and I'll walk home from downtown; I could do with a walk."

He was entirely himself again; as we drove he talked, a little, but I couldn't talk; I had said all I wanted to say; I existed in nothing but a vacuum of waiting. Even the mechanical things I did—stepping into the car, finding the ignition with its key, turning it, pressing my foot to the starter, following the driveway to the street, finding the streets toward

206

the hotel—seemed somehow distant and muffled. And he too, after a while, fell silent; it wasn't until we had left the car at the curb and he had taken me into the hotel lobby—deserted and lit only by one shadowed globe behind the desk—that he once more spoke.

He said, "You're a brick, Cathy. But I don't have to tell you—you know what I think of you, don't you? Always and forever, Cathy." He stood looking down at me as I looked up at him; in the dimness I could see only the shape of his head, the shadow of the hair that was really so bright, the arches of his eye sockets, the strong line of his nose and mouth. He hadn't kissed me since I was fifteen, and only lightly and carelessly then, but he swiftly bent to kiss me now, not carelessly but still lightly, our lips barely brushed. I should have felt something; I stood there in my woodenness trying to feel things, but all that existed inside me was the new isolation that had begun when I was sitting on Sylvia's sofa.

After the brief kiss he left quickly; I stood where I was near the foot of the Admiral's stairs. In what, I don't know. Maybe a kind of wonder. Then I half turned to look upward.

I knew what I should do; I should climb those stairs, rap until Mother heard me, get into bed, sleep for at least what was left of the night. There would be plenty of time, in the morning, for me to look where I must look. Only it wouldn't do me any good to ascend those stairs; I could get into bed but I never would sleep; until I had explored this one remaining possibility there couldn't be any rest for me. Mother didn't know I was back at the hotel; if she was restless and wakeful she'd think me still with Russ. Outside, it was still full dark, but dawn soon would be breaking. . . .

I didn't do anything, really; the few vague and disconnected excuses for what I wanted to do weren't excuses or even arguments. My mind was already made up, had been made up ever since that moment on the sofa. Within two minutes after Russ had gone out through the Admiral's door I was out through it too, I was crossing the sidewalk, lifting my face to the fresh chill air that was such a contrast to the air of the lobby, sliding into the front seat of the car I had just left. I still felt almost nothing; certainly I felt no fear; I recognized that what I was doing was dangerous, maybe; I recognized that the way of safety had been up those hotel stairs to the room with Mother, I realized how empty our house must be, with no one in it and no one expecting anyone to be in it, but all that made no difference. Neither danger nor safety, right then, seemed to mean much; I seemed to be beyond fear, in the same way that people fear death all their lives and then, when the moment comes—I saw it with Father—they're no longer afraid.

In that predawn hour which is perhaps more still, more close to a lapse of all motion and all living than any other hour of the sun's turn, our neighborhood was very quiet. The street stretched long and unused from one corner light to the next, holding nothing but a few quiescent parked cars and the half-visible houses sunk under their trees in a wood-slumber of their own. No house lights showed anywhere; Rose Gamble's house was as dark as the rest. This was one night when, if she got up, she wouldn't so much as glance toward us, expecting us to be at the hotel.

When I had run the car along the side porch I did hesitate, not because fear had begun rising, but because my mind recognized so well the folly of what I was doing. I still could turn back. But the pull into the house was much stronger, and actually, I told myself, it couldn't be too dangerous; no one could know I was being visited by this necessity. I moved. The kitchen door was well locked as we'd left it, the room beyond dark; when I'd made my dash I stood on its threshold, sending antennae out. No sound anywhere except the perhaps quickened flow of my breathing, the rustle of my body; Mother had had a fire again yesterday and there still was a faint warmth, steadying warmth, coming from it. No reason for tiptoeing but, moving away from that threshold with the door relocked behind me, I tiptoed; tiptoed over the terrain I knew so well—waxed surface of kitchen linoleum, icebox waiting to catch me with its corner at the left, pale loom of sink at the right. Diningroom threshold, narrow aisle between table and plants. Livingroom carpet, a rocker to catch at my knee, hallway, the stairs, and then my room.

Once more I stood waiting and listening, listening to a night in which there was nothing to hear, nothing, again but the sounds and motions that existed in my own person, nothing but the faint settle and stir of an old wood house slowly decaying, nothing but an even fainter lift and drift of air and leaves beyond window and wall. I was alone in the house. Of course I was alone.

Before I did anything else, then, I pulled down the window shade, turned on the light. Before me at once, sharply and clearly, was my little, familiar, homely room: the single white iron bed that I'd had since I was seven, with the worn chenille spread over it, the marble-topped walnut dresser with the carved side brackets beside its mirror, the forget-me-not-sprigged wallpaper over the angled ceiling and the walls, the closet door open on my dresses and shoes, the two gray shag rugs on the gray-painted softwood floor, the one rocker, the one window with its crossed and ruffled curtains, the old treadle sewing machine holding the octagonal red box—all so well known, all so intimately, achingly well known, and yet, under the circumstances, so strange.

I stepped toward the sewing machine and the red box.

Coming, I hadn't been afraid. Entering, I hadn't been afraid. But I was afraid then. My stomach cramped, my mouth dried, my hands iced. Not because of anything outside. But because of what I might find in the red box.

Only two days ago I had put the merry-go-round back into this box, broken as it was. Mending it had been something to leave for later. I took it out again now, and it was exactly as it had been when I'd set it away: top torn, supporting ribs snapped like broken bones. The rough-

bright spot of solder still showed where the little Italianate man had balanced, the paint flecks were still gone from the base.

Not only I, but Waslewski too, had recently looked at this thing, turning it over and over in his big hands. The night before that the intruder who nearly killed us had been so close to what he sought that he too had held this thing in his hands, dashing it in anger at the floor.

I set the thing down on the corner of the dresser, where Sylvia had set it. This was the way she had stood beside it, just as I was standing now. Her one hand had been on the key, turning, when I returned to the room; she'd wound the spring all the way, then stepped back to listen . . .

My own hand touched the key, too, but I didn't turn it; I couldn't stand here alone to see the top twirl and the riders circle, as Sylvia had; I couldn't have the quiet around me broken by the scratchy little tune, not now. Instead I once more picked it up. Brass pole in the center, much too slender to be hollow. A track for the much too small ponies, the much too small riders. But the base—the octagonal base held the spring, held the music box. That base must somehow open, in case the springs or the music box needed repair. Whoever sold this toy to Sylvia had very likely showed her how that base opened.

Slowly I tilted the thing to its side. The unpainted wood bottom, all in one piece, bore nothing but a purple stamp, "Haley's toys, No. 3068." Tiny nails, set close together, rimmed the entire octagon.

Not there. I tipped it back to sit upright. It must be the sides that moved, the alternately green- and red-painted sides of the base. Against my exploring thumbs, though, those sides stayed firm. Maybe my thumbs were damp, maybe they were weak.

I began all over. Began more methodically, this time, and a little more strongly. Began with the panel from which the winding key protruded, pushing first to the left, then to the right. The split sides of that panel refused to move. I went on to the next. To the next . . .

It was that third panel that moved. Moved, at first, very little. So little I couldn't feel it. But my eyes saw the thin line of unpainted wood appearing along the left edge.

I must have stopped breathing, bending over that toy. I don't think anything went on in my body at all. I pushed again with one thumb against the surface of the panel and this time even my hand felt the slide of the thin wood in its groove. I pushed again . . .

No need to wonder any more, then. No need for more hunting. I slid in my fingers and there it was, the small pile of papers.

I held them in my hand, knowing that insistently as I had been driven I hadn't really wanted to find them. Maybe it had begun while I was helping search Sylvia's apartment—the deep, pulling unwillingness to find the thing I yet was forced to discover. I stood with that little packet in my hand, the light overhead making a brilliance all around me. But a kind of blindness was settling over me; when I looked at the brilliance it darkened. In my body there was only one impulse toward movement, an impulse that would have taken me downstairs to the kitchen stove and thrust these papers within it.

Only that wouldn't do either. What I held was cause of murder. I could burn what I held, so I'd never know. So almost everyone else would never know. One person, though, would still know. One person would never believe I had destroyed without looking.

How long it was before confusion lessened enough for me to look I don't know. There came a time, though, when I was looking at what I held. Looking at the one sheet of note paper with the handwriting in blue ink, which was on top. It had been folded once but some of the handwriting was on the back, and I wouldn't have needed to open it.

I stood there then, knowing. Knowing so much there was very little more I needed to be told later. Knowing why, when Mother had asked Sylvia if she were in danger, Sylvia had come to me. Knowing why Sylvia had chosen my room for her hiding place. Knowing what she would have told me if she had lived to see me on that Saturday.

Knowing about Ada and Ada's frantic belief and her searching, knowing about Ada's whole last ten years. Knowing who had stood inside our diningroom door. Knowing who had killed Hector.

The note, in the familiar handwriting, began:

Sylvia, sweet,

You know you're my only love—the only woman I love now, the only woman I'll ever love. I wouldn't ask this of you again if there were any way out of it, Sylvia; I swear it's the last time. I can't possibly keep up connections on the pay I draw in this Army; I've had to juggle accounts a bit—not much, it seemed perfectly safe. Now it looks as if top brass is out for me . . .

I didn't turn over the page. I looked, instead, at the first of the cancelled checks beneath it. A check for fourteen thousand dollars, signed by Sylvia, made out to Major Russell Bennert.

Once more I had nothing to feel, nothing at all. Not horror, not sickness. Not surprise. I might always have known. I stood there and I didn't want anything, didn't regret anything. I had no horror, no sickness . . .

No surprise as I turned for the opening of my door, or Russ as he appeared. No surprise for the hand over my mouth, no surprise for what he said: "I'm sorry, Cathy. You know I'm sorry."

I didn't struggle. I don't think I wanted to struggle. I thought, "I wonder if this is the way Sylvia felt." There must have been a moment when Sylvia, too, knew she would have to die; a moment when even Sylvia knew how dangerous danger can be. Sylvia too must have loved him once; this was what she and I had in common, only she wanted him enough to take him ruthlessly and against all decency, her own sister's husband. Even if she tired of him, even if at last she was throwing him

212

away, even if she was threatening to reveal him to me, even if she was threatening to cut him from what he wanted, her money, still she must have remembered she loved him. Maybe Sylvia too had stood quietly with his one hand over her mouth and his other sliding something about her throat, just as I was. I thought, "I wonder how much of his decision to kill Sylvia came because it was to me she threatened to reveal him, how much because of the money."

He said, "I'll have to take those, Cathy; you can see I have to have them." From my fingers the checks and the note slid easily, gently. He said, "Ada's got the money now, and that note and those checks are the only things in this world that stand between me and the things I've got to be; I wouldn't have had any chance in the legislature, I wouldn't have had any chance for anything else, if they'd come out. You know what I've got to be, Cathy; one of the things you've liked about me is my ambition; you know I'm able. Ada may suspect me, but she won't stand out against me, not really, not long. You know how I hate doing this, Cathy, but I've got to be safe; just you now, just you and maybe your mother, if she gets too inquisitive . . ."

He was behind me; I hadn't tried to turn. But then, abruptly, he wasn't behind me. I was facing him. The soft length of fabric was about my throat, tightening. I knew there was no use in fighting him; we were entirely alone in the house; I could see the street as I'd come into it—the long deserted stretch of blacktop, the parked cars, the empty sidewalk, the houses asleep under trees. In my own house there had been no breath and no stir; no one could come to my rescue. Just the same I was fighting; he had released my mouth and I opened it for screaming, though no scream came out; I had no breath for screaming. But some strength still lived in my body, a little; I got my arms up; my fingernails raked once over his face. Not strength enough, though. This time when light faded, it faded rapidly. I fell through deep space, twisting and twirling . . .

But then, abruptly, that downward swirl lessened. The darkness

213

too changed in quality, not increasing, not decreasing, but swaying back and forth. I still was falling, I still had no breath and no strength, but the fighting went on. I fell under the fighting, something struck my side; my hands that had been so powerless could slowly creep up to gnaw at the fabric about my throat; I gasped—somehow it didn't seem the first gasp—and air pressed in my chest; I struggled upward, only to be struck again violently and go down once more. This time, though, my hands were free, so were my throat and my eyes. . . .

By the mere operation of opening my eyes I could see again. See a room that dizzily circled and swam, a room crowded to bursting with men knotted and wound in the fighting which now drew away from the spot in which I lay aside and fallen, my head on the treadle of the sewing machine. I was alone, but then I wasn't. Mother bent over me, shaking me, crying, "Cathy, Cathy, Cathy——"

Who solved Sylvia's murder? Who first guessed at her murderer? Not I, though I found the checks and the note. Not Lieutenant Kopp or Waslewski, though they were both there, willing and eager enough, at the end.

Not even Long Meadow. But Mother and Pete. They were the ones, sitting in Pete's cell, doing nothing but talk. Mother who from old disaffection was quite willing to concentrate on Russ, Pete who was ready to follow her lead.

Mother hasn't hinted why she was so willing to suspect Russ; that's a topic she manages always to avoid. She merely says, "Every time Russ Bennert's name came up, we'd say, 'Of course, he's clear; he had an alibi, and the murderer sent that anonymous note against him.' I don't know how we ever got around to asking, 'Suppose he sent that note himself,' but as soon as we'd done so the perspective changed. Instead of throwing suspicion on Russ, that note actually did the opposite— made him look innocent and falsely accused, just as he must have

214

planned it should. And more than anything else, it brought out his alibi. We began looking hard at that alibi. Out of the whole lot of us—I'd noticed this at the time—he was the only one who had a neat and tight alibi at all. Cathy had talked to him at her desk about eight-thirty; he'd asked her to bring him coffee. At nine or a little later he was sitting on the edge of her desk drinking that coffee, and from then on he was with Dr. Diebuhr. The only time he could have killed Sylvia was between eight-thirty and nine. I talked to Laura Firbeck but she was still certain it was his car she'd leaned against during a good part of that half hour. We tried figuring out how he could have used someone else's car, maybe Dr. Diebuhr's, but even Dr. Diebuhr doesn't leave his key in the ignition. Then after Ada broke into the garage——"

At this point Pete takes it up. "What Laura identified the car by was that license, the B7000. I finally got thinking, though, how easy it would be to switch plates from one car to another, and then we had it. Russ Bennert bought a red Studebaker last spring after Dr. Diebuhr bought his—maybe he began planning as far back as that. He parked at the hospital's side entrance every time Dr. Diebuhr didn't beat him to it. On this one night, though, he got there first but didn't park by the door—he parked quietly somewhere along the street. All he had to do, then, after Dr. Diebuhr turned up, was slip down the side corridor, unhook his license plates from extra plates he'd picked up somewhere, hook them over Dr. Diebuhr's plates, and be off. When he got back he just reversed. He could go right in to your desk, Cathy——"

Mother breaks in soberly, "Poor Ada. I can't get away from what this has been for her. She must have suspected; that's why she hunted so. It was to see if they had extra plates around that she broke into that garage——"

Pete says, "Your mother did the selling job; she went to Waslewski and Lieutenant Kopp. They didn't want to see it at first, but then after a while they did. Anyway they bought enough to begin watching. When you told your mother that Russ was asking you to help hunt—that cinched it, even for them; they could guess then how pushed he was. When he killed Sylvia he probably thought she had those checks right where he could pick them up quickly, maybe in her desk. He must have gone through her place again and again, beginning with the night he killed her . . ."

That meticulous hunting I had done. That Russ had done. Was that why there'd been no surprise? Had I known, somehow, that for Russ it wasn't a first hunt?

Pete again. "From what you said at the inquest, Russ knew Sylvia had gone ahead at least part way with her threat to expose him; he must have thought when he couldn't find what he wanted that if he got you started you might get hot. When you did get hot you probably turned queer enough so he guessed: he hung around the hotel long enough to see you leave. He missed out in just one thing—your mother had already called Waslewski, as soon as you left her. Waslewski let me out. The bolt of Sylvia's door into the Gainer house was cut as soon as Russ shot it; Lieutenant Kopp was right there in Sylvia's living room part of the time you were upstairs. Waslewski and your mother and I waited here, in her bedroom——"

Mother shudders. "It wasn't fun, Cathy. All that long, long night. Hearing you come in, not daring to breathe. Hearing him creep after you——"

I shudder too.

Pete says, "I got first crack. That much I had, anyway."

I was in bed a few days; not sick, just staying in bed. People were nice to me, the way people can be nice in Long Meadow. They came to see me. Pete. Doris. Dr. Diebuhr. Rose Gamble and Agatha Pence and Mrs. Meerus and Mrs. Upsher. They brought cakes and rolls and casseroles. Clint and Nila Boyce came before they left for New Jersey;

probably they'll never be out this way again. Lieutenant Kopp came with Doris, manfully apologetic; Lieutenant Kopp doesn't know it yet, but in an astoundingly short time he is going to find himself facing a minister with a wedding ring in one hand. People tried to touch only the spots that wouldn't be too sore. They said soberly, "At least it's over now. Nice not to be locking our doors any more. . . . " They seldom mentioned Ada, seldom mentioned Russ.

After the few days I got up and went to work; there wasn't any reason why I shouldn't. I'd lost something I'd had a long while, but amputation is different from illness; after a thing is cut away you begin healing.

In the evenings, now, often, I ride or walk past the Gainer house. Pete picks me up at the hospital at ten; the Shore Road is the prettiest drive we have, and we're not going to avoid it. Sometimes there are lights in Gainer House; Ada's lights; I look up at those lights in the house which maybe I once envied; the house still sits high, white, and nested on its terrace amid its cedars; it's a beautiful house, but I don't covet it, not any more. Maybe Lucy Hague, whom I so much misjudged, is still fond enough of soft living to comfort Ada as much as she can be comforted; I hope so.

I don't have to use tact with myself; I can think about Russ. For Russ it wasn't enough to be loved by one woman; Russ never wanted to give anything up; he married Ada but kept Sylvia; perhaps he chose Ada in the first place because he thought she was the one who would get John Gainer's money. But I don't think it was money alone that made him keep Sylvia, any more than it was money alone that made him kill her. No money was concerned in the ties he kept between himself and me. He didn't encourage—not too much—but he also never let go.

Then, again and again, I think of Sylvia. Sylvia who in a way brought about her own death. "Maybe he's what I'm still looking for," she'd said with her hand on the little toy man from my merry-go-round, the man who was an open door away from dull reality, the man who stood for a life illicit and exciting and forbidden and unknown. But if Sylvia had had such a symbol, so too had I; Russ was my beckoning door; the things I wanted had been different than the things Sylvia sought; what I had wanted was stability and security and strength, and because I'd thought Russ opened a way toward these I'd never broken the dream.

Mother has had a letter from a Mr. Abt, a lawyer; it says that a check in Mother's favor, found among the effects of Miss Sylvia Gainer, has been admitted to probate. We don't know yet, though, if we want that money; if Sylvia was giving it to me to make sure I'd be away from Long Meadow, and Pete, then I don't have it coming. I seem to be feeling differently about money than I did before. I feel different about Long Meadow. Maybe it wasn't the debt and Long Meadow I so hungered to be away from, maybe it was just myself. Maybe I have to find in myself the capacity to pay off those debts; maybe the trouble with me is that I've rested back, waiting, wanting other people to open doors for me, when I should have done my own opening. Maybe capacity and ability aren't all a matter of training. What's been happening to me is a story; maybe I can write it so people will want to read it.

The other night Pete and I were out as usual. Pete said, "It's almost all clear now. Hector too—he tried blackmailing Russ, just as we guessed. Up to the point where things sort of started running away from Russ, he had me all sewed up for the verdict, even way back to sapping my reputation by dropping sleeping powders in my drinks and getting me in a fight with Clint Boyce. I suppose I should have told you about that fight— it was because Clint said once that you were Russ Bennert's girl."

I'd have interrupted but he still had too much to get off his chest.

"You don't have to say it. There was supposed to have been one more clue against me too. A matchbook. One Russ picked up at the Kitchen, and carefully dropped under Sylvia's hand when he'd killed her. Anyway so he says to Waslewski. No one's ever seen any such matchbook, but that's what he says. Try figuring that one out—why should he lie now, and if he isn't, what became of that matchbook?"

I looked at him. We'd been driving for half an hour, that particular night; it was almost eleven. Late, but not too late. Pete had parked the car in one of the lookouts on the west side of the lake; it was October, cold but not too cold; some leaves, especially oak leaves, still clung to their branches; they rustled in the small breeze like taffeta; the lake rustled too. Cars purred on the highway behind us, a thin scimitar of moon was out. Behind the wheel Pete lounged, relaxed and easy, hands linked at the back of his neck, elbows wide. He was a dark-haired, peak-browed, ruminant Pete, the leopard in him far down under. He didn't look as if he ever had said, "Two things I drooled about, all those long months on Saipan, smoked spareribs and you." He didn't look, yet, as if he thought life was going to be either fun or funny. He didn't look as if he could be lighthearted. Or dynamite.

Now that I'm out from under the restraints and disciplines I've kept myself in for so long, I'm afraid another of the things I'm going to feel different about is Pete.

I lifted my handbag to my lap from the seat beside me and opened it. I got out first the billfold and then the matchbook, and held it out to him.

All he said was, "Cathy." But it was a good thing the car was parked.